# THE BOOK KNIGHTS

## by J.G. McKenney

Library and Archives Canada Cataloguing in Publication

ISBNs:

| | |
|---|---|
| 978-0-9876823-6-9 | Hardcover print version |
| 978-0-9876823-7-6 | Paperback print version (Createspace) |
| 978-0-9876823-8-3 | Amazon Kindle ebook version |
| 978-0-9876823-9-0 | Smashwords epub version |
| 978-0-9959299-0-6 | Kobo ebook version |
| 978-0-9959299-1-3 | Nook ebook version |

Cover art by Ivan Zanchetta (ivanzanchetta.com)

Typeset in *Sabon* at SpicaBookDesign

Printed and bound with www.createspace.com

*To my parents for sharing the power of words.*

# ACKNOWLEDGEMENTS

First off, I'd like to recognize the efforts of all those authors and researchers whose past work on the King Arthur legend was invaluable to me in creating this new spin on a timeless tale. Having borrowed elements from many of the fable's incarnations, my purpose was to create an entertaining and original story. I hope I've succeeded.

Many people took the time to offer opinions and feedback on this book at various stages of its development, and I'm very grateful to those "book knights" for their help. A big thank you goes out to Ellen Brock, Madison Cassidy, Rowan Duff, Heidi Lucas, Owen Cunningham, and Madelyn Burt whose input helped shape the story. Arthur aficionado Brent Murry's notes were very concise and encouraging. Stephanie Spencer's thoughtful comments and enthusiasm have been an inspiration; I can only hope the book is discovered by more readers like her.

Finally, I owe the deepest debt of gratitude to my wife, Wendy. Her patience and support have never waned. Without her love and devotion, I would never have completed this quest.

# CHAPTER 1

The door exploded from its hinges, and a platoon of Incendi troopers armed with electroshock batons scrambled through the twisted frame, separating into squads to search the upper and lower floors. The husband and wife who resided in the humble two-story unit were pushed against the wall at the base of the stairs, awaiting judgment. Terror flashed in their eyes as the police ransacked the home, toppling furniture and smashing belongings.

A young officer approached the couple, looking at them with a strange mix of sympathy and loathing. Tall and thin with a chiseled jaw and icy blue eyes, the captain was clad in black like his men and wore a fedora tilted forward on his brow. A gold flame insignia pinned near its peak flickered as the overhead light played upon its polished surface.

"Your daughter. Where is she?" The captain spoke softly, his words laboring under the weight of concern. He stepped past them toward the kitchen, awaiting an answer. One of the squads was finishing its search there, cupboards

1

were open, a pile of shattered dishes on the floor. The captain scanned the place settings on the dining table: two cups, two dishes, a knife and fork each.

"S...she's out with a f...friend," the man stammered. "She hasn't come home yet." Finding his courage, he added, "Why are you here? What do you want?"

The Incendi captain shook his head in disappointment. He hated to bear witness to such resistance, such denial. It was even worse, knowing a child was involved. He approached the man, whispering as he moved. With an open palm, he struck him square in the chest, hurling him back against the wall. The man crumpled to the floor in agony.

"Stop!" shrieked the woman. She went to her husband and cradled him in her arms. With pleading eyes, she looked up at the officer. "Please. We've done nothing wrong."

The captain turned toward the battered front door. "That's not what I've been told."

She followed his eyes to her next-door neighbor standing in the shadows beyond the threshold, arms crossed to shield her against the cool night air and the guilt of betrayal.

"Mrs. Tulley?" The words caught in her throat, and she began to sob. "What have you done to us?"

Just then, a voice rang out from the second floor: "Captain Mordred! Here!"

Mordred sneered in disgust at the man and woman huddled together on the floor. "You have no one to blame but yourselves." He nodded for them to be taken away, before striding up the stairs.

Near the far end of the second-floor hallway, two troopers stood at attention next a rectangular waist-high opening in the wall. Hanging from an enclosed vertical hinge, a false radiator matching the cavity's dimensions was suspended between them. Calling for a flashlight, the Incendi captain removed his fedora and crouched low, edging his way through the narrow passage.

It opened into a thin windowless room. Particles of dust hung in the air, glowing embers caught in the shaft of light emerging from his hand. Mordred pointed the beam at the floor, and concentric circles of gold marked the worn carpet like a target. Still crouching, he moved slowly, carefully, pausing after each step, studying the floor's surface, knowing that readers often left traps for Incendi. Seeing no evidence of subterfuge, Mordred straightened and raised the light. He couldn't believe what he saw.

The walls were covered by shelves filled with books! Halfway down the outer wall was a standing lamp with two high back leather chairs on either side. After careful inspection of the reading light's mechanism, Mordred switched it on and called to the two men waiting outside. Entering the space, their eyes widened.

"We will perform the Lighting as soon as I've examined the contraband," said Mordred. "CEO Fay will be proud of our work tonight. Praise the Corporation."

"Praise the Corporation!" repeated the troopers.

The Lighting ceremony was completed exactly as prescribed, the same words, the same rituals, just as Morgan Fay had instructed her first Incendi two and a half decades before. With his lieutenants standing at attention behind him, Mordred reached for a small gold case buckled to the wide leather belt of his uniform. Flipping back its lid, he pulled out a match and struck it against the case's side. A flame hissed into existence, and he straightened his arm, holding the burning match out in front of him.

"With this flame, I bring light," he intoned. "With this heat, I cleanse."

He waited a moment before letting the tiny torch fall on a pile of crumpled pages at his feet. Then, dropping his arm to his side, he pivoted in place and led his men out.

The fire crept across the floor, devouring paper and carpet, gaining momentum as it spread. A thick, black smoke filled the room, rolling over itself like a storm cloud, ravenous flames growling hungrily as they climbed. A moment later, there was another sound: a deep, drum-like thudding, barely audible above the burning tempest. A lower section of the shelf separated from the wall, and a row of hard covers slapped the floor. More books cascaded to the carpet, and a groping hand emerged.

The girl coughed violently, retching as she labored to breath amid the thickening blanket of smoke. She squeezed out from behind the book case, reaching back to pull a duffel bag from the cavity, pushing aside the dish, cup, and utensils her father had cast into the void in the rush to hide her. The bag held provisions, preparations made for a day they prayed would never come.

Making sure her vidlink was in her pocket, she lifted the hood of her sweatshirt and with eyes clenched shut, crawled across the floor, dragging the duffel bag. Scalding heat seared her throat as she gasped for air, her face and hands feeling like they were on fire. Gulping a mouthful of acrid smoke, an intense wave of nausea washed over the girl, and she fell against the wall of books. She was helpless now, certain she was going to die.

As the firestorm raged, her mind floated away from the horror. She was a young child again, sitting on her father's lap, following his finger as it traced words on the page. She giggled and squirmed with excitement as the story unfolded, peeking ahead, eager to find out how the tale would end. Her mother leaned toward her from the adjacent chair, her smiling face awash in the light of the reading lamp. *This is our secret, Arti. You can't tell anyone.* She could hear herself answer, *I promise.*

When the story was done, she reached across with her tiny hand and closed the book's cover. She smiled up at her parents expectantly, waiting to say the ritual words together.

*And they lived happily ever after.*

From somewhere in the cloud of her delirium, Arti Penderhagen heard the books on the shelves call to her, drawing her back to the present. Words echoed from their pages, guiding her hand along their bindings, showing her the way out.

# CHAPTER 2

Arti's memory of her escape from the burning home was as cloudy as the smoke that stung her eyes and filled her lungs. She wasn't sure what happened in those last desperate moments, incapacitated as she was by the raging inferno. The fact that she *thought* she heard the books speak to her was an indication of just how impaired her judgment had been. She wondered what she would have done if they had summoned her toward the flames. *Would I have followed? Would I be dead?*

She didn't want to think about it. All that mattered was that she made it out of the burning library, finding her way to the window at the end of the upstairs hall. Propping it open with a piece of wood that was resting on the sill, an inrush of fresh air poured over her, and she coughed violently, throwing back her hood, taking several deep breaths. Once her head was clear, she threw the duffel bag out and scrambled over the sill, hanging precariously by her fingertips until she found the courage to let herself drop to the lawn below. The height was greater than expected; she struck the ground hard and rolled onto her side. Looking toward the front of the house to make sure no one was watching, she scrambled to retrieve the bag and crossed the backyard to a rickety cedar fence barely visible in the darkness. Momentarily snagged by a protruding wire as she straddled the barrier, she pulled herself free and melted into the night.

Arti alternated between a fast walk and a jog, all the while wrestling with the awkward weight of the duffel bag and bouts of convulsive coughing. She threaded her way along a series of dark, deserted backstreets, avoiding the main thoroughfares still likely to have pedestrians and traffic, putting as much distance as she could between herself and the flames that devoured a life she could never return to. After walking for over an hour through a suburban maze of homes and apartment buildings, Arti found a narrow alley between two rows of townhouses where she could rest and examine the contents of the duffel bag.

Loosening the rope around the mouth of the canvas sack, Arti peered inside. It was too dark to see what was there, so she plunged her hand in and felt around. As luck would have it, the first thing she touched was a thin, metal flashlight. When she pulled it out and switched it on, she was surprised to see how black her hands were, guessing the rest of her probably looked the same. She shook soot from her hair and brushed away ash and grit still clinging to the baggy hooded sweatshirt draped over her thin frame. Stifling a cough, she examined her torn pants, gingerly touching a lacerated knee, the product of her battle with the fence. She coughed again, the heaviness in her chest and a wave of nausea reminding her that the minor wound was the least of her worries.

Shining the light into the bag, she inspected the rest of her supplies. There were a few cans of food, a small jug of water, a knife in a plastic sheath, a blanket, a lighter, and a red Corporation credit chip worth fifty flash. She saw something else: a letter.

Propping the flashlight on her leg, Arti unfolded the paper slowly, noting the rough edge that ran down one side. She guessed it was from one of the books in the library. In the ever-shrinking world of print, scribes were forced to cannibalize the blank pages found at the front and back of manuscripts; there were simply no other sources of paper available to them. Pens were even rarer, as was the ink they used. This was one of the few examples of pen writing Arti had ever seen.

She knew that her mother and father had learned the skill when they were very young, in the final years before the practice was abolished in schools, but she could count on one hand how many times she had seen them do it. The characters on the page appeared to have been applied in hesitant and uneven strokes, but the words they formed were legible. Arti wondered which of her parents' hands had crafted the message.

*Arti:*

*If you are reading this, it means the library has been found, and the Incendi have taken us. We know how frightened you must be, but try to be strong, and remember everything we told you.*

*The Incendi will be hunting you now. Get to Isle as fast as you can. Stick to the plan, and <u>trust no one</u>.*

*Be safe. We love you.*

*Mom and Dad*

Arti's parents had always warned her that such a day could come, making her rehearse the escape plan from the time she was old enough to understand their instructions. The secret library, if found, would be a deception in itself. They were correct in thinking the police would not search behind its shelves, but they didn't expect the collection of books to be burned immediately upon discovery. Had they known this, they would never have put their daughter at such risk. Normal Incendi procedure involved cordoning off homes where contraband had been found to allow for Network coverage and a full Corporate investigation. That usually took days, more than enough time for their daughter to slip away unseen. Arti could only imagine the horror her parents must have felt knowing the house was being burned with her inside.

Tears welled in her eyes making the words a watery blur on the page. After a few minutes and another coughing fit, she stood and gulped some water from the jug, then returned it to the duffel bag. Switching off the flashlight, she pocketed it along with the letter.

"Stick to the plan," she whispered, pulling the hood over her head, "and trust no one."

Arti had hoped to arrive at the West Bridge before midnight, but nearly two hours into the trek her pace had slowed considerably. She had never been to this part of the city before, and she lost her way more than once in the labyrinth of backstreets and boulevards crisscrossing its southern reaches. Precious time had been lost, and she knew that every minute that passed increased the likelihood of capture.

Listening through a tiny speaker plugged into her ear, Arti feigned interest in the ads scrolling across the vidlink's screen. The latest Corporation lottery was worth ten million flash, the sound of cheering accompanied an explosion of colored pixels. Barry Briton, star of the highest rated linkshow, *Eyes on the Prize,* pointed at the viewer and shouted, "You could be next!"

The lottery ad faded away, and another took its place. This one featured a beautiful young woman with long auburn hair and skin like porcelain. Her green eyes sparkled above a toothy smile as the newest line of Fay Industries products—vidlinks, eyecams, and spylids—danced around her. "A picture is worth a thousand words," she said, pulling one of the devices magically from the air, turning its tiny screen toward the viewer. "Show, *don't* tell. *You* are the Corporation."

Another blaze of light filled the screen, introducing a "newsflash". It was no coincidence that it shared the same name as the Corporation's currency, since the announcements almost always featured rewards given for turning in readers and, on rare occasions, the even more dangerous and elusive scribes.

A line of troopers stood at attention in front of a burning home. A crowd of people bathed in the light of the fire cheered. A child with his back to the camera extended an arm to a tall Incendi officer. The captain in his fedora smiled as he shook the boy's hand. The words "Ten thousand flash!" echoed in Arti's ear.

The camera panned across the home's burning façade, and Arti immediately recognized it through the flames. *That's my house!*

The crowd cheered again, and the boy turned to face the camera, smiling. When Arti saw who it was, her heart skipped a beat.

*Robb.*

Arti had never told her neighbor about the library; that secret was too dangerous to share with anyone. But betrayal feeds on smaller morsels, crumbs of fear and suspicion—food that Robb Tulley apparently had an appetite for. Arti tried to remember what she might have said or done to give him reason to suspect her family had books. Nothing came to mind, but it was clear by what she was watching on the vidlink that he had reported them. Robb had been the closest thing to a friend Arti ever had, and now she feared that her trust in him was responsible for destroying her family.

The crowd cheered again, and the newsflash ended with a picture of Arti's face filling the link screen. The voiceover boomed: "REWARD!" Everyone, everywhere, was looking at Arti's image right now; she recognized it as her grade nine school picture taken less than a month before. Straight blonde hair hung to her shoulders, framing a face devoid of expression. The portrait lingered for an eternity before finally fading into another ad.

Rounding a corner past a low-rise apartment complex, Arti breathed a sigh of relief at the sight of the bridge, lamp posts sticking up like quills from its arching back. But her celebration at seeing the glowing path to freedom was cut short when she noticed two black Destrier sedans parked up the street. If it had not been for the light cast from the bridge, Arti wouldn't have noticed them.

With their high, curved fenders and wide running boards, the vehicles had "Incendi" written all over them. It was impossible to tell if there was anyone in the cars; even in daylight, the thick tinted glass would have shielded the occupants from prying eyes. Arti knew that turning back now would be pointless; they would easily run her down. All she could do was pretend to be passing by the bridge, then make a run for it.

Continuing along the street, Arti stared down at her vidlink, trying to look casual, just another person on her way to work the night shift. *Keep moving,* she told herself. *Don't look up.*

The bridge was approaching on her left, getting closer with each step. *Almost there.* Her heart was racing, and her breaths came in short gasps. Without lifting her head, she glanced up at the cars only a few hundred feet away.

*Now!*

Arti stuffed the vidlink into her pocket and sprinted toward the bridge, the sudden acceleration throwing back her hood. The Destriers' engines rumbled to life, their tires screeching on the asphalt as they raced after her. Cradling the duffel bag, she ran as fast as she could up the bridge's gentle incline, but the span was deceptively long; there was no way she'd make it across before the cars caught up. Then Arti heard the vehicles squeal to a stop behind her. Still running, she looked back, wondering why they had ended the chase. When she faced forward again, she had her answer.

A tall figure stood at the apex of the bridge. Arti stopped suddenly, her feet skidding across its slippery steel surface.

The man approached Arti, hands raised in a gesture of calm. Passing through an island of light cast down from one of the bridge lamps, the flame insignia on the man's fedora shimmered, and his face was revealed. Arti recognized him immediately, the angular jaw, the piercing eyes. It was the Incendi captain in the newsflash, the one who had given Robb Tulley his reward.

"There's no reason to run away," said the man. It was the same hard, sharp voice she'd heard from behind the bookshelf of her family's library. He was only thirty feet from Arti and edging closer.

"Your parents are safe. They're getting the help they need. I'll take you to them," he added, extending his arm to her.

*Twenty feet.*

"It's not your fault, Arti." Hearing the Incendi speak her name sent a chill up her spine. He knew who she was. He knew everything.

*Ten.*

Arti backed away from the man, and he stopped moving toward her. "Please," he begged. "I just want to talk to you."

Arti heard car doors slamming behind her. Four troopers, big men carrying electroshock batons, were standing beside their vehicles. They didn't look like they just wanted to talk.

The Incendi captain spoke again, but this time the words that came from his mouth were of a language she didn't recognize, possessing a lyrical quality, a strange intonation and rhythm. In a blur of movement, he closed the gap between them, driving his index finger into Arti's chest. The focused strike sent her tumbling backward onto the bridge platform. She landed hard on the steel surface, and the duffel bag flew from her arms.

The officer raised a hand, signaling his men. "Take her."

Arti rolled onto her side, unable to rise. The blow had knocked the wind out of her, and she gasped for air. As the troopers trudged up the bridge to collect her, she forced down her panic and looked for a way to escape. The only option was to roll into the canal; the edge was near. But a voice from below the bridge platform offered a better plan.

"This way," it hissed. A grate lifted not three feet from where Arti was lying. From the narrow opening, a hand emerged, pulling the duffel bag down. "Hurry!"

Though still reeling from the blow, Arti managed to crawl across the bridge deck and squeeze through the gap. A shout rang out from above: "Stop her!"

Light filtered down through the latticework of the bridge's steel platform, illuminating the substructure of beams and girders in a checkerboard pattern. Through the flickering ribbons of light, Arti could see the back of the stranger who had come to her aid. The boy was smaller than her, and thin, wearing a wedge-shaped cap and dark clothes that blended with his dark skin; it was hard for Arti not to lose him in the shadows. He moved like a cat, scampering across the narrow framework of bridge supports with amazing agility, holding the bulky duffel bag in front of him as he ran. In contrast, Arti was slow and awkward, picking her way clumsily behind, feet sliding through mounds of powdery pigeon droppings.

"Stay with me," ordered the boy. Throwing Arti's duffel bag over his shoulder, he jumped to a ladder attached to a thick vertical column. Arti could hear the splashing sound of water below and wondered where he could be leading her. *Are we going to swim for it?*

The noise of the churning current grew louder as Arti descended. She could smell the water now, a wet sliminess filling her nostrils. The farther below the bridge deck she climbed, the darker it got. She was surprised and relieved when she saw the figure of the boy standing below her at water level, balancing on what appeared to be some kind of raft. Arti stepped from the last wrung of the ladder onto the craft, a mishmash of wooden planks and timber pieces bound together with wire and rope. It shifted under her weight, and water splashed over its edges. For a moment, Arti was sure it was going to sink.

A yell from above echoed through the steel skeleton of the bridge; the troopers were almost to the ladder. The boy untied a frayed rope holding the raft to the foot of the bridge and pushed off. The craft jerked as it was grabbed by the flow, slowly picking up speed, leaving the bridge—and the troopers—behind. They could only watch as Arti and the boy drifted away into the night. High above them at the bridge rail, Arti could see the tall Incendi captain's dark silhouette.

# CHAPTER 3

The raft came to rest against the half-submerged frame of a dock jutting out from a small boathouse leaning precariously over the island's rocky shore. Tying the raft off, the boy jumped free of the waterlogged platform and without looking back, called tersely to Arti, "Come on."

Arti lifted the soaked duffel bag and followed, noting that those were the first words the boy had uttered since their narrow escape from the bridge. The rusted hinges of the boathouse door groaned as the boy forced his way inside. He reached into a cupboard and pulled out a candle and matches; a moment later, the small room was alight. It was the first opportunity Arti had to get a good look at her rescuer, and it was then that she realized *he* was a *she*.

"I thought you were—"

The girl cut her off, "I don't care what you thought." Below her wedge-shaped cap and close-cropped curly black hair, she had a delicate caramel face with large hazel eyes topped with long lashes—an appearance that contrasted sharply with the way she moved and talked. She wore layers of clothing, the cuffs of her shirt sleeves and pant legs frayed and dirty, a pair of boots with the toes torn out completing the ensemble. The girl crossed her arms and scrutinized the dripping duffel bag.

"Let's see what you got. Dump it." The girl's speech had a hard edge to it, her words crammed together as if syllables were expensive.

Arti hesitated, unsure of the girl's motives. "Why?" she asked. "I...I can pay you for helping me."

The girl sighed, as if Arti was stating the obvious. "I'll get to that." She nodded at the bag. "Now dump it."

Not knowing what else to do, Arti obliged, tipping the bag slowly so its contents spilled onto the sagging wooden floor. The girl scanned the supplies, making quick calculations in her head.

"Fifty flash, not bad. The lighter I can use, the knife and blanket will be easy to sell." She lifted the jug. "And the water's a bonus."

"But I'm not—"

"What else have you got?" She looked Arti up and down. "Pockets."

"Wait...I—"

"Empty your pockets!"

Even though she was a head taller than the girl, Arti didn't put up a fight. Maybe it was all she'd been through this night that stifled her resistance and made her comply. She reached into her pocket and offered her flashlight and vidlink to the girl, careful to keep the letter from her parents concealed.

When the girl saw the vidlink, she was utterly appalled. "You idiot!" She grabbed it from Arti, wrenched open the door and ran outside. Arti followed, looking on helplessly as the girl tossed the device as far out into the water as she could. It bobbed for a second on the surface then disappeared into the murky depths of the canal.

"What did you do that for?" protested Arti. "Are you crazy or something?" She followed the girl back inside the boathouse, waiting for an explanation.

The girl tilted back her cap and glared up at Arti, eyes narrowed, words dripping with sarcasm, "You have no idea how dumb you are. Why do you think the Flames were waiting at the bridge for you?"

It took a moment for Arti to understand. *My vidlink. They were tracking me.*

"I...I didn't know they could do that," Arti confessed, trying to wrap her head around it. The admission was yet more proof of how ill prepared she was to survive on her own.

"Why are the Flames after you?" asked the girl.

Arti was reluctant to answer, but the girl had saved her and deserved the truth. "We had books and...the Incendi found them."

The girl's eyes widened. "You're a reader?"

Arti nodded, extending her hand feebly. "My name's Arti, Arti Penderhagen."

The girl ignored the gesture, searching Arti's face for something that would confirm her extraordinary claim of literacy. Not finding it, she replied coolly, "I'm Gal."

"Gal what?"

"Just Gal."

"Okay...um...I really appreciate you helping me...Gal.

But I need my stuff." Arti nodded at the contents of the duffel bag on the floor, "It's all I have." She cautiously leaned over and picked up the flash chip, holding it out to the girl. "Like I said, I'll pay you."

The offer of money seemed to appease Gal. "Yeah, you will," she said matter-of-factly. "I stuck my neck out, and you owe me—big time."

"How much do you want?" asked Arti meekly. "I mean, what do you think is fair?"

Gal laughed. "You ain't gonna last long in this town, dealin' like that. You're lucky you made it this far. I coulda took your stuff back at the bridge and left you for the Flames."

The girl was right, and Arti knew it. She was an easy mark for anyone who wanted to take advantage of her. But there was something about Gal that told Arti she was not one of those people, that she was the exception to her parents' rule.

"But you didn't," Arti said, with a disarming smile.

Gal started pacing back and forth in frustration, the weak floorboards of the boathouse creaking under each light step. "Maybe I'm the idiot," she said. She looked at Arti with a mix of contempt and sympathy. "You got no idea how hard it is to live in this rat hole of a town. It ain't nothin' like Main. You got everything you need over there—made for good scroungin' too. But now I can't even cross the bridge, thanks to you."

"You can have the money," said Arti. "I just need somewhere to stay until I figure things out. Until I can go back."

"Go back? Are you nuts? You can't go back. The Flames will be watchin' the bridges. Go anywhere near them, you're dead meat." Gal looked at Arti like she had two heads. "Why would you even think it?"

19

"The Incendi have my parents. I...I have to...."

"What? Save them?" Gal shook her head. "You're crazy if you try."

The wounded look on Arti's face made Gal regret her words, and she puffed out a breath in frustration. "I'll take the fifty flash and fence it for Isle coin. Should be able to get twenty bucks for it to buy some food. The rest of your stuff we split down the middle—keep, trade, or sell. I'll help you for a bit, but I ain't makin' no promises. That's the deal. Take it or leave it."

"Alright," said Arti. "It's a deal."

Gal took a step toward Arti, with her finger raised. "And if you make things hard for me," she said, poking her, "the deal's off. Got it?"

Arti nodded, caressing her shoulder, "Got it."

Gal gathered Arti's supplies and stuffed them into the duffel bag. She extinguished the candle and returned it to its place in the cupboard, leading Arti out of the boathouse and up from the canal's rocky shore toward a narrow road running alongside the waterway.

"Where are we going?" asked Arti.

"My place," answered Gal, without turning. "Now be quiet."

They crossed the road next the canal and began weaving their way through a series of connecting alleys. Navigating through the pitch-blackness, Gal never slowed, only changing course once when they encountered a handful of people in a small courtyard crowded around a fire burning in a barrel. She grabbed Arti by her sleeve and pulled her through a hole in a high mesh fence to avoid the encounter.

Arti stumbled blindly in Gal's wake until they arrived at a long single-story building that spanned most of a block.

Gal led Arti through a large open window concealed behind a copse of evergreens, the soles of their shoes crunching on fragments of glass strewn across a polished marble floor. Safely concealed inside the building, Gal produced the flashlight from the duffel bag and shone it ahead of them. A wide hall led past a room that had once been encased in glass, a high counter with a doorway dividing the space.

"This was a school, back in the day," explained Gal, stepping past the counter.

They walked through another hall leading out the rear of the first room, rounding a corner past a pile of legless plastic chairs until they were facing a wide steel door covered in dents, beneath a drop ceiling. Deep gouges on the door's jamb hinted at many unsuccessful attempts to jar it open, and a long silver handle with a bend in it protruded from its right side just above waist height. Handing the flashlight to Arti, Gal removed her cap and pulled a thick twine necklace over her head; a shiny silver key dangled from its end. She inserted the key in the handle's scarred lock and turned it, at the same time pulling down on the curved lever. A hollow "click" could be heard, and the heavy door swung open with an eerie squeal.

"This is it," declared Gal proudly. "Home."

A few steps from the door, Gal reached for a lamp sitting on a table and pressed a button on its metal base, igniting it. There was a whispering sound and a sweet metallic odor as the fuel burned, filling the space with a soft white glow.

It was a large room, one side covered in a series of open metal cabinets with nothing on them but a few stacks of blank paper and cardboard file folders. The other half of the room was empty, save for a small table and chair against the wall, and a narrow bench with a grimy blanket and pillow at one end. Wedged between the tines of a large ventilation grill above the bench was a glossy advertisement featuring a man, woman, girl, and boy—laughing together. The happy family's clothing and hair styles looked old fashioned, and Arti guessed the ad was from a long time ago when they used print for such things.

"Just somethin' I found," said Gal, referring to the picture. "Couldn't get nothin' for it." She shrugged, "So I stuck it up there to block the draft."

After checking that the door was pulled tight and locked, Gal added Arti's supplies to a pile of canned food stacked next the table. She chose one and, lifting an opener from a nail on the wall, removed its lid.

"Hungry?" she asked, offering it to Arti.

Arti nodded and took the seat next the table. "Thanks," she said, wondering how she should go about eating from the can.

"Watch your lips, the edge is sharp," Gal warned. "I need to get another spoon. Well, two, I guess, now that you're here. Traded my last one for lamp oil." Gal lifted the back of her shirt and pulled a knife from a leather sheath clipped to her belt, setting it on the table. She plopped down on the bench and wedged the pillow between her back and the wall.

Arti pretended not to notice the weapon, commenting on the food instead. "It's good," she lied, slurping down the contents of the can, a slimy mix of what might have been chicken and noodles. But she was hungry, and it was better than nothing.

Gal lifted Arti's jug of water from the duffel bag and pushed it across to her. "Try not to drink too much; clean water's hard to find. And it ain't cheap." She pointed to a large pail near the door. "Don't drink that; it's for the crapper. I'll show you tomorrow." She squinted. "Unless you gotta go now."

Arti looked at the pail, her expression a mix of curiosity and dread. "No...I'm okay."

Although she was dead tired, Arti felt compelled to tell Gal her story. The anger and aggressiveness Gal had displayed at the boathouse were gone, and she listened intently to the harrowing account of the Incendi raid and Arti's narrow escape from the burning house. Arti expected Gal to be impressed by her dramatic getaway, but she seemed more amazed by Arti's knowledge of books.

"So, you can *really* read?"

"Yes," said Arti. "I learned when I was little. My parents taught me."

Gal's eyes narrowed. "Everyone says readin's a black art, and that people that know their letters are dangerous."

Arti leaned toward her. "Do I *look* dangerous?" She reached for the jug and took another sip of water. "And reading isn't a black art. That's just what the Corporation wants everyone to think so they *don't* think. My parents explained it all to me."

"How many books have you read?" asked Gal.

"Lots." Arti tipped her can back and swallowed the last of the noodles. "We had hundreds in our library," she said, staring down at the empty container in her hand. "My parents work at one of the plants near the canal." She paused, realizing that everything about their lives was in the past now. "They knew a trucker who brought in shipments from the Docks. They traded him for books—when he could get them. The hard part was making sure no one at the plant noticed what they were doing. There's always someone willing to report you to get a reward." In her mind, she saw the smiling face of her neighbor, Robb Tulley.

"My parents collected books for a long time and built a secret library in our house to hold them all. But the Incendi burned everything and...took them away."

There was a long silence before Arti spoke again. "It's your turn, Gal. What's your story?"

Gal was a closed book that couldn't be pried open. She wouldn't talk about her childhood, but it was clear to Arti that she'd lived a very hard life—and a lonely one. She was twelve years old—just two years Arti's junior—but her small size and wiry build made her appear younger. Until you looked at her eyes. They didn't belong to a child; they'd seen too much to hold on to any kind of innocence. And though they regarded Arti with curiosity and interest, there was suspicion hiding behind them, a wariness that made trust difficult. The only thing Gal was willing to share was the story of how she discovered her pride and joy, the room they were sitting in.

It was almost two years ago while out "scrounging"—Gal's term for finding or stealing anything she could use or sell—that she found her home in the abandoned school. She expected the building to be stripped of its valuables but was surprised to find one locked steel door that hadn't been breached. It became her mission to find a way in, and after days of trying, she did.

It was like entering an undiscovered tomb of some ancient king with all its contents still in place—except there wasn't any gold or silver or jewels. For Gal, it held a treasure even more valuable: a place where she'd be safe from the outside world.

24

"And when I got inside, I found the key up there." Gal pointed at one of the shelves. "Pretty lucky, eh?" She reached for the twine necklace under her collar, pulling the key out and kissing it.

As impressed as Arti was by Gal's achievement, she felt sorry for her. "It must have been hard being on your own."

"Pfeww. Bein' alone don't bother me none," said Gal, her eyes betraying those words. She knocked her empty can off the table with the back of her hand and kicked it across the floor. It clattered and bounced against the base of one of the shelves before spinning to a stop. "You're just lucky you had parents that cared about you."

*Cared.* Arti refused to think about her mother and father in the past tense. She swore again that she would go back for them. As soon as she could. No matter what. The weight of that pledge added to her exhaustion. She slumped from the chair to the floor and reached for her blanket. "I'm really tired. I need to get some rest." She was nearly asleep when Gal spoke again.

"You never asked me how I got in here with the door locked."

"Don't tell me," said Arti, keeping her eyes closed. "Secrets should be kept."

Two matching marble pedestals stood in the middle of Morgan Fay's expansive tower suite, facing the thick iron door, the only entrance into the circular room. One pedestal supported a massive leather-bound book while its naked twin revealed only the swirling gray veins of polished stone and the dark telltale scars of a fire long since extinguished.

25

Lifting the huge book from its place, the CEO of Fay Industries cradled it in her arms, crossing to the ornate oak desk below a window on the tower's curving outer wall. She set the book down gently and took her seat, carefully turning the tome's broad pages until she found her place.

For twenty-five years, Fay commanded her company from her office high atop the restored ancient castle overlooking the city of Tintagel, Main and Isle, the Avalon River to the south, and Lake Ogden to the east. She was almost sixty but had the face of a woman half that age. Her jet-black hair never grayed, her sky-blue eyes never clouded, her ivory skin never succumbed to the wrinkles of time. Those privileged enough to be allowed in her presence—the top executives in her company that did her bidding—never dared speak of her ageless appearance. Concerned only with maintaining their own wealth and position, and fearing nothing so much as Fay's wrath, they refused to question the strange magic that kept her young. They didn't know about the power of words.

Fay watched intently as a tiny tendril of ink curled and twisted its way into existence. The magic of a letter's birth never ceased to amaze her, and she was elated by the rate at which the characters were coming. It wasn't long ago that a single word took months to form. Now ten times that many materialized in a day, the process accelerating with every book threatened by the flames of another Incendi Lighting.

The language was Old Ferencian, and the words had no apparent relationship to those around them, isolated entries bourn of countless events occurring at once. Even so, Morgan Fay read them with religious zeal, drinking in each syllable like drops of a life-sustaining drug, knowing they would soon fill all but the last of *The History's* blank pages—the one *she* would write.

Her thoughts drifted back to the day it all began, the day she made her decision to choose a new path, to change the future. It started in the very room she was standing in now, in what was then the greatest library in the world.

She was supposed to be alone. Her mentor had been called to Hynal, some thirty miles north of Tintagel, to collect ten volumes of North Verinese poetry that a farmer had discovered hidden in an attic. The Order said it would take at least a week to catalogue the substantial find, pay the farmer, and return the prize to the library. But eager to get back to the castle, he completed the transaction in just four days.

And returned to flames.

Fay could still see his face, the utter disbelief, the terror. "He wasn't supposed to be here," she whispered, but the regret in those words was quickly smothered. "Fool. He was afraid of them."

Another word appeared on the ancient tome's page, completing a phrase that miraculously mirrored the inferno of her memory...

*From the flames...*

Fay gasped as she translated the emerging message. Never before had words in *The History* been connected. She watched in amazement as the sentence continued.

*...to the Isle of Avalon,...*

There was only one place that fit the description; she could see it from her castle tower. Fay rose from her chair and looked out through the narrow window cut into the thick blocks of stone. Except for the soft glow coming from the Docks on its far shore, the old city was asleep.

*Isle of Avalon?* Her mind raced. *Why has the tome named you?*

A knock at the iron door startled her. "Come," she said, turning away from the window, angered by the interruption.

Her Incendi captain, Mordred, entered the room. The tall young man's movements were measured and formal. He removed his black fedora and bowed his head to Fay, looking down at the granite floor, afraid to meet her eyes.

"What is it?" she asked.

"You wished to be informed of any important events," he said. Mordred glanced nervously at the tome spread open on Fay's desk. "I performed a Lighting this evening—the largest in years. Hundreds of books. They were destroyed immediately, as you requested." He looked up at her, eager for approval. "We have two readers in custody, a husband and wife named Penderhagen. But..." he swallowed nervously, "their daughter has eluded us. We lost her at the West Bridge. She...made it to the island."

The Incendi captain withered under the look Fay gave him. The escape of *any* reader was regrettable, but the news of the fleeing girl affected the CEO in a way Mordred hadn't witnessed before. It was the first time he'd ever seen her look truly worried.

"Question the parents," she said, taking a deep breath and sitting down at her desk. "But keep them alive until you're sure they've told you everything they know. I want their daughter found."

It was then that Morgan Fay noticed the sentence that had been forming on the tome's page was complete. A wave of panic washed over her as she read the words.

*...the Challenger has come.*

# CHAPTER 4

Arti woke with a start, throwing off her blanket and rolling to her side, searching the room for something familiar, something to quell her panic. The inky darkness amplified her fear, her heart pounded in her chest, and she gasped for air.

"What's wrong?" came a voice from above her. Arti saw a form move in the blackness, then heard a click and was momentarily blinded by a flash of white light. She squinted past the lamp at Gal staring down at her from the bench where she had been the night before. Like images streaming across a vidlink screen, it all came flooding back to Arti: the raid, the chase, the rescue.

"I forgot where I was," said Arti. She combed her fingers through her hair and rubbed her eyes. "And I had some bad dreams." The face of the Incendi captain still lingered in the recesses of her mind, along with the heat and the smoke and the dread. "Didn't you sleep?" she asked.

"Yeah, I woke up a while ago," said Gal. "I've been thinkin' about our deal."

Arti's heart sank. "You haven't changed your mind? About letting me stay, I mean."

Gal looked insulted. "'Course not. A deal's a deal. I was just wonderin' if you'd…" the words caught in her throat, "if you'd…teach me how to read."

Arti smiled. "Sure, Gal. I'd like that."

Gal pushed back her cap, beaming with delight. "Really?"

"Yes," laughed Arti, amused by her reaction. "But it's not going to be easy without anything *to* read."

With a surge of excitement, Gal spun around and plunged her hand behind her pillow, retrieving a small book. "Remember I told you about findin' the key to the door up there?" She nodded at the shelf behind Arti. "This was under it." With a mix of trepidation and hopefulness, Gal offered the book to Arti.

Arti recognized it immediately. *"The King's Errand*, by Eldon Sears. We had this story in our library," she said, running her fingers over the embossed crown on its mustard-yellow cover. "It's one of my favorites."

"Really? What's it about?" asked Gal, encouraged by Arti's enthusiasm.

"A boy who has to look after his little brother when their mother dies," explained Arti, turning to the book's title page. "His name is Ward Weatherington, and his brother's called Petey. They don't have any food, and no one will help them. They're almost starved when Ward finds the Wizard's Gem, a magical blue stone that makes him invisible. Ward uses it to take food and money to survive, then the king offers

30

a huge reward to anyone who can steal a map from the evil wizard, Rancoram—he's the one who lost the gem that Ward found. The king needs the map to find out where the wizard's imprisoned his daughter."

Gal was enthralled. "Does Ward steal the map? Does he get the reward? Does the king save his daughter?"

Arti saw an opportunity. She reached for a piece of paper from the shelf next to her bed, folding it over on itself. "You'll have to wait and see," she said, closing the book on the mark. "I'll read you one chapter every night—all but the last one."

"Then I won't know how the story ends," protested Gal.

"Yes you will," said Arti, "because you're going to read the final chapter on your own. I'm going to teach you how, but you have to teach me, too."

Gal was perplexed. "Teach you what?"

"Everything I need to know to rescue my parents."

Gal threw back her head and groaned. "I told you, you're crazy if you try. Scroungin' on Isle's one thing, messin' with Flames is another. You're gonna end up—"

"I don't want to hear it." Arti didn't raise her voice, but her tone was firm. "I'll teach you how to read, if you teach me how to survive on the streets. When I know enough, I'm going to cross back into Main and find them. That's the deal. Take it or leave it."

Gal rolled her eyes and grumbled. Finally, she thrust her arm out. "Fine. Deal."

As they shook hands, Arti grimaced.

"What's wrong?" asked Gal, afraid Arti was going to add something else to the contract.

Arti's face flushed with embarrassment. "Last night you said something about a washroom. I *really* have to go."

Making sure the door was locked behind them, Gal, carrying the sloshing pail of water, led Arti down a hall to another room with white tiles on its walls, many of them broken or missing. A narrow corridor divided it from the hallway, and sunlight cascaded down through a small window high on the outer wall, revealing a square-shaped pattern of rusty metal brackets on a dingy green marble floor. Centered between the metal brackets bolted to the floor, there were three round holes where toilets used to sit.

"Use the one over there," Gal pointed at the hole farthest from the doorway. "It drains the best." She dropped the pail of water next to the opening, and it splashed back and forth. "Pour in some water to wash it down. You don't need much. Bring the rest back when you're done. And don't spill any; it's a long walk to the canal to get more." She grinned mischievously. "I hope your aim's good. Welcome to Isle."

Arti stared at the hole in the floor. "You've got to be kidding. This is disgusting!"

"No, disgustin' is crappin' in a corner or behind a tree," said Gal. "This way it don't stink to high heaven. I'll wait for you in the hall. Hurry up."

"But how do I...you know?" Arti raised her hands.

"Oh, I forgot," said Gal. She reached into her pocket and pulled out two pieces of crumpled paper and handed them to Arti. "That's all you get."

That morning, after a breakfast of canned soup and water, Gal showed Arti around the rest of the old school— bypassing the washroom. Twenty-five years had not been kind to the building. Everything that could be salvaged or burned had been stripped from it offices, halls, and classrooms, leaving little but peeling paint to bear witness to the institution's proud past. High on the wall of what had been the gymnasium, large faded block letters spelled out its name:

TINTAGEL PUBLIC SCHOOL

HOME OF THE DRAGONS

Arti had heard the name before, and she felt stupid for not making the connection sooner. The halls, the classrooms, the gymnasium; all had been visited in her childhood imagination, brought to life through her parents' stories. Separated by a grade, this had been their school, the last place they had been free to read, write, and learn in a world that would forever change.

Arti told Gal what the words on the wall said, explaining that if she wanted to learn how to read, she would first have to learn all the letters and the sounds they made.

"How many are there?" asked Gal, then cursed when Arti told her. It was a stroke of luck when, while exploring one of the classrooms, Arti noticed the alphabet painted above a shattered blackboard. That morning, Gal was given her first lesson.

"I'll never remember them all," Gal complained, leading Arti out of the back door of the school after the session. "There's too many."

"You will," promised Arti. "It'll just take time." She remembered how mysterious the letters had seemed when she was first introduced to them and the triumph that came when she finally broke their code. It was the greatest gift her parents could have given her—outside of their love. It reminded her just how much she missed them, and the promise she made: *I'm going back for them.*

They crossed the street to a row of dilapidated houses, their worn wooden facades leaning out over the buckled sidewalk overflowing with tall grass and crawling weeds.

"Where are we going?" asked Arti.

"For a tour," said Gal, leading Arti down to the nearest intersection and a warped street sign with the words "Hill" and "High" crisscrossing it. The existence of the sign made Arti realize just how different this place was from home. Writing of any kind was forbidden in Main. To see words hoisted high on a street corner was unthinkable, and Arti couldn't help but stare at the spectacle.

"You need to learn your way around the island," continued Gal, ignoring Arti's fixation on the sign. "If we get split up, you gotta be able to find your way back."

They spent the day walking the streets of Isle, heading east on High Street past Waverly and Bay toward Park Avenue. This part of town was quiet, and they only passed a handful of people on the way. Doubling back along Center Street, Gal explained how she made a living here.

"I scrounge. Find, trade, or steal—whatever it takes. I figure since most people got more money than me, they can afford to give some away." She looked down proudly at her upturned palms. "Best hands in Tintagel. Ain't a pocket I can't pick." Her expression became more serious. "But you gotta be smart about your marks. Your best bet's someone you ain't likely to see again: sailors and traders who wander too far from the Docks or that are in their cups. Steer clear of the locals; they don't appreciate anyone takin' money from them or their customers." Gal continued the lesson by assessing passersby based on dress and behavior, sharing her deductions with Arti.

"Dockers wear overalls and hard toe boots. They ain't rich, but they can do alright if they don't blow it all on booze and gamblin'. It's the shop and bar owners who make most of the coin, and they dress the part—Ferenci silk and Astengi leather. Most got places on Johnson and Center, with a few runnin' the bigger joints down on Water Street near the Docks. Owners carry lots of clout. 'Course, even they hafta answer to Big Billy Johnson.

"Big Billy runs this town. Nothin' comes ashore without his say; all the food and clothes and booze go through him. He gets a cut of everythin', and the Corp'ration pays him to make sure supplies get across the bridges. Billy's the boss, lets everyone know it, too. Each month he brings in fighters from all over to his warehouse on Water Street, the Cauldron. When you're ready, I'll take you there."

Arti's first full day on the island was long and exhausting, making her realize just how much she had to learn from Gal. Returning to the safety of the records room, they shared a loaf of bread so stale Arti thought she might chip a tooth. Then, under the white glow of the gas lamp, she honored her agreement with Gal, reading the first chapter of *The King's Errand*.

Gal was captivated by the story of Ward Weatherington and his world, utterly amazed that a city full of people could inhabit a few thin pages, that some simple marks on paper could describe a life so vivid and real. She could see, feel, and smell everything Ward did, even sharing in his thoughts. Gal studied Arti's face as she read the tale, awed by the strange alchemy of its words, an eager apprentice to its magic.

"It ain't fair," said Gal, after Arti finished the opening chapter, closing the book on the mark. Gal's lip quivered as she stared at the floor, unable to shake the image of Ward and his little brother weeping over their dead mother. "They're just kids."

"It's only a story," said Arti. "Don't worry; things will get better for Ward and Petey." She caught herself, "Well, after a while, anyway."

It wasn't enough to put Gal at ease. "Why would he write somethin' like that?" she asked. "Why would he want to make people feel bad?"

"So you'd remember what it's like to feel happy, I guess," answered Arti. "Bad things have to happen for you to appreciate the good things."

"But what if you ain't had many good things?" asked Gal.

This time, Arti didn't have an answer.

# CHAPTER 5

Over the next several days, Arti and Gal's routine was the same. The morning started with Gal's lessons in front of the broken chalkboard, Arti her patient teacher. In the afternoon, their roles were reversed, Gal showing Arti how to survive on Isle's mean streets. And every evening ended with another chapter of *The King's Errand*.

The hardship experienced by Ward Weatherington and his little brother, Petey, was almost too much for Gal to bear. At the end of chapter three she declared she'd had enough, that the story was stupid, the author was full of crap, and she didn't want to hear any more. The next evening, she begged Arti to continue.

After Ward found the sparkling blue Wizard's Gem in chapter four, Gal talked for over an hour about all the things she'd do if she could be invisible. Most were illegal. When Ward left the king on his mission to steal the map from the evil wizard, Rancoram, Gal hugged her pillow so hard it would never regain its shape. She was utterly silent for three straight chapters, listening breathlessly as the hero made his way through the pitch-blackness of the Blood Monster's labyrinth, knowing the horrible eyeless creature could be waiting around the next corner, ready to pounce in a flash of fangs and claws.

And though she'd never admit it, Gal developed a serious crush on the book's young protagonist. A handsome and witty thief with a magic gem that made him invisible, what wasn't to love?

As she listened to the tale unfold, it became apparent to Gal how great a gift Arti was giving her. She wanted more than ever to be able to read stories on her own, to accompany other characters on other adventures in other worlds. And to that end, she was making great progress.

Arti was impressed by Gal's intelligence and the speed at which she learned. The twelve-year-old made her share of mistakes along the way, but in no time, she knew the alphabet and the sounds the letters made. What really pleased Arti was how much pride Gal took in her education. One afternoon while walking down Driftwood Avenue in the west end of the city, she looked up at an old, rusted shop sign and sounded out the letters, "S...m...i...ths—Smiths." Arti had never seen a smile so full of joy. And though she could still get frustrated at times (needing to be reminded that cursing didn't make things easier), it was clear just how much the gift of reading meant to Gal.

Arti was also proving to be a good student. Isle was no longer the disorienting maze it had once been. She could now remember the location of places—the shops, buildings, and landmarks—and could navigate her way around the island without getting lost. Gal had shown her every part of the city numerous times, and Arti realized how distinct each area was. North of Center Street, a wide road that ran east and west, dividing the island, was mostly residential. Or, at least it was a quarter century ago. Now most of the homes, town and row houses of wood and brick, were vacant shells missing doors and windows, stripped of anything that could fuel a fire, be traded, or sold. The few dwellings still inhabited by Isle residents were piecemeal creations, a mishmash of salvaged materials plundered from neighboring abodes, monstrosities sewn together with scraps and wire.

The western part of the city—from Mill to Cobden Street—was much more spread out. Homes sat on larger lots with retail parks plunked in between. Abandoned car dealerships and building supply stores were a testament to the city's first years of consumerism and expansion in the days before Main was born. On the westernmost tip of the island, a high rocky cliff jutted out into the Avalon River like the bow of a great ship. Known as the Lookout, it had once been used as a vantage point by smugglers to signal ships approaching from upriver, telling them it was safe to come ashore at Smugglers Bay or warn them of a Shore Guard cutter lying in wait.

Learning about the city wasn't enough; Arti had to know how to survive here. Her education took a giant leap the first time Gal had her act as the "bumper" for a pick-pocketing run on the end of Market Street, close to the Docks.

Gal selected the targets, and it was Arti's job to distract the unwary victims. An "accidental" bump followed by an indignant protest worked best, but Gal warned Arti that marks had to be chosen carefully. Communication and teamwork were vital if they were to avoid getting caught.

"Never steal from a local," she said. "They'll remember you. Be careful pickin' your marks, and always be ready to run if things go to crap." Then Gal made Arti repeat "The Rule" if ever a bump and grab went wrong: "Get away, and get home."

Their first partnership in theft went off without a hitch. The shift whistle had just sounded across from the Cauldron and a steady stream of workers flowed up from the Docks, some heading home, most making a beeline for one of the many watering holes on the way. Amidst the shuffling mass of overalls and work boots, Gal spotted a young wide-eyed, wispy haired sailor looking around as if he was lost. Facing Water Street, Gal was leaning against the wall next the front door of The Sea Dog, a dirty old saloon plopped on the corner of the block with a boarded-up side entrance on Market Street. From under her tilted cap, she watched as the sailor approached, satisfied he was a good mark.

Gal walked past the corner a few steps ahead of the sailor then stopped to tie her shoe. The moment her fingers touched the laces, Gal looked to her right and winked to a hooded Arti who waited a few paces down the saloon's wall, hoping she would remember the instructions: "You don't move 'til I touch my shoe laces. Then three steps, and you're into him. Make it look like you're surprised, and give him crap to throw him off. One, two, three, bump. Got it?"

Arti timed the contact perfectly. Stepping between Gal and the corner of the building, the young sailor stiffened at seeing Arti appear from nowhere. His thin arms came up defensively, and he shuffled to the side, unable to avoid contact with her. Arti pretended to be offended by his clumsiness, throwing insults at the red-faced youth as he apologized profusely. In a kind of ballet, Gal swiftly rose to her feet, moving in close behind the young man, shadowing him as he spun to avoid Arti, small hands deftly working his pockets. Oblivious to Gal's handiwork, the sailor never looked back, quickening his pace down Water Street, eager to escape the confrontation.

Gal kept her eyes on the mark as he scurried down the street. "Two Crenchy silvers," she whispered, jingling them in her pocket. She winked at her accomplice, "Not bad."

Arti's first theft was both a triumph and a tragedy. Her technique had been sound, and she and Gal would eat well tonight. But the thought of the young sailor discovering his misfortune plagued her. She didn't like what she had done to him, and her shame lingered.

An hour after their success with the young sailor, they returned to work the same corner. Gal was against the wall, eyeing the action on Water Street, when she noticed a group of men approaching. Two of the men walked together, with another trailing behind, not part of the group. The front pair looked like dockers, probably finishing their shift late. They were locals, not to be messed with. The third man seemed out of place. Gal thought he might be a trader or a passenger on one of the freighters. He staggered a little, already in his cups and probably heading for more. That meant he'd have coin. He wasn't very big, and the drink would make him less of a threat. Gal marked him.

She walked ahead of the first two men and, clearing the corner, dropped to one knee, waiting for them to pass before giving Arti the signal to advance on the third. *You don't move 'til I touch my shoe laces.*

It didn't register with Arti that Gal's hands had not yet fallen to her foot. Forcing thoughts of the young sailor from her mind, she took a deep breath and started to move, her heart thumping with each step.

One. Two. Three.

Gal tried to wave Arti off, but the warning went unnoticed. Arti arrived at the corner, just as the first two men came around it. The contact was more violent than she had planned. She ploughed into the man closest to the wall; he was big and solid and gave no ground. Instead of avoiding Arti, he grabbed and held her. Arti cast a panicked look at Gal, and the big man followed her eyes, immediately making the connection.

"Why you little rats! Thought you'd try my pockets, eh?"

The big docker clenched his hands tightly around Arti's arms, forcing her back against the wall. He hollered to his friend to grab Gal, but she was already running—not away, but toward him. From behind, she kicked the big man between the legs, and he folded over, releasing Arti.

"Run!" yelled Gal. Arti didn't need to be told twice. She rounded the corner and raced east down Water Street, her hood bouncing behind her.

"Get her!" screamed the man from his knees, and his friend was off. He then turned to Gal, eyes red with rage. "As for you, you little beggar…"

He surprised her by quickly gaining his feet and began to chase Gal with a speed faster than his size suggested was possible. Gal sprinted across Water Street, heading south toward the Docks, the big man close behind.

Thanks to Gal, Arti knew the island well, including the best places to lose someone. Even so, it took a while to evade her pursuer. It wasn't until she crossed First Street, slipping through a narrow gap in a broken fence beside Warren's Odds and Ends, that her pursuer decided she wasn't worth the trouble. But the chase had really scared her, almost as much as the night she escaped the Incendi on the West Bridge. Gal had saved Arti that night, and now her friend's words kept her feet moving: *Get away, and get home.*

Gal had been chased many times before, but never with as much determination. The big man followed her south across Water Street and even climbed under the pier after her. But it was a lost cause for him from that point on. Gal's surefootedness on the wooden substructure made it impossible for the angry docker to keep up. It was like a bear chasing a squirrel through a tree. He finally gave in with a curse and a warning.

"If I ever see you on the street, you're dead, kid!"

Arti waited for over an hour outside the records room, her thoughts darkening with the halls around her. *I messed up,* she thought. *I messed up, and Gal got caught.* With her face buried in her hands, Arti imagined all the terrible things that might have happened to her friend, each more horrible than the last. Then, like an apparition, Gal silently emerged from the shadows, stern-faced as she reached for the key around her neck.

When Arti saw her, she sighed with relief. "Thank god, you're okay. I...I thought—"

"No you didn't." Gal scowled as she inserted the key in the lock. "And it almost cost us—big time!" She pushed hard on the door and stormed past Arti. A moment later, lamplight filled the room.

"I'm really sorry," pleaded Arti, following Gal inside. Her hands were raised as if that would help her cause. "I should have waited. I wasn't watching...I..." her words trailed off, then the admission came: "I don't like stealing from people."

Gal looked at Arti as if she had two heads. "Do you think I *like* stealin'? Do you? I do it cuz I hafta. I do it cuz I gotta eat." She lifted the water jug from the table and took a swig. "Ward Weatherin'ton got it right: Steal or starve."

For the rest of the night, Gal refused to speak to Arti, and *The King's Errand* stayed closed. It was a hard lesson, but Arti knew Gal was right. Life on Isle was not about what was right or wrong; it was about survival. You did what you had to do to make it to the next day—plain and simple. It made Arti realize just how impossible her goal of saving her parents was. Taking coins from sailors' pockets was difficult enough. How could she ever think she'd be able to rescue prisoners from the Incendi?

As hard as Arti and Gal worked the streets, they were barely able to keep their food and water stores stocked. They needed a bigger score and, lucky for them, an opportunity was coming to scrounge the richest and most dangerous hunting grounds of all. After a particularly light supper that left their stomach's growling, Gal leaned over the table and shared the plan with Arti.

"We're gonna try the Cauldron," she said. "But there's some things you need to know."

"The Cauldron?" repeated Arti, "The big warehouse on Water Street where they have the fights?"

"That's it," said Gal. "Right across from the Docks. Big Billy's holdin' a match there tomorrow night. Heard a couple dockers talkin' about it. They said Big Billy's got somethin' special planned. It'll be *real* crowded, everyone pressed up against each other, most of them pissed to the eyeballs. We could play dice in their pockets, and they wouldn't notice."

"Sounds easy," said Arti.

Gal frowned. "Not if we get caught. It's a rough crowd—not to mention Big Billy's goons. A couple months ago they caught a kid stealin' and cut one of his fingers off. We're gonna hafta be real...s-m-r-t." Gal tried to keep a straight face but couldn't. "Just kiddin'," she said. "You taught me better than that."

# CHAPTER 6

Gal's plan was to work the crowd outside the Cauldron's main doors. She knew from experience that the fights always drew big numbers, and it would take a while for all the spectators to squeeze their way inside. Those waiting to enter would be in close quarters, so a fair bit of jostling was to be expected, a perfect opportunity to separate the patrons from their money. And being outside offered Gal and Arti a chance to flee, should anyone notice what they were up to.

"It'll be a regular bump and grab," said Gal. "But this ain't Market Street. We gotta be extra careful pickin' the marks. One mistake could cost us a finger—or worse."

To their delight, the scrounging outside the Cauldron went better than Gal and Arti could have dreamed, though the close contact with so many people—most with breath that smelled like turpentine—made Arti cringe. The girls waited for the line at the main door to build before working the crowd from one end to the other. On a signal from Gal, Arti, hair and face hidden within her hood, distracted the marks with a push, while her smaller partner deftly liberated coins from their unprotected pockets.

One pass proved to be enough. Gal and Arti made more money in those twenty minutes than they had in two weeks. The throng of patrons had become so large and the ability to move among them so difficult that another pass would have been too risky; they wouldn't be able to get away if they had to.

"Can't wait to see how much we made," said Gal, patting her bulging pockets. "What a haul!"

"Let's go," said Arti, "before someone wonders why we're just standing here." She noticed that one of the bouncers at the door was taking an interest in them.

"We ain't goin' home yet," said Gal. "Follow me."

Gal led Arti around the back of the Cauldron to an old metal ladder attached to the warehouse wall. It ran up the side of the building to a small platform and what appeared to be a sliding door with a padlock on it. Without explanation, Gal started to climb the ladder, leaving Arti below.

"What are you doing?" Arti hissed, looking around to make sure no one was watching. She heard a low roar come from inside the building.

"I wanna see the fights," came the answer. "Come on!"

"It's locked," Arti protested. But again, she had underestimated Gal. Her partner in crime removed the dummy padlock and waved it at Arti in that *Don't be an idiot* way of hers, before pushing open the door. Arti rolled her eyes and started to climb.

Arriving at the platform, she stepped through the opening, and Gal slid the door closed behind her. The air was stifling, carrying a pungent mix of sweat and alcohol, and the buffeting noise of thousands of men eager for violence.

Gal turned and started walking along a wide steel girder about forty feet above the sea of spectators until she came to another platform suspended over a central raised ring around which the crowd was densely packed. Watching her scamper across the beam reminded Arti of the night she first met her at the West Bridge, how easy the girl had moved among its spider web of supports. *She's had lots of practice.*

Gal waved Arti on, and balancing with her arms held out from her sides, she carefully crossed the span to the platform.

"Best seats in the house," Gal declared, sprawling on her side and looking down at the ring below.

"I don't know if I want to see this," said Arti, taking a place beside Gal with some hesitation. "I'm not big on fighting."

Gal looked at Arti like she had two heads. "What? The fights are one of the only good things about this town." She paused, seeing the squeamish look on Arti's face. "It won't be that bad, just a bit of blood. Look away if you hafta."

A ribbon of tobacco smoke hung in the warm, moist air. Through the wispy cloud, strings of incandescent lights dangled from rusty steel girders, bathing the canvas stage in a warm yellow glow, illuminating the faces of the restless audience crowded around it. There were so many people crammed into the warehouse that most found it difficult to move. A push or a shove often resulted in an elbow or a punch, brawls breaking out like bubbles in a boiling pot. Any prolonged wars over territory were extinguished by the bouncers, but occasionally, a particularly enthusiastic patron would receive a good clubbing before being dragged to the door and tossed into the street. The stench and heat only added to the throng's discomfort and aggression. Arti wondered how many of the angry outbursts were the result of men reaching into their pockets, only to discover that their money was gone—now in the possession of the two girls sprawled on the platform high above them.

A bell rang, and the restless crowd answered it with a deafening roar of approval. Bodies ebbed and flowed like waves washing against the sides of the raised ring. A tall, gangly referee with grey stubble on his head and chin stepped through the ropes onto the canvas stage, escorting the first pair of combatants.

They were small, wiry men about Arti's size. One was fair-skinned, the other a shade darker than Gal. Barefoot and dressed only in baggy shorts that hung to their knees, they bounced up and down, swinging their arms back and forth, faces frozen in steely determination, animal ferocity burning in their eyes. The crowd became quiet as the referee pointed to the fair-skinned fighter, his raspy voice rising above the din of the crowd.

"In this corner, from Crent, with ten wins and one loss, Mori 'Little Tiger' Igumi!"

Half of the spectators screamed their approval, apparently backing the slender easterner.

"And in this corner, from the Astengan port of Valeeza, with twenty-six wins and two losses, Neeka 'The Viper' Cominell!"

A second explosion of cheers erupted from the Astengan's supporters. More pushing and shoving ensued, and another small riot next the ring was beaten down by the bouncers.

With a signal from the referee the bell sounded again, and the tiny gladiators flew at each other. Arti couldn't believe how fast the two men moved. Flurries of kicks, chops, and punches came in lightning flashes. The combat carried them back and forth across the ring; first one was the aggressor, then the other. Each man had his own style. The Little Tiger employed a formal martial art—balanced kicks and punches—while the Viper spun, bent, and cartwheeled around his opponent, delivering strikes from all angles. The action continued for a few minutes without pause, and no quarter was offered by either combatant.

"Who do you think's gonna win?" asked Gal, without lifting her eyes from the ring below.

Arti was so absorbed in the action that it took her a moment to acknowledge the question. "I...I don't know. They're both so fast."

Just then, the fighter from Crent kicked the Astengan square in the jaw, sending him sprawling on the mat. The crowd roared again, and Arti immediately amended her statement.

"He is. The Little Tiger."

Gal turned to Arti. "Wanna bet?"

Arti looked at Gal, puzzled by the challenge. Couldn't she see what was happening? The Viper was down, and he would have to concede the match or risk further injury. Ignoring the little voice in her head that warned of another Gal trick, Arti accepted the gamble.

"Okay. What's the wager?"

"The loser's gotta fill the bucket for the crapper the next three times," replied Gal. She held out her hand, waiting for Arti to accept.

Arti almost laughed out loud. If there was one chore she hated, it was lugging the bucket full of water all the way from the canal to the school.

"Fine," she said, shaking Gal's hand. But as soon as the contract was sealed, a devious smile appeared on her young friend's face.

After a celebratory lap of the ring, arms raised in triumph, the Little Tiger moved in to finish off his injured adversary, leaning over the Astengan's prone body, slowly raising a leg above the helpless man's head, playing to the crowd. Arti covered her face with her hands, not wishing to witness the strike, but curiosity got the best of her, and she peeked through her fingers. A chant was now echoing through the warehouse: *Tiger! Tiger! Tiger!*

There were other voices below the clamor, warning the Little Tiger that he was leaving himself open for attack, that his overconfidence was a mistake. The caution went unheeded, and just before the Crentian could answer his fans and deliver the final blow, the Viper rolled backward into a somersault, kicking out his legs in a scissor movement, ratcheting them around the Little Tiger's neck. With a sudden jerk, the Crentian was hurled to the mat, his back hitting the floor so hard the slap of skin against canvas could be heard by everyone in the building. He remained motionless as the Viper sprung to his feet, raising his hands in victory. The referee, kneeling next the unconscious man, concurred, pointing to the Astengan. A new chant reverberated through the warehouse, so loud it seemed as if the roof might collapse on top of Arti and Gal: *Viper! Viper! Viper!*

"Will he be okay?" asked Arti, above the din.

"He'll be fine," said Gal, nonchalantly. Under the care of the referee, the Crentian was now stirring, confused and disoriented. "See, he just got his bell rung."

Arti turned on Gal. "You knew it was trick. Didn't you?"

Gal started laughing. "The Viper did the same thing to a Verinese fighter a year ago. Can't believe the Crenchy fell for it."

"That's not fair," protested Arti. "You cheated!"

"I didn't cheat," replied Gal, shrugging off the accusation. "I just did what you always tell me to do. I made an... etchacated guess."

Arti smiled and rolled her eyes. "Call it what you want, but I'm not filling the pail the next three times."

"Twice then," offered Gal. "I wasn't *sure* the Viper was fakin'."

Arti relented. "Okay, twice. But I'm going to get you back." She narrowed her eyes at Gal. "When you least expect it."

The following two fights, although not nearly so dramatic as that of the lightweight match, were even more brutal. One featured two North Verinese middleweights exchanging heavy blows for a full twenty minutes before the bell sounded, and the referee declared the fight a draw. The warriors staggered from the ring on the arms of supporters, each vowing loudly to finish the fight—inside or outside the ring. The next bout, a heavyweight grudge match between two Isle dockers, was conceded when one of the fighters received a bone crushing knee to his ribs that resulted in a punctured lung. The loser was lifted from the ring spitting mouthfuls of blood and gasping for air, causing the final match to be delayed while the crimson puddles were mopped away. Arti was sickened by the sight and had to avert her eyes and breathe slowly to quell her nausea. When she recovered enough to speak, she pleaded with Gal to leave, but her protests fell on deaf ears. The next match was the big event, the one Gal heard the dockers talking about. She wasn't going anywhere.

On the thick arms of two rough looking brutes, a round, stunted man was lifted to the ring, bending awkwardly between the ropes.

"That's him," hissed Gal. "That's Big Billy."

Billy Johnson, the undisputed boss of Isle and proprietor of the Cauldron, waddled to the center of the canvas stage and lifted a stubby arm. A hush fell over the crowd.

"It's time for the main event, friends!" he shouted in his heavy North Verinese accent. The pitch of the little man's voice rose as he spoke, the last word ending on a high note that soared up through the rafters where Arti and Gal were sitting. "And I promise you won't soon forget it." A smile crossed the little man's face, and his eyes sparkled with delight. "Even the Cauldron has yet to see two throwers the likes o' these."

He pointed to one side of the ring. "In this corner, from the highlands of Parmell, with a record of fifty-three wins and no losses, all by knockout, 'The Canvas Scourge', Rangal 'The Mountain' Rogan!"

A man of unbelievable proportions squeezed through the ropes. Even those onlookers too drunk to string three coherent words together were suddenly sobered by the sight of the giant from the East. With arms the size of tree trunks and a barrel chest rippling with muscles, he towered over Big Billy like an oak tree next a shrub. The Mountain's face was covered in scars, and the crooked remnant of a nose divided a pair of heavy lidded eyes. At first, he smiled, displaying a mouth devoid of teeth. Then he roared—for that was surely what it sounded like—as he flexed his muscles for the astonished crowd.

Big Billy pointed to the corner opposite The Mountain's, waiting for the crowd to quiet down.

"And in this corner, a newcomer to the ring, from the Ferencian island of Maren," Billy's eyes lit up with joyous anticipation. "The Poet!"

There was a confused murmur from the spectators as a lean young man stepped nimbly into the ring, shirtless beneath a black leather jacket. As handsome as any linkshow actor, he had slicked back brown hair and smiling blue eyes that regarded the audience with a mix of curiosity and humor.

"Gotta be some kinda joke," said Gal, glancing at Arti. "He's gonna get pounded."

Arti didn't know much about fighting, but it was obvious how mismatched the two were. No one in his right mind would believe the young Ferencian had a chance against an opponent as massive and powerful as The Mountain. She knew she should leave rather than witness the slaughter but couldn't lift her eyes from the ring.

The Poet slid the leather jacket from his arms and laid it carefully over the ring's thick iron corner post. His tan skin glowed under the lights, and a large tattoo glistened on his back. From Arti's vantage point high above the ring, she could see it was some kind of cup covered in swirling black lines. The young man ran through his warm-up routine, odd stretching movements that drew laughter and insults from the belligerent crowd.

"This ain't no ballet, boy!" yelled one onlooker.

"Rogan's gonna have fun with you, kid!" bellowed another. "Better run home to your momma!"

The bell rang, and the young man walked toward the center of the ring as calmly as one might stroll through a park. The Mountain was waiting for him there, a sadistic grin etched on his mutilated face.

"Yer a real priddy boy, arn ya?" said Rogan. A deep, rumbling avalanche of laughter spilled from The Mountain's lips. "Ya wone be priddy when I'm dun wid ya."

The Poet answered the threat in verse, a translation of Old Ferencian, the words strangely melodic and gentle: "Into the eyes of evil, a knight must peer. Holding fast to his honor, shedding all fear."

Arti couldn't hear what the young man said to the Parmelese giant, but whatever it was, she could tell it enraged him. He lunged at The Poet, but the young man evaded him with an impossibly quick sideways movement. When the referee tried to intervene, The Mountain flung him out of the way with a sweep of his massive arm. Landing in a tangled heap against the ropes, the official started to rise, but a murderous look from Rogan made him decide that it wasn't a good idea. With a curt shake of his head, the referee signaled Big Billy that he would not return, and a roar from the crowd supported his decision. This would be a fight without authority, without rules, without mercy.

The Mountain lumbered after The Poet, fists raised in front of him like battering rams. The young man mouthed something and spun away from the charge, landing a powerful kick to the giant's knee. Rogan staggered for an instant, more inconvenienced than hurt by the strike. He growled at The Poet and, with surprising speed for a man so massive, swung around at him with a backhand blow that narrowly missed its mark. The young man arched his back, dropping below the strike. Then he rolled across the floor, rising again with arms crossed, a contemplative smile on his handsome young face. The ensuing laughter from the crowd only made The Mountain angrier.

Rogan moved in on his quarry again, this time ensuring that escape was impossible. The Poet cautiously backed away from the giant and was soon out of canvas, his tattooed back pressed against the ropes. There wasn't one person watching who thought he had any chance of surviving the avalanche of Parmelese flesh that now loomed over him. The cheers and taunts that had filled the warehouse faded away in anticipation of the young Ferencian's demise. For Arti, this was even worse than seeing the blood spilled in previous matches. She was sure the handsome fighter was going to die in front of her.

Then she saw his lips move again.

Although their vantage point was the same, Arti and Gal would argue over what happened next. Gal was sure the young Ferencian used a weapon against The Mountain, something carefully concealed in his fist. Arti disagreed; she saw something else, something much stranger and harder to explain. It happened very fast, but she was sure she saw a faint aura envelope the young man, a cloak of energy barely noticeable against the backdrop of the cream-colored canvas. Somehow, The Poet focused it through his fist into the broad chest of his opponent, throwing the huge man backward across the ring, following the punch with a spinning kick so powerful it drove Rogan through the ropes, leveling the first three rows of spectators.

"That's crazy," barked Gal, sliding the door closed behind her, quieting the raucous cries still echoing through the Cauldron. She replaced the dummy lock and waited for Arti to start down the ladder. It was not yet dark, and having checked that the alley was clear, the girls were eager to get home and count their coin.

"I'm just telling you what I saw," said Arti, carefully placing her hands and feet on the rungs as she descended. "I know it sounds weird."

"You're just sayin' that cuz you thought he was good lookin'," teased Gal. "I saw how you stared at him."

Arti felt her face flush and was glad Gal couldn't see her embarrassment. "You thought so, too," she said, covering for herself. "Admit it."

"He was alright," said Gal, "but not my type."

"And what type is that?" laughed Arti, arriving at the ground.

Gal landed like a cat beside her. "Rich," she said.

Arti lifted her hood and walked with Gal toward the front of the warehouse, wading into the river of people that flowed out from the main doors of the building. They arrived at the sidewalk with the departing crowd, one stream of patrons crossing Water Street south toward the Docks, the other heading east and west. Carried along in the human current, the girls moved in the direction of the setting sun toward Hill Street and home.

As they neared the corner, Arti noticed a tall, slender figure standing on the raised step of a tackle shop studying the passing mob. Strands of blonde hair poked out from beneath his flattened cap. He wore a loose grey jacket, ill-fitting pants, and a pair of polished black leather boots that shone in the twilight. The man's eyes moved back and forth, scanning each face as it passed. They were eyes Arti had seen before—once on the West Bridge over a month before and numerous times since in the dark recesses of her dreams.

Arti stopped suddenly, grabbing Gal's arm. "It's him," she hissed. "The Flame!"

As one man grumbled at them for blocking the sidewalk and another cursed and pushed them aside, Gal took over, leading Arti back the way they had come, weaving through the crowd, guiding her into a darkened doorway sheltered from the street.

"Flames ain't supposed to be on this side of the canal," declared Gal. "Big Billy don't allow it."

"Well, he's here," objected Arti. "And he's looking for someone."

"Who?" asked Gal.

Arti collapsed against the door with a fearful sigh. "Me."

# CHAPTER 7

Floating like an angel in front of the glowing green screen, the pretty young woman smiled and reached out, pretending to pluck something from the air, extending her hand toward the camera.

"A picture is worth a thousand words. Show, don't tell. *You* are the Corporation."

The red light went out, and the director skipped across the granite floor, fists raised in triumph. "You nailed it, Gwen. You are a star, baby!"

She resisted the urge to laugh at the chubby little man in his ridiculous cap and scarf. *What's so impressive about saying the same stupid lines for the millionth time?* But she held her smile and swallowed her pride. As much as she detested her celebrity image, she knew it was a part she must play.

"We'll break for lunch," announced the director in a high-pitched squeal. "I want everyone back in half an hour. We have the *Eyes on the Prize* promo to shoot this afternoon, so I expect everyone to be their best." He winked at Gwen, making it clear his pep talk wasn't directed at her. Victor Herrat may have been eccentric, but he wasn't stupid; he would never risk offending his star performer. Like Gwen's parents, he used every opportunity to capitalize on her fame and better his own position. He softened his voice, "Will you join me for lunch, Gwen? I've had Reginald prepare something special."

"Thank you, Victor," Gwen replied with as much arrogance as she could muster, "but I need a little time."

"Of course, of course," said Herrat politely. "I understand completely." He clapped his hands. "Out! Out! Let's give Ms. Degan some peace." Gwen smiled appreciatively at the director, perfectly masking her disdain.

The entourage hurried to leave the studio, and when Gwen heard the clanging sound of the elevator doors closing, she grabbed her shoulder bag from her dressing room cupboard and made her way into the hall. There were three separate areas on the third floor of the old castle, a level below that of CEO Fay's expansive tower suite. The studio was the one nearest the main building, and the Incendi laid claim to the other two, identified by the gold flame insignias painted on their inky-black doors.

The larger of the spaces occupied by the Corporation's secret police functioned as its headquarters, the nerve center that received decap and reader alerts, dispatching Incendi on raids and arrests. Black-clad troopers came and went at all hours by way of the tower's spiraling stone staircase, original to the ancient structure. There were rumors that it led all the way down to a dungeon deep beneath the castle, a dark and damp place where the most dangerous readers and scribes were imprisoned—before they disappeared entirely.

The narrow second room wedged between the police headquarters and the studio was called the Archive, off limits to all but the Incendi captain, Mordred. No one was to access it without his permission, and no one ever did—except Gwen Degan.

She walked casually to the door, checking the hall again to make sure no one was coming. Gwen felt the familiar rush of adrenaline, the fluttering heart and shallow breaths that always accompanied these risky forays. The door had no lock; it didn't need one. No one else was crazy enough to defy Mordred's orders.

Established by Morgan Fay when her company was formed, the Archive contained a collection of the world's most dangerous books and was not a place that someone in her right mind would choose to go. Gwen first found the courage to enter it four years before, shortly after her acting career began, and every time she stood in front of the black door with its golden flame, she remembered that day and how her life changed forever...

*Using the soft light of her vidlink to guide her, Gwen edged her way inside, careful to make sure the heavy door didn't make a sound as it closed. She knew she shouldn't be doing this; it was insane, suicide.*

*Just beyond the threshold, something caught her eye. Lying flat on a shelf, it was square in shape and not much larger than her hand, covered in strange symbols and bright, colorful images: an apple, a ball, a cat. Similar objects of varying sizes and thicknesses were stacked next to it, leaning against one another along the length of the shelf, disappearing into the darkness. Her throat constricted with fear, and she felt as if she might faint.*

Books!

*The tiny tome with the apple, ball, and cat on its cover
called to Gwen, begging to be taken. She reached out to it,
caressing its surface gently with her fingertips, wondering
how anything so delicate and pretty could be threatening.
She lifted it from the shelf and turned it over in her hands.
A lifetime of warnings echoed in her mind, fourteen years of
fear and paranoia surfacing at once. People caught with books
vanished, never to be seen again. It made her decision to slip
the little book into her pocket all the more remarkable.*

*That evening, alone in her bedroom, Gwen stared at
the book for over an hour before finding her courage again.*
I'll just look inside. Nothing bad will happen. *She carefully
pried open the cover and was relieved when she suffered no
sudden bout of illness or pain. That initial success gave her
more courage, and moments later, she was leafing through
the tiny tome's pages.*

*There were twenty-six of them in all, each inscribed
with a picture and a group of strange symbols. They were
like puzzles to Gwen, mysteries to be solved. She studied the
figures under the soft glow of her vidlink screen, still afraid
that the illicit activity would somehow be discovered, that her
parents would become suspicious and confront her, or that a
squad of Incendi troopers would smash down her bedroom
door and take her away.*

*With her ability to instantly memorize images and
shapes, it took less than two weeks for Gwen to crack the book's
code. She guessed that the first symbol on each page stood for
the beginning sound in the corresponding picture's name. It
followed that the remaining symbols, together, sounded out
the rest. Gwen studied each page, all twenty-six characters, in*

*order, and the sounds they made. Her dedication and desire to learn were without limit, and though she knew what she was doing was a serious crime with grave consequences, she couldn't stop. After many hours of experimentation, trial and error, failed theories and accidental triumphs, fourteen-year-old Gwen Degan taught herself to read.*

*Once she had learned everything she could from the tiny book of letters, Gwen returned it to the Archive, trading it for another. Week after week, month after month, year after year, she secretly paroled one incarcerated work after another. At first, she chose books with colorful covers and large print, their stories filling her with joy and amazement. Each night she would read until tired eyes betrayed her. Then, hiding the book in her closet, she would live out the stories in her imagination. Heroes, wizards, princesses, and queens; all were roles she assumed with wondrous abandon in the ethereal universe of dreams.*

*As Gwen matured, so did her tastes. Fiction was her greatest love, but she also became fascinated by works of philosophy, history, math, and science. She enjoyed exploring new landscapes of ideas, discovering something precious on each journey. Her astounding memory allowed her to recall every word and phrase long after she'd read them, and she would often cross-reference one author's words with another to construct her own understanding of the subject matter. But that was more a side effect than a motive for reading. To Gwen, books were doorways into worlds of wonder, every work possessing its own magic, its own reason to risk everything to visit its pages...*

She closed the door quietly behind her, holding the vidlink like a lantern, its weak light pushing back the darkness.

As always, she was greeted by the tiny book of letters in its place nearest the door, an old friend welcoming her back. She edged her way down the narrow corridor between the three levels of rainbow colored bindings, looking for the small wedge of paper she had left as a marker the week before. Locating it halfway down the second shelf, Gwen removed *Villion's Ethics* from her shoulder bag and carefully returned it to its place. The two-hundred-year old text, a translation from the original Crentian, had been a fascinating read, with its perspectives on freedom, choice, and liberty—concepts strangely foreign to the world Gwen lived in. It gave her an appetite for something older.

Her eyes went to a stack of worn leather-backed tomes at the end of the bottom shelf farthest from the door. One grabbed Gwen's attention, the strange symbols on its spine making her wonder what ancient secrets awaited her inside. The book's cover was stuck to those beside it, and it took some effort for her to pull it free. She placed the paper marker where the book had been and adjusted the adjacent volumes to fill the void.

Slipping the book into her shoulder bag, Gwen quietly shuffled back to the Archive door. She put her ear to the cold steel and listened for any activity in the hall, voices or footsteps on the stone floor that might indicate someone's presence there. Hearing nothing, she opened the door a crack and listened again, peeking through the narrow opening to make sure the corridor was empty. With only the hum of the lights on the hall's ceiling disturbing the silence, Gwen was convinced it was safe to depart. In one fluid motion, holding her bag with its hidden treasure, she stepped into the hall and quietly closed the heavy black door behind her.

Back in the studio, Gwen set her bag with its precious contents in the cupboard of her dressing room. Relieved that her mission was complete, she sat down at her make-up table and closed her eyes until her heart stopped racing. Even though she had entered the Archive hundreds of times, she would never consider it routine, knowing what the consequences would be if she was caught. Gwen checked herself in the mirror, took a deep breath, and walked back to the set to wait for the director and his staff to return. Standing next the green screen was the last person she wanted to see.

Mordred looked at Gwen with amusement, knowing he had surprised her. She recovered from her initial shock, meeting his look with a submissive calm. Beneath the usual dread she felt in his presence was a question even more frightening: *Did he see me leave the Archive?*

"Hello, Miss Degan." Mordred smiled and nodded, the gold flame on his fedora shimmering under the studio lights. "It's been a while."

"Yes, Captain," was all Gwen could say. She felt a strange mix of relief and terror. *He doesn't know.*

"I hope I haven't caught you at a bad time," said Mordred. "I know how important your work is." He moved closer to her. "I'd hate to interfere."

"No," said Gwen, hiding her discomfort. "Your timing couldn't be better. The director and crew are at lunch, and I'm getting ready for the afternoon shoot."

"As professional as always," said Mordred. "We are much alike in our devotion."

Gwen smiled at the compliment. "My role is not nearly as important as yours, Captain. I feel safe knowing you are protecting us. Praise the Corporation."

It was a masterfully executed lie. She knew how dangerous the Incendi captain was, had heard the stories of his strange powers. They had come from reliable sources, troopers who witnessed them first-hand, hard men and women not prone to exaggeration. She would have dismissed them, otherwise. They all spoke of their captain's refusal to carry an electroshock baton, how he uttered strange words, disarming and disabling suspects with a speed and efficiency that seemed impossible.

"Praise the Corporation," repeated Mordred. "It is very kind of you to say…Gwen. I'm happy to know that I've given you comfort. Maybe we can—"

"Captain Mordred? Is that you? What a wonderful surprise!" Victor Herrat clapped his hands as he entered the studio, bouncing across the floor.

"Dear Director," said Mordred, calmly turning. "Good to see you again."

"To what do we owe the pleasure of your company?" asked Herrat, smiling as he frantically waved his entourage away.

Mordred never missed a beat. "CEO Fay has planned a very special event," he explained, "in celebration of our glorious Corporation's twenty-fifth anniversary." He looked at Gwen and smiled. "I was just discussing it with Miss Degan. I'd like her to share the good news with our citizens."

Herrat giggled. "A special event? How exciting! What has our beloved CEO planned?"

"A Lighting like no other, my dear Director, one that will burn more brightly than all that have come before." The studio lights danced across Mordred's golden flame, pleasure igniting his eyes. "This Corporation Night, the Archive will burn."

The Incendi captain's declaration staggered Gwen. The books in the Archive were the most important things in the world to her, and the thought of the collection being burned was too horrible to imagine. She pictured the little book of letters engulfed in flames. It made her want to scream.

"The Archive!" gasped Herrat. "It...it will be the greatest spectacle ever linked." The director could hardly contain his excitement. "Where will the Lighting take place?"

"On the clifftop," said Mordred, "so everyone in Tintagel—Main and Isle—can see the flames." He leaned toward the director and whispered, "CEO Fay will strike the match."

Herrat's eyes widened, and his mouth fell open. It was the first time Gwen had ever witnessed the man at a loss for words.

"And what will my role be in this?" Gwen asked feebly, breaking the silence.

Mordred smiled down at her. "You will tell the world that the day they have long waited for has come." There was a fanatical glow in his eyes. "The dawn of a new era."

Gwen hardly remembered leaving the studio. The Incendi captain was still discussing the details of the Lighting with Victor Herrat when she asked to be excused. Had she stayed a moment longer, she was sure she would have broken down in front of them.

Luckily, her parents were once again away on business and had left Gwen their car so she didn't have to call for one of the company limousines. She barely remembered stopping at the two gated security checkpoints on the curving drive leading down the hill from the castle. All she could do was look up dumbly at the Incendi guards and nod. Once they saw the linkstar's pretty face, the gates were quickly opened.

Gwen drove to her home in Rockcliff Park, an upscale neighborhood on the eastern edge of Main, exclusive to Fay executives and their families. A sleek new highway linked the gated community to the castle, so Gwen's commute took only minutes.

The house was a modern amalgam of stone and timber that reclined against a stony hill covered in tall pines. Gwen activated the automatic garage door opener and parked the car inside. Unlocking the door that joined the garage to the house, she passed through the kitchen on the way to her bedroom, slapping her vidlink down on the granite counter top, ignoring the red message light flashing on the refrigerator panel next a still image of her mother's smiling face.

The last thing she wanted to do was facelook with her parents; she knew how the conversation would go. First, they'd tell her how wonderful her last vidad was, and how countless people at the conference had requested her private link address so they could leave her a fanloop. Then they'd ask how her day at the studio went, addressing her as "Honey" and "Dear" to convince her they cared. They'd start talking softly in a tone one might use with an infant, but then they'd become more forceful and direct. Before long, their compliments and praise would morph into advice and criticism, leaving Gwen feeling more like an indentured servant than a beloved daughter.

Her father would tell her how important it was to network with as many of the studio executives as possible. "Your future depends on it," he would say, but Gwen was certain that he meant *his* future.

Gwen's mother was no better. She would tell Gwen to watch her diet, reminding her that beauty was everything in her line of work. Gwen knew the words by heart: "You've been blessed with good looks, Dear. Make them count, you won't be pretty forever."

The years of control and manipulation made Gwen realize she was just an investment to them, a piece of property whose value was expected to appreciate. Her parents didn't know who she really was, and they didn't care. As long as her fame kept them feeding at Morgan Fay's trough, they were content.

After turning on the bedroom light, she pulled the book from her bag and set it gently on the bed. Its cover was beautifully crafted in soft sheepskin dyed an earthy green. The bottom third was embossed with a cup of shimmering gold, and above it floated a tiny three-dimensional silver sword fastened tightly by a brass stud, the tip of its blade pointing up at the title, *The Knights of Maren*. Gwen wondered what it was about, feeling the same excitement that came every time she started a new book, the powerful mix of curiosity, anticipation, and wonder. Propping a pillow between her back and the headboard, she settled down for a long read, knowing it might be her last.

According to its title page, the book was over three hundred years old, a translation from an Old Ferencian original written by Guillaume de Lac. Gwen always tried to picture what an author looked like and how he might speak. "De Lac" had a wealthy, aristocratic ring to it, so she imagined a foreign noble with a neatly trimmed beard and manicured fingernails, elaborately dressed and formal. As she read the introduction, she could hear his accent and crisp diction, every word uttered with the precision and skill of a master orator.

Gwen read through the night, unable to put the book down. Compiled from over a thousand years of historical records, it was the story of a powerful warrior sect sworn to protect the most precious artifacts ever crafted by human hands: a pair of books written in antiquity on the Ferencian Island of Maren.

Identical in every way down to the smallest detail, they were known as the *Grail Tomes*, so called for the elaborate cup that adorned their covers. The tomes were the property of the Order of Librarians, an ancient guild of academics dedicated to the protection of the written word. The Order believed that every book possessed magic, its spell-like potency a product of the writer's craft. Fearing that a day would come when the very existence of books would be threatened and their magic lost, they began the laborious process of collecting all the great works, in every language and discipline, preserving them in libraries where their legacy could be shared.

And they commissioned the *Grail Tomes*.

Attributed to a pair of renowned scribes from Astenga and Crent, most of what was contained in the books remained a mystery. The first Knights of Maren were only permitted by the Order to study one of their chapters called *The Verses*, a collection of poems that greatly enhanced their fighting skills. In Old Ferencian, the martial art was called *farapenne de moets*, or *the strike of words*, but de Lac did not provide specific details about the method, saying only that the poems and the technique were passed down orally from one generation to the next. Governed by will and intention, words became an extension of a knight's body, a weapon precise and powerful— literally, poetry in motion. De Lac made the extraordinary claim that a single unarmed Knight of Maren could defeat ten armed men in combat. Gwen would have dismissed it all as the stuff of myth and legend, the romantic ramblings of a man in love with the past, had she not heard of something eerily similar happening now.

*Mordred.*

The Incendi captain's assaults on readers and scribes were just as de Lac described. "Farapenne de moets," she gasped, closing the book. "He does it with words."

Gwen stared down at the book's cover, at the silver sword and the golden cup. If she was right, it meant Mordred knew *The Verses*. But how? The Knights of Maren existed centuries ago, and even if they were still around, Gwen was sure they wouldn't share their secrets with someone like him; the Incendi captain didn't protect books, he burned them. There could only be one explanation.

*He has a Grail Tome!*

# CHAPTER 8

The girls' take at the Cauldron far exceeded their expectations, but they didn't feel like celebrating. Arti was sure she'd seen the Incendi captain, the same one who had taken her parents and burned her home. If he was still after her, she and Gal were in serious danger.

"I don't get it," said Gal, twisting the lid on a can of mixed vegetables until it snapped free. "He has to really want you bad to risk comin' here. It don't make no sense. You're sure it was him?"

"Yes. It was the Flame who was waiting for me at the bridge—the same one. I'll never forget him. He's scary, Gal. Really scary."

"He won't be so scary if Big Billy finds him on the island. The Corp'ration ain't supposed to mess with us. That's the deal Big Billy made with...whatsername."

"Morgan Fay."

Gal nodded. "Yeah, everyone calls her the Witch on the Hill. They say she spends all her time up there castin' spells."

Arti frowned at Gal, "You don't really believe that, do you?"

Gal reclined on the bench with her hands behind her head. "I ain't sayin' I believe it. I'm just tellin' you what people say."

Arti was going to add that there was no such thing as magic, but then she remembered what the Incendi officer did to her on the bridge. And what about her escape from the burning library? She only found her way through the smoke and flames because she thought she heard the books talk to her. What if it hadn't been her imagination?

"The bottom line is we can't let the Flame find you," said Gal. "So the Docks are off limits for a while. We'll scrounge the West End. There ain't as much coin to be made around Cobden and Driftwood, but it ain't likely he'll look for you there. And we got enough to last us a while." She mumbled through a mouthful of vegetables. "Now you know why I said your plan to go back into Main's crazy. Go anywhere near the bridges and you're dead meat. I ain't never heard of a Flame chasin' a reader like this; he must be real mad you got away."

"There has to be more to it than that," said Arti. She looked up at Gal with steely determination. "But I'm still going back."

"But it ain't...but you can't..." Gal realized it was useless. "Just give it a while," she relented, "'til the heat's off."

Winning the argument did little to raise Arti's spirits. Gal was right, if the Flame was still hunting her, the chances of getting off the island were bad enough. How could she think she'd be able to get to her parents, let alone save them? And what if it was already too late?

It was a possibility Arti refused to accept. *They're still there*. She couldn't let go of that last thread of hope, knowing that if she did the whole fabric of her life would come apart.

Arti looked up at *The King's Errand* resting on the shelf. There was only one chapter to go before she'd hand it over to Gal to finish. "I hope you don't mind," she said, "but I don't feel like reading tonight."

Unsettled by her sighting of the Incendi captain the night before, Arti slept late. It was almost noon by the time she and Gal arrived at Cobden Street near the island's western shore. Vacant lots covered in tall grass and saplings divided fields of crumbling asphalt backed by low rise buildings, shops and malls long since abandoned.

As they turned down Center Street, Gal pointed to a building with a towering steeple atop its arching front facade. All of the structure's windows were gone, and a tree was growing through the concrete base anchoring the large sign at its entrance. She read the words on the sign, pronouncing each syllable as Arti had taught her.

"The...Cam...el...Lot."

"That's right," praised Arti. "You're getting good." Gal winked back at her proudly.

Below the name, there was a cartoon image of a camel with an undulating back, words emerging in a bubble from its open mouth: "Buy at the Humps, Save at the Pumps." A couple old wrecks sat adjacent to the building, windshields smashed, hoods, doors, and wheels missing.

"They sold cars," said Arti.

"No kiddin'," chirped Gal. "How'd you figure that out?"

Arti stopped and put her hands on her hips in mock disgust. "You can be a real pain, you know that?"

They stepped over the low sill of one of the building's large front windows and began searching for anything of value that might have escaped the eyes of previous looters. The place had been stripped clean, only bits of wire and cable remained, hanging from its ceiling like metallic spider webs. While Gal explored one of the rooms, Arti walked down a long hallway until she came to an exit that opened onto a back lot. The steel door had been pulled from its jamb and hung precariously by a single rusty hinge.

A garage with three large open bays faced the broken door where Arti stood. Two of the cavernous spaces were empty, save for a few tangled birds' nests stuffed into crevices where the roof trusses and the block walls met. Arti was surprised to see a vehicle parked in the third bay, a box-shaped motorhome staring out from the shadows. Surprisingly, it appeared to be in good condition, with headlights and windows intact, and front tires that looked to be full of air. She guessed that it couldn't have been there long, or it would have been stolen or stripped.

As Arti pondered the unexpected presence of the motorhome, she noticed a man crossing the back lot, heading toward it. He looked to be in his late twenties or early thirties—though Arti had never been good at guessing people's ages—and he was dressed in a knit sweater and khaki pants. His hair was neatly cut and combed, and a small goatee adorned his chin. He looked around cautiously, then knocked on the motorhome's narrow side door, before entering the vehicle.

Curiosity trumped caution, and Arti crept stealthily across the lot to investigate. She ducked low with her back pressed against the side of the motorhome and edged her way toward the vehicle's large side window. She could hear two men arguing.

"Is this some sort of joke?" said one.

"No, I assure you," said the other, in a voice that sounded older.

"I came here because I was told you were offering a serious commission with a significant advance. Instead, you want to play parlor tricks?" It was the man with the goatee, concluded Arti.

"This is no trick. It's a simple question: What do you see?"

"Ridiculous!" protested the younger man, his anger rising. "I don't appreciate having my time wasted."

Arti could feel the vehicle shake against her back; there was movement inside. She was about to hide but hesitated when she heard the older man speak again.

"That was not my intention, sir. I'm simply looking for someone who can answer my question. Apparently, you cannot." There was more shuffling. "Take this payment for your troubles. And please, tell no one about our meeting—for your own safety."

"You're mad!" said the younger man.

The motorhome shook again, and Arti scrambled behind it as the side door opened. The young man emerged, glancing nervously at his surroundings before walking quickly around the main building toward the street. Arti crept back along the side of the vehicle and crouched below the window again. She was surprised to hear the old man still talking— apparently to himself.

"Maybe I am mad," he grumbled.

Arti straightened from her crouch, stretching just high enough to look inside. The man held his bald head low, chin against his chest, gloved hands covering his face. A massive book covered a small table in front of him.

"Who's there?" asked the man, dropping his hands suddenly.

Arti crouched down, frozen with fear.

"I don't appreciate being spied upon." There was a pause. "I know you're there," said the man, a little louder, so he could be sure she could hear him. The vehicle vibrated, and a moment later, its side door opened, and he poked his head out. "I don't usually offer hospitality to strangers who peek in my window, but I just made tea, if you'd like some."

Arti knew she should run. That she should race back into the building, find Gal and get away from this place as fast as her feet could carry her. But there was something in the old man's demeanor, the gentleness of his invitation that made her hesitate. There was also the book. *Could he be a reader?*

"How do I know I can trust you?" asked Arti, breaking her silence.

"How do I know I can trust *you?*" came the man's reply. Watery blue eyes smiled through a web of wrinkles. "My name is Merl. What's yours, young lady?"

"Arti," she answered, immediately angry at herself for volunteering the information.

"Arti," he repeated, thoughtfully. "And your friend?"

"Friend?"

"The one hiding under my home," he said, nodding at the ground. "You're both welcome to join me inside; the tea's almost ready."

Arti bent down and peered beneath the vehicle, surprised to see Gal there, sprawled on her back, knife in hand, a puzzled look on her face.

Against Gal's objections, Arti was determined to take Merl up on his offer.

"He seems harmless enough," whispered Arti. "And there are two of us; what could he do?"

"*Seems* and *is* ain't the same thing," hissed Gal.

Arti started up the van's steps and turned. "Coming?"

Gal shook her head in frustration and reluctantly followed.

Arti paused again at the top step. To her left, below the level of her feet, was the driver's compartment: a bucket seat behind a steering wheel, separated from the passenger seat by a wide center console. To her right was a ten by six box crammed with all the amenities of a modern home. Along one side, next the window, was a line of tiny cupboards suspended above a miniature cooktop, sink, and refrigerator. Along the other, beneath a yellow dome light on the ceiling, was a U-shaped booth with high backed seats covered in vinyl that wrapped around a small circular table holding three white cups and a dented silver tea pot. The rear of the van held more cupboards suspended at eye level and, below them, a wide cushioned bench with a blanket and pillow resting on it. The large book Arti had seen through the window was gone.

"Come in, come in," said Merl. He had a kind manner, and the tone of his voice was gentle and disarming. "How do you take it?"

"We didn't take nothin'!" blurted Gal.

Merl laughed. "No, I mean how do you take your tea?"

The girls looked at each other for help. "The same way you're having it would be fine," suggested Arti.

"Black it is," said Merl. He looked up at the girls and gestured to the booth wrapping the round table. "Please, sit."

Merl poured the tea and passed the cups carefully to Gal and Arti. "This is the last of my Crentian Herb. I hope you enjoy it as much as I." He smiled again, waiting for them to try it.

Gal looked down at the steaming drink. "You ain't tryin' to drug us, are you?"

Merl was appalled. "Of course not!" He frowned at Gal and traded cups with her. "Just to put you at ease," he said. The old man lifted the swapped mug to his lips and gently blew on it. Then he closed his eyes and took a sip. "Mmmm, wonderful."

Arti lifted her own cup to her mouth and breathed in the tea's aroma, a sumptuous blend of fruit and spices. Working up enough courage, she also drank.

"It's really good," she declared. "I've never tasted anything like it."

"One of the benefits of travel," said Merl, grinning. "You discover such delicacies." He grunted, "But then you can't live without them."

Gal ignored the small talk. "What's with the gloves?" she asked.

"Gal!" Arti hissed with embarrassment.

Merl continued to smile, but the joy in his eyes was gone. "It's alright, Arti. I don't mind." He set his cup down and adjusted the tea pot on the table. "I was injured…in a fire, many years ago. My hands were burned quite badly." Merl flexed his gloved fingers. "They still get a little stiff sometimes, and they can be tender, so I wear these for protection. In fact, there are days when it feels like I just pulled them from the flames." He stared at his hands for a moment, before looking across the table at his guests. "What brings two young ladies to this end of town? Do you live nearby?"

"We were just looking around," said Arti. Her tone became apologetic. "I'm sorry for spying on you. It's just that I saw the other man come inside your…" she looked around, "…home, and I was curious."

"I understand," said Merl. "No harm done." He brushed his gloved hand across the table, as if wiping away crumbs. "Just forget about it. We'll pretend it never happened. Okay?"

"Who was he?" asked Gal.

Merl's expression darkened. Gone were the grandfatherly warmth and the welcoming smile. "I don't wish to be rude, but I'd appreciate it if you could finish your tea. Sorry to rush you, but I have some important matters to attend to."

"It has something to do with the book, doesn't it?" asked Arti. The question seemed to suck all the air out of the motorhome.

Merl stood up, nearly bumping his head on the cupboard above the booth. "I'm sorry, but you have to go."

Gal frowned at Arti. "What book?"

"There was a big book on the table," explained Arti. She nodded at Merl. "He asked the man to tell him what he saw, but he couldn't. He thought it was a trick." She

80

searched Merl's icy blue eyes. "He must not have been able to read."

Merl was flustered. "I don't know what you *think* you heard or saw but—" He stopped in mid-sentence, realizing what Arti just said. Moving very slowly, he returned to his seat and placed his gloved hands on the round table as if to steady himself. The intensity of his stare was unsettling.

"What...did you see?"

"I told you," she said, looking down. "There was a big book open on this table. The page had some writing on it—a bit on the top and more in the middle. It looked like a poem or something. I was too far away to make it out."

Merl was astonished. "You can read?"

"She sure can," said Gal. "I can, too," she added proudly.

Merl scrambled to his feet, hastily squeezing past the girls on his way to the back of the compartment. He lifted the lid on the wide rear bench, casting away the pillow and blanket that were resting there, revealing a hollow cavity filled with books. On top was a huge tome over two feet across and so thick that Merl's gloved hands could barely grasp it.

He lugged the huge book to the round table, leaning it on its spine as he frantically set aside the cup and tea pot. The tome's back cover was missing, a number of pages were also gone, and those that remained looked as if their edges had been burned away. The scent of charcoal wafted in the air as Merl gently arranged the book on the table, rotating it for Arti. The thick, yellowed pages made cracking sounds as he slowly turned to one of three places marked with gold string.

The old man was shaking. "What do you see?" he asked, holding his breath.

Arti looked up at Merl, then down at the huge page in front of her. "It's written in a language I don't understand," she said. "I can't read it."

"What do you mean? 'Cept for the top bit, it's just a bunch of letters all over the place," said Gal, looking at Arti like she'd lost her sense. "'Course you can't read it!"

Merl ignored the younger girl. He wetted his lips and swallowed. "Try, Arti."

"What part? The line at the top or the ones in the middle?"

Gal tried to interrupt again, but Merl raised his hand for quiet. "The middle," he said. "Read what you see there."

Arti obeyed, carefully pronouncing each strange word. "Ca litera ede castere. Ca stiva ede rizer. Ca crisa ede essent."

Gal frowned at her. "Where do you see that?"

Arti looked at Merl for an explanation. The old man smiled like someone who had finally arrived at a destination after an incredibly long and arduous journey. There were tears in his eyes.

"We can all see the first line on the page," explained Merl. "It's Old Ferencian and, translated, it means: *Whoso pulleth the words of this tome shall challenge for the write of History.*" He glanced at Gal. "But whereas the rest of the page appears as a jumble of random letters to you and me, for one person there is a message hidden there. The young man who just left is a local author of some renown. I thought it might be him, but I was wrong." Merl wiped his eyes with the back of his gloved hand, smiling victoriously at Arti.

"*You* are that person, Arti, and the words you have just uttered are in the same ancient dialect. You said: *The book is my shield. The pen is my sword. The ink is my blood.* It is the oath of the Knights of Maren."

Merl sighed deeply, as if he'd just shrugged off the weight of the world. "After all these years of searching, I've finally found you."

# CHAPTER 9

It was the first time in many years that Morgan Fay felt the curious mix of uncertainty and apprehension she recognized as fear.

*The Challenger has come.*

In the days following the appearance of those four words she couldn't lift her eyes from the tome, watching hour after hour, day after day, as each character slowly materialized on the page, praying the usurper's whereabouts would eventually be revealed. But *The History* would divulge nothing, and with her patience wearing thin, Fay decided to act. What one part of the *Grail Tome* denied, another might reveal. She would consult *The Meditations*—and wield her pen.

Fay knew how dangerous it was. All words have inherent power amplified through a scribe's imagination and skill. Flowing from a master's hand they become greater than the sum of their parts, affecting the world beyond them in ways one would not think possible. The ultimate expression of that power was *The Meditations,* a collection of ancient passages so sublimely crafted that after decades of careful study, Morgan Fay was still wary of their potency.

Though her mastery of them was tenuous at best, *The Meditations* had served Fay well. Through them she had infused her ubiquitous Network with a drug-like quality, hypnotic and compelling in its effects. Not long after its inception, most of Corben's citizens were addicted to the continuous flow of images streaming across their vidlink screens. The magic embedded in the Network's video weakened their will, making them more compliant and obedient until they finally submitted to Fay's authority, surrendering a great deal more than their country's name.

*A picture is worth a thousand words. Show, don't tell. You are the Corporation.*

Without protest, new laws were enacted. Vidlinks were to be carried by citizens at all times, and owning books was a crime. Schools banned novels and texts, signs were removed from streets and store fronts; almost overnight, all forms of writing vanished north of the Coin Canal.

Some readers and scribes resisted, discovering their literacy offered protection against the debilitating effects of Fay's technology. Risking their lives to keep reading, they hid books in basements and attics, behind walls and under floors. To root them out Fay created her Incendi police, armed platoons of black-clad troopers that raided, arrested, and "cleansed" in the Corporation's name. Financial rewards and Network fame were offered to citizens who informed on others they suspected of keeping books. Neighbor turned on neighbor, friend betrayed friend, and families were torn apart. After forcing tortured confessions from them in the cold, dark depths of the castle dungeon, Incendi police executed readers and scribes by the thousands. Their books died along with them, burned in celebratory Lightings broadcast to the mesmerized masses.

Fay was close to achieving the goal she had set so long ago, *The History* was nearing its final page, and soon the power of words would be hers. Every eventuality had been anticipated, every contingency accounted for. Save one...

*The Challenger has come.*

The golden sheen of Wyzera's pen caught the light as Fay withdrew its tip from the ornate well. She held it above a piece of paper next to the open tome, preparing to write, drawing the power of the great book's words into her consciousness where she could focus it on the question like a search light. But as she tried to draw a response from the page, something impeded her will, hiding the truth, denying the answer she sought. In a quarter century of using *The Meditations* to realize her goals, she never experienced such resistance.

"Where is the Challenger?" she asked, her voice quivering, perspiration beading on her ivory skin. She held the question in her mind and lowered the pen to the paper as she read the first line of the passage before her, a short piece entitled *The Maze*.

The words were perfect, each syllable flowing into the next with melodic precision, creating an image so clear, so precise, so beautiful that Fay had to catch her breath. The image and question mingled together in her consciousness, and she labored to bind them there, her hand tightening on the pen like a vise, the veins on her temples throbbing with the intense pressure created by the effort.

The resistance was distant but strong, fighting to destroy her focus and deny an answer, but Morgan Fay would not relent. Her face reddened with exertion, and she leaned over the broad oak desk, unwilling to surrender. The lights in the wall sconces dimmed, and she was nearing her breaking point when an image crystallized in her mind. The tip of the pen's blade sliced through the paper, digging into the desk's polished surface, scarring its woody grain. Bleeding ink, it carved out the word *DRAGONS* just before Morgan Fay collapsed.

Disheveled and confused, she was awakened by the gentle nudge of a hand on her shoulder.

"Are you well?" Utter despair darkened Mordred's face. His eyes darted back and forth from Fay to the pen to the paper's ragged message.

"Mordred," Fay mumbled, straightening herself in the chair. She frowned at the Incendi captain's fingers still touching her, and he pulled his arm away. With a dignified lift of her chin she returned the pen to its case and combed her fingers through her long black hair. "I'm fine." She took a deep breath to center herself. "Any progress in your search for the Penderhagen girl?"

Mordred swallowed. "No. If she's still on the island, someone must be helping her. So far, her parents have given us nothing." He lowered his head, expecting to be chastised for his failure.

Fay did not look at him. Instead, she brushed away the sheet of paper, studying the word chiseled into the desktop. *DRAGONS.*

"Oh, she's still on the island," said Fay. "And I think I know where she's been hiding."

"Me?" asked Arti. "I...I don't understand. Why would you be looking for me?"

Gal nudged Arti below the table and nodded toward the motorhome's narrow door. It was clear she thought the old man was crazy, and she wanted to leave. Now.

"Don't go," pleaded Merl, noticing Gal's signal. "Please. I'll explain everything." He stood and reached for the pot. "But it's going to take a while; I'll make more tea."

The story Merl recounted was as fantastic as any Arti had read in her family's library. "Before the Corporation," he began, "I was a member of the Order of Librarians, a group whose sworn duty was to protect the written word in all its forms. The Order believed the power of words kept evil at bay, that it was a gift belonging to everyone, a shield against the sword of oppression.

"I was very young when my talents garnered the attention of senior members of the Order, those who wanted to ensure that the rarest and most valuable books would be found and protected. It was the Order's wish that people have access to the knowledge contained in those works; they were to be shared with the world." Merl smiled proudly. "I was as surprised as any when I was given the honor and responsibility to be the Master Librarian for the collection. There were many in the Order who thought I was too inexperienced for such an assignment. They were probably right." Nostalgia warmed his face. "But I was full of energy, and my faculty for languages far surpassed any of the other candidates.

"The library was here in Tintagel at the castle on the hill, in what is now the headquarters of Fay Industries." Merl expected to surprise Arti with this information, but she only nodded. "You knew about the library. How?"

"My parents went there on a school trip when they were little," replied Arti. "They told me all about it. They said it was amazing."

Merl smiled again, remembering the many tours he had given to schoolchildren. "I must have met them. Isn't that strange?" he muttered. "And they were right, the library was a very special place. But it was also too much for any one person to manage.

"Thousands of books came to me each year, and the Order wanted the older texts to be translated, so they could be studied and enjoyed. It took so much of my time just maintaining the volume of works—collecting and cataloguing everything—that I had little time left for academic matters. I needed help, but finding someone fluent in ancient dialects was not easy. For many months, the Order searched near and far for a person qualified for the job—without success.

"Then one bright autumn day, a young woman came to the castle. She was pretty with long black hair, and I noticed her reading a yet-to-be translated Old Ferencian manuscript. Dumbstruck, I asked her how she had learned such an obscure dialect. She told me that she had worked at a small library in her home town, a tiny hamlet in East Corben on the North Verinese border. They had two works in Old Ferencian, and she claimed she used them to teach herself the language!

"I didn't believe her, of course," snorted Merl. "No one could learn Old Ferencian alone with only two works as reference. So, I tested her." He shook his head. "I was shocked to discover that her skills rivaled my own." He took another sip of tea. "By the way, if you haven't figured it out yet, the young woman was Morgan Fay."

"The Witch on the Hill?" gasped Gal.

89

Merl nodded. "The same, though she was much different then." The old librarian stared into his cup. "We became very close, Morgan and me. We were a team. Together we made the library at Tintagel the greatest in the world."

"So what happened?" asked Arti. "What went wrong?"

Merl caressed the thick book's cover with his gloved hand, tracing the embossed gold and silver cup's curving lines. "The *Grail Tomes* happened. The books came to us from a private collection in East Crent. The details of their provenance were a little fuzzy, but we didn't ask questions; we were just happy they'd survived. It was a homecoming of sorts, since the Order had commissioned them when it first formed over two thousand years ago. They were the crown jewels of our collection, the most beautiful and important books ever written." Merl looked down at the tome with reverence, remembering a time when it had stood on a marble pedestal in the library's castle tower. "Even in this sorry state, it's still a treasure."

"You said *tomes*. There's more than one?"

"Yes, Arti. This book has a twin, identical in every way, down to the smallest detail. When the tomes came to us, we couldn't believe our good fortune. But they arrived with a warning, a very odd set of instructions. Morgan and I were told we could only read one particular page from the books, and only on two specific days of the year." The old man saw the confusion on the girls' faces. "Yes, I thought it was strange, too—some bizarre superstition handed down through the ages. But as I discovered later through my research, the *Grail Tomes* had a very strange story to tell.

"They were written by a pair of mystic scribes who delved deeply into the magic of words. Yes, *magic* I say, for the books have a power that cannot be explained by logic or reason." He delicately lifted the tome's thick leather cover, revealing a title page decorated with intricately scripted letters, hand painted jewels of shimmering gold around deep rich hues of cobalt blue and dark forest green.

"There are four chapters in all, beginning with *The Meditations*, forty-four passages whose imagery is so wonderfully rich they possess spell-like power. I have studied them for twenty-five years—very carefully, I should add—and only scratched the surface of their potency. They are very dangerous, and you must never look at them. Understood?" He stared at Arti and Gal until they nodded.

At the first of three string bookmarks, about a quarter of the way down the scorched binding, Merl carefully wedged his gloved hand into the tome, turning to another brightly painted page featuring another title and an intricately decorated gold and silver cup, matching the one on the book's cover.

"The second chapter, *The Verses*, contains one hundred and twelve individual poems, works that ebb and flow with a grace and movement that is breathtaking. *The Verses* were used to train a select group of warriors charged with protecting the *Grail Tomes*. They were called the Knights of Maren, and they swore fealty to their king and the Order of Librarians."

Arti's eyes widened. "We saw someone with a tattoo that looked just like that." She pointed at the cup in the center of the page and looked at Gal for confirmation.

Merl sounded doubtful. "A Knight of Maren? Here? Now?"

"He fought in the Cauldron," said Gal. "Kicked The Mountain's ass."

Merl frowned. "'The Mountain'?"

"That was the name of the other fighter," explained Arti. "He was *real* big."

"I see," said Merl. "If there is a true Knight of Maren here on the island, we may have a worthy ally for our quest."

"Quest? What are you talkin' about?" asked Gal.

"Let me finish," said Merl. "Where was I?"

"*The Verses*," said Arti.

"Yes, yes, *The Verses*—I've explained that. The third chapter is *The Test*. That's the part you read today, Arti. *The book is my shield. The pen is my sword. The ink is my blood.* It is the ancient oath of the Knights of Maren. I had no idea what message was hidden on the page, but by pulling the words from the tome, you have named yourself the 'Challenger.'"

"'Challenger?'" Maybe Gal was right, thought Arti. Maybe the old man *was* crazy. "Challenger for what?"

"The answer to that question is found in the final chapter." Merl heaved the tome on its back, exposing several singed and missing pages. "As you can see, this tome has been damaged, some of it burned away. The same flames that did this nearly consumed me." He paused as if what he was about to say was difficult.

"Remember how I told you that Morgan Fay and I worked together in the library? She..."

As the old man struggled to find the words, Arti looked at the partly burned book and Merl's gloved hands, making the connection. "She started the fire."

"Whoa," whispered Gal.

"Yes," said Merl. "Morgan was always curious, always wanting to learn—I loved that about her. But after a while she became obsessed with knowing what secrets the books held.

I tried to make her realize the danger, to remind her of the vow she had made."

*Only twice a year, on the equinox, when light and darkness are in balance, may we open the Grail Tomes. To read The History. To count the words.*

"She thought I was being overly cautious but promised to obey my wishes. Months later, I happened upon her reading *The Meditations* and knew that vows meant nothing to her. She denied everything, but I could see that the books had changed her. The Morgan I knew and loved had left me." Tears welled in Merl's blue eyes. "Then came the flames.

"She took the other *Grail Tome* and set fire to the library. I arrived at the castle just in time to save this one." Merl gently patted the book with his gloved hand. "Morgan thinks I'm dead, and that it died with me. That is to our advantage." He sighed, "Ah, but I'm getting ahead of myself.

"The last chapter is called *The History,* but unlike the other three, it is still being written."

"Who's writin' it?" asked Gal. "You?"

"No, Gal. Not me."

Merl spun the heavy tome on the round table and flipped a swath of empty, singed pages to one that had a few lines of elegant, swirling script at its top, words written in the same Old Ferencian found in the preceding chapters. "Look," he said.

The girls stared down at the page but didn't notice anything. Finally, Gal's patience ran out. "What? I don't see nothin'. Just a bunch of words I can't read." Ignoring her, Merl studied the cup in his hands, waiting.

"Hold on," said Arti. "Something's happening." She leaned closer to the page. "A letter! It just appeared!"

Gal, having also witnessed the phantom character materialize, stared wide-eyed at the page. "And there's another," announced Arti. "It's making a word." She shook her head in disbelief. "*The History* is...writing itself."

"Yes," said Merl. "And the words are coming faster with every book threatened with destruction, bringing us ever closer to the day."

Arti searched the old man's eyes. "What day?"

"The day our destiny is written," said Merl.

"Our what?" asked Gal.

"I think he means the future," said Arti.

"That's precisely what I mean," said Merl. He watched as another letter snaked into existence on the tome's broad page. "The ancient scribes who created this book knew the power of words was humankind's greatest gift, that it must be shared among everyone if the forces of evil were to be kept at bay. Fearing a day would come when its power would be stolen, they created *The History*.

"Its purpose is to warn us when our connection to the power of words is being threatened. The faster the words appear on *The History's* pages, the more of its power we've lost, and the closer we are to our doom." The old librarian offered a weak smile. "Luckily, it also provides a way to restore the balance, to take the power of words back."

Merl nodded at the book, just as another word finished forming. "When they arrive at *The History's* final page, the words will stop coming, the revelations will end."

Arti frowned. "But you said our destiny will be written."

"Yes, it will," said Merl, "but it can only be crafted by a human hand, by a scribe capable of wielding one of the great pens." Arti was even more confused, now.

"Don't you see?" continued Merl. "That's been Morgan's purpose all these years. She's been robbing us of the power of words, banning and burning her way to the final page, knowing that when it's all that remains, the future is hers to write. And when she does, she'll have the means to find every scribe and reader in existence. No one anywhere will be safe." Merl glared at Arti. "She'll burn every book... and kill us all."

He set his cup down on the edge of the table and sighed. "When I realized what she was planning, I knew I had to stop her. I broke my vow to the Order and began to study the tome." His face softened. "And to search for you. The world is a big place, and I'd almost given up. I had no way to know where the Challenger would be found. The words that appeared in *The History* had never offered any help. They were isolated, disconnected, their purpose and meaning incomprehensible.

"Then, two months ago, something miraculous happened." He reached out and turned a couple of the book's huge pages. "Here it is," he said, pointing at a line of curling script, reading it slowly. "*From the flames to the Isle of Avalon, the Challenger has come.* It was the clue telling me where to find you." He smiled, reflecting on the day's events. "Or where *you* would find *me*."

The old librarian gently closed the broad leaves, exposing the tome's tattered binding and the stubs of other pages that had been burned away. "There would have been eight pages left before the final one."

"But they're gone," said Arti. "You won't know when they're full."

"That is the dilemma we face." He took his seat again. "*Whoso pulleth the words of this tome shall challenge for*

95

*the write of History*. Arti, *you* are the one who can deny Morgan Fay what she most desires. You've passed *The Test*." He reached across the table and gently patted the burned and battered book. "But this *Grail Tome* is useless to us now. You cannot write on a final page that isn't there."

Arti understood. "We need the other tome, the one Fay has. That's our quest."

"*We? Our?*" Gal threw her head back and groaned, "Aw, crap!"

# CHAPTER 10

Arti had to admit the whole thing sounded crazy. A quest to steal a magical book with the ability to dictate the future? From CEO Morgan Fay, the most powerful—and dangerous—person on the planet? A mission into the headquarters of the Incendi police, the Flames that had taken Arti's parents and were still hunting her? No one in her right mind would risk it.

But as dangerous as Merl's plan was, it gave Arti hope. Hope that what he had said was true, that she might be able to alter the course of history—and save her parents in the process. It still wasn't enough to conquer her doubt.

"Don't get me wrong," said Arti. "I want to help. It's just that...I'm not special. I don't know anything about being a knight or a scribe or what the future should be. What if I wasn't supposed to pull the words from the tome? Maybe I just got lucky. Maybe it made a mistake."

"I understand your misgivings," said Merl, "but it's no good questioning the tome's decision. Any good librarian knows the reader doesn't choose the book, the book chooses the reader. The *Grail Tome* picked you; the task is yours. When the final page is all that remains, *you* must write it."

Arti blew out a long breath. "How long would it take for the other pages to be filled—if they weren't burned away, I mean?"

"I can't be sure," said Merl. "The words are coming faster with each passing day. At best, we have a few weeks. Not near as much time as I'd hoped to prepare you."

"Prepare me? What do you mean?"

"I must teach you how to scribe. After we take the book from Morgan, you have to write *The History*'s final page."

"But the *Grail Tomes* are written in Old Ferencian. I don't know that language."

"You don't need to." Merl lugged the damaged book away, setting it gently inside the rear bench of the motorhome before sitting down on its cushioned lid.

"In the years following Morgan's betrayal, I looked for a way—any way—to set things right. I researched the Order and the scribes who penned the *Grail Tomes*. My investigation took me to the four corners of the world: North and South Verin; Astenga, and Crent; to the Great Hall of Parmell; and, of course, the Scriptorium in Ference where the books were born. Fact and myth are history's bedfellows; it's hard to wake one without disturbing the other. But, bit by bit, I pieced together the story of the tomes—and the two pens that wrote them.

"They were wielded by the most gifted scribes of the ancient world—an Astengan mystic named Merrill and a Crentian called Wyzera, or *The Wizard*. The pens translated their writers' thoughts into Old Ferencian, each word and phrase and sentence perfect. But a pen of power will answer to only one living writer. It was true then, as it is now.

"Morgan has a *Grail Tome*, so we must assume she has Wyzera's pen and that she's able to wield it. The other has been safely hidden by the Order for millennia. It's here on the island, Arti, and I'm going to take you to its keeper."

Gal had heard enough. "We ain't goin' nowhere but home. You're nuts!"

"You can't go home," countered Merl. "It isn't safe. You're just lucky I found you before Morgan did." He patted the bench below him and mumbled, "It must have worked, after all."

"But I have to go back," insisted Arti. "I need to get something—it's really important. Please."

Merl saw the desperation in the girl's eyes and puffed in frustration. "Alright," he relented. "We'll stop there after you get the pen, but you'll have to be quick about it." He waived his finger at them. "In and out."

Arti sat in the passenger seat, Gal propped between her and Merl on the wide center console. The motorhome's engine rumbled to life, and blue smoke bellowed from its rusty tail-pipe, filling the garage. Even with the windows closed, oily fumes assaulted their senses. Arti coughed, eliciting memories of the night she escaped her burning home, echoes of fear and sadness and loss. She choked back the emotions with the exhaust, energized by the renewed hope Merl had given her. If she could take the complete *Grail Tome* from Morgan Fay and write its final page, she could change the future and save her parents. She prayed it wasn't too late.

"Her name is Vivian, and she's the oldest surviving member of our Order," said Merl, driving the vehicle slowly from the garage, careful of the large protruding mirrors on each side. "She has a little shop at the end of the island on the lakeshore. She...doesn't like me very much. Blames me for all Morgan has done." He paused, clearly troubled by the verdict. "I told her that if I ever found the one who could pass *The Test*, I would send him..." Merl glanced apologetically at Arti, "I mean *her* for the pen. I expect she'll want to question you." He frowned. "To make sure I haven't made another mistake."

The motorhome passed the dealership's main building, burping more smoke as it rolled onto Center Street's bumpy asphalt. Two more left turns had them heading east on Water Street. The narrow beach at Smugglers Bay appeared on the right, just below a hill peppered with reeds. A little farther on, warehouses replaced the vegetation, trucks loading and unloading goods in steady streams from long docks jutting out into the wide Avalon River. Traffic flowed to and from the main arteries of Hill and Bay Streets, the most direct routes from Isle's southern shore to the East and West Bridges that crossed the Coin Canal into Main.

Halfway down Water Street, they passed the Cauldron, Big Billy Johnson's arena where Arti and Gal had seen the young man fight. Arti remembered how handsome he was and how he moved like a dancer.

"That's where we saw The Poet," she said, pointing across the street at the huge warehouse. "The one with the tattoo." Merl glanced out his side window at the massive building but said nothing, his silence making Arti believe he thought the young man's presence on the island was mere coincidence.

Passing Billings Bay and the old Fisherman's Wharf, the street narrowed to one lane. A large tilted sign marked the final intersection at Park Avenue. Gal read the words out loud: "Dead. End."

They drove to the very tip of the island where the Avalon River opened into Lake Ogden. An old home stood at the water's edge behind a pair of towering oaks. It was a neat two-story board and batten painted bright blue with white shutters. A sign hung from a post at the end of the walkway leading to the house: *Lakeside Antiquities.*

As Merl turned the motorhome around—a task made difficult by the narrowness of the roadway—Gal pointed to a car parked next the house.

"Holy crap!" she said. "That's a F'rencian Charger! I ain't never seen one before—'cept in pit'chers." The sleek white sports car sat low to the ground, wide tires hugging chrome rims, angled windows tinted black, its contoured body exuding shark-like grace and ferocity.

"They gave one of those away on *Eyes on the Prize* last year," said Arti. "They're r-e-a-l expensive."

Merl took note of the car as he edged the motorhome up to the end of the walkway, stopping in front of the sign. "What are you going to tell her?" he asked, for the third time.

Arti sighed. "That you sent me for the pen."

"And?"

"I should answer all of her questions."

"Good," said Merl, nodding anxiously. "We'll wait for you here and keep watch."

"You're not coming in?"

"No," said Merl. "I told you, Vivian wouldn't be very happy to see me. I'd just be in the way."

Gal shuffled across the seat behind Arti. "I'm goin' with her."

"That's not a good idea," growled Merl. "You'll only—" Before he could finish, Gal had already jumped out of the vehicle, winking back at him as she slammed the door.

Arti paused next the signpost and took a deep breath. The last time she was this nervous she had to do a presentation in front of her class at school—and it had not gone well. Gal waited beside her, pretending not to notice how uneasy her friend was. As a distraction, she pointed her finger up at the sign and asked, "What's that word?"

"An-ti-qui-ties," said Arti. "It means old things. She sells them."

Gal scowled, "Who'd wanna buy somethin' old?"

Arti smiled at her and started toward the house. She knocked on the white paneled door and was answered by a woman with a thick accent. "Come in. We're open."

The entrance led to a hallway with a hardwood floor covered in old rugs. There were objects everywhere, pottery and lamps, wooden trunks, and pieces of blown glass. A tall grandfather clock was nestled in the corner just below a set of stairs leading up to the second floor. A brass pendulum swung back and forth behind an etched glass window below the clock's gold face.

An archway framed by painted moldings joined the hallway to the next room. Small tables were scattered about the space, covered in an assortment of merchandise made of metal, wood, and porcelain. It took a while before Arti noticed the woman leaning over a long, narrow counter adjacent to the far wall with a large aquarium at its end. Bubbles percolated up through the water, and brightly colored fish dodged between rocks and weeds sticking up from the glass tank's pebbled bottom.

The woman was no taller than Gal, with silver hair tied back at her neck. Her attention was on a gold ring propped on the counter which she inspected through a tiny lens held over one eye. With her other hand, she grasped a small tool, guiding a sparkling red gem pinched at its tip toward the ring's setting.

"I'll be with you in a moment," she said, concentrating on the task.

As they waited, Arti noticed Gal eyeing a glittering blue sapphire pendant with a delicate gold chain hanging from a hook next the archway. She had seen the same look in her friend's eyes on many occasions—just before something of value disappeared into her pocket. Arti glared at Gal, shaking her head slowly and mouthing the word, "NO."

"A beautiful piece," said the woman. "I can see why it caught your attention." Emerald green eyes smiled up at Arti. "Would you like me to take it down for you?"

"Um...no thanks."

"Well, if there's anything I can help you with, please ask. My name is Vivian."

"I know." Arti's throat was suddenly dry. "Merl sent me for the...pen."

The woman's demeanor changed immediately. Kindness became caution, warmth suspicion.

"Has he now?" Without lowering her eyes, she set the lens and tool aside. "What's your name?"

"Arti. Arti Penderhagen."

"And your friend?"

"That's Gal."

"And where is Merl?" asked Vivian.

"He's waiting outside," answered Arti. "He thought I should see you alone. But…Gal…um…insisted on coming with me."

"He's afraid of you," blurted Gal. Vivian couldn't help but smile at her candidness.

"Come closer, Arti," said Vivian. Arti did as she was told, carefully navigating among the tables until she was standing next the counter.

"You say Merl sent you for the pen. That means you passed *The Test*." Vivian's eyes narrowed. "Tell me, what did you have to do?"

"I had to pull the words from the tome, the book Merl saved from the library."

Vivian leaned toward Arti. Although small in stature, the movement made her as intimidating as a giant.

"And what did you see that others have not?"

Arti took a nervous step back. "It was the oath of the Knights of Maren…in Old Ferencian. I didn't know what it meant until Merl told me."

"The oath! Of course!" said Vivian. "So simple. So… perfect."

The old woman studied Arti, appraising her, searching for a hint of deceit. Finding none, she smiled and said, "Well then, there's no sense wasting time."

Vivian edged her way along the counter and passed behind the aquarium. With her features distorted by the water and glass, she reached down and retrieved a small wooden box. Setting it down on the counter, she waived Arti closer.

"I've kept the pen for a very long time. It once belonged to Merrill of Astenga, one of the *Grail* scribes." She removed the box's lid. "This is Excalibri." Vivian lifted the pen from the container, offering it to Arti. Gal squeezed in beside her to get a better look.

Made of bright, shining silver, it was shaped like a miniature sword, with a tiny pommel, hilt, and guard at its top, the "blade" tapering to a sharp vented nib. Arti reached out to take the pen, and the instant it touched her hand she felt a sudden pulse of energy, a warm burst of light that startled her. Gal felt it too, jumping back as if she'd been shocked.

"W…what was that?" asked Arti, afraid to move. "What just happened?"

"There's nothing to fear," Vivian assured her, satisfied with the result. "That was the final proof I needed. The bond is made. The pen and your will are one."

Arti turned Excalibri from side to side, examining it from every angle, admiring its beauty and craftsmanship. It felt so light and balanced, as if it had been made for her hand. She held it out for Gal to look at.

"Cool," she said.

"You hold it well," approved Vivian. "Like a true scribe of old." She retrieved something else from below the counter. The small spherical container was made of the same silver as the pen, with a hinged top. On it was engraved a cup identical to the one found on the *Grail Tome's* cover.

"This is Excalibri's well," said Vivian. "But the ink inside lacks one important ingredient. Do you remember the Knight's oath?"

"Yes," said Arti. "'The book is my shield, the pen is my sword, the ink is my blood.'"

Vivian pulled back the inkwell's lid. "Give me your hand."

Gently grasping Arti's index finger, and holding it over the mouth of the container, Vivian withdrew a pin from a drawer beneath the countertop. "Just a little prick," she warned. "It won't hurt."

Arti pulled away. "What for?"

"The ink is your blood, Arti. Without it, Excalibri cannot write."

Arti offered her hand again, wincing as Vivian poked her fingertip, directing a small drop of blood into the silver sphere.

"There. Done," she said, closing the lid. "That wasn't so bad, now was it?"

Arti sucked on her finger as Vivian returned the pen to its case, setting it beside the inkwell.

"The pendant comes with them," said Vivian. She smiled at Gal and nodded at the archway. "Well, go ahead."

Gal hastily weaved her way through the cluttered tables to where the jewel was hanging. She carefully took it down, coiling the delicate gold chain in her hand, admiring the sparkling blue gem.

"Thanks," she said. "I won't sell it. I promise."

Vivian ushered the girls to the door. "You have much to do, and little time. Best you were on your way." She looked out at Merl waiting in the motorhome, and Arti could see her regret.

"I've been pretty hard on him. Would you do me a favor and tell him I'm sorry? He found you, after all."

Arti nodded, and Vivian hugged her. Afraid she might be subjected to the same treatment, Gal stepped back and stiffly offered her hand. The old woman laughed as she shook it.

As Arti and Gal walked from the house, Vivian called after them. "Good luck, girls." She watched until they were almost to the road, then she spoke to someone standing behind her at the top of the stairs.

"Were you listening?"

"Yes."

"Follow them."

As soon as Arti and Gal got back in the motorhome Merl started spewing questions. "Well? What happened? What did she say? Did...did you get it?"

Arti cradled the pen and inkwell in her lap. "I got it. The pen *and* the ink.

"Ink? Yes, off course, I never thought of that."

"And she says she's sorry," added Gal.

Merl turned the key in the ignition. "She said that? Really?" He looked back at the house, but the door was closed.

His questions continued, and Arti told him everything, repeating every detail of the short visit with Vivian—between Gal's directions to the school. Merl was particularly impressed by the blood ritual.

"I never came across anything about that in my research. I wonder how she knew."

A cough from Gal interrupted his musings. She pointed down the street. "That's it up there. Go by a bit. We'll go in the back way."

"I don't like this," said Merl. "Make it fast."

The motorhome rolled up to the cracked curb next an overgrown yard at the rear of the school. Arti placed the pen and inkwell inside the glove box and jumped out, with Gal following close behind. Entering the building through the squeaky rear door, they hurried down the hallway past the gymnasium, turning toward the main office and the records room in back of it. Gal untangled the key from the sapphire pendant hanging around her neck and bent to unlock the heavy steel door, pushing down on its warped handle. As soon as it swung open, she went straight to the lamp on the table and lit it. Then she grabbed a canvas bag from the floor next her bed.

"I'll pocket the coin," she said, "and bring some food. We're only takin' what we need; everythin' else stays."

Arti nodded, but it was the letter from her parents she had come for. *We love you. Mom and Dad.* She removed the letter from a folder on the file cabinet and carefully slid it into the front pocket of her hoodie, before stuffing some supplies into the duffel bag.

Holding the lamp in one hand, her tied-off canvas bag in the other, Gal paused in the doorway, looking back at the room that had been her home for over two years. Arti could see how hard it was for her to abandon it.

"We'll come back someday, Gal," she promised.

"Ain't no big deal," said Gal, her voice unsteady. She shut off the lamp and set it gently on the floor, pulling the door closed behind them.

As the girls turned the corner to the main hallway leading outside, they saw a tall figure standing at the exit. Arti's heart leapt into her throat. That same dark profile had blocked her way once before.

"It's him! It's the Flame!"

The Incendi captain wore no disguise, his presence in the jet-black uniform and fedora a clear violation of the truce between Morgan Fay's Corporation and Big Billy Johnson's island syndicate. Gal spun around, ready to lead Arti back the way they'd come, knowing the window next the main office offered another way out. But a quick glance around the corner revealed three more Incendi troopers armed with lighters closing on them from that direction. They were trapped.

As he passed through a wide shaft of light coming from one of the classrooms, Arti could see the officer's face below the angled cap. It looked as cold and hard as marble. "You must be the one who helped her get away last time," he said to Gal. "You'll pay for that."

Gal ignored the threat, too busy weighing her options. Their only hope was the classroom halfway between them and Mordred. Cradling her bag, she grabbed Arti's arm.

"Come on!"

The Incendi captain reacted immediately, giving chase. He yelled to his troopers, "Go around! Cut them off!"

Navigating through an obstacle course of broken desks, Gal led Arti to a large window devoid of glass on the classroom's outer wall. She tossed her bag out, and Arti followed suit, casting her duffel bag through the framed opening. They jumped through the window, landing in a tangle of arms and legs on a sprawling vine-covered juniper. Freeing themselves from the prickly shrub, they scrambled to their feet, recovered their bundles and sprinted toward the motorhome a few hundred feet away. Like a black panther, Mordred leapt from the window, nimbly touching down on the grass behind them.

When Merl saw what was happening, he frantically slammed the vehicle in gear and accelerated down the street toward the girls, turning sharply, jumping the curb in a shower of sparks. Arti reached the motorhome first and, fumbling with her duffel bag, threw open the passenger door.

As Gal waited for Arti to climb into the vehicle, she looked back. Mordred was coming fast. She threw her bag through the open door and spun around to face him, knife in hand.

"Hurry, Arti!" yelled Merl. "I have to get you out of here!"

"Hold on!" screamed Arti. "We can't leave Gal! Do something!"

Out of the corner of his eye, Merl noticed the other troopers running across the field toward them, brandishing their lighters. He knew the weapons were powerful enough to short out the vehicle's electrical system.

"There's nothing I can do."

"Go!" commanded Gal. "Now!"

The motorhome's engine revved loudly as Merl slammed his foot down on the accelerator. As it lurched forward, the vehicle jostled and bounced, and the passenger door slammed shut knocking Arti against the center console. She rebounded, clawing at the window, just as Mordred arrived.

"Gal!" she cried.

Gal didn't see the blow that shattered her fingers, sending the knife clattering to the asphalt. There was only the Incendi captain's whisper and a stab of pain. She staggered back, cradling her hand, trying to understand what had happened.

Mordred cursed at the motorhome as it sped way, his body vibrating with rage. For the second time, he had failed to capture the Penderhagen girl. Failed Morgan Fay. "Bring the car around!" he yelled across the yard to his troopers. "We'll go after them. This one will tell me where they've gone."

"I ain't tellin' you nothin'," said Gal. With her good hand, she reached down for the knife.

Mordred uttered another lyrical phrase, backhanding Gal above her left eye, tossing her like a ragdoll onto the roadway. She landed on her back, arms splayed like an angel.

A moan came from her lips, and she tried to get up, but the world spun wildly, forcing her back down.

Mordred was angry at himself for hitting her so hard. If the girl died, she was useless to him. It was then that he heard a deep rumbling sound and noticed a sleek white car approaching at high speed. As it raced toward him, its brakes locked, and it skidded sideways. It was still moving when the driver's door flew open, and a young man launched himself at Mordred. The Incendi captain murmured something, just as a powerful kick landed squarely on his chest, sending him reeling.

Making sure that Mordred was down, the young man removed his leather jacket and covered Gal with it. He reached for her hat and stuffed it in his pocket, then delicately lifted Gal from the roadway and carried her to the car. Opening the passenger door, he set her down gently in the seat.

"Tenera," he whispered. *Hold on.*

Taking his place behind the wheel, he slammed the car into gear. The Charger's powerful engine roared, and slick wide tires devoured the asphalt. As he sped away with the injured girl in the seat next to him, the young man looked up at the rearview mirror and was amazed by what he saw. The man in black was standing!

The young man wiped a greasy hand on his pant leg and glanced down at the girl with concern. At least he knew the captain and his troopers wouldn't be coming after them. It would be a while before they got their car running again.

"Let's get you to Aunt Vivian," he said, in an accent identical to the proprietor of Lakeside Antiquities. "When you're able, you can tell me where your friends have gone."

Gal tried to speak, but her words were barely a whisper.

"Ca…mel…Lot."

# CHAPTER 11

Gwen woke up coiled in her blanket, fully clothed, the bedroom light still on. A corner of *The Knights of Maren*, the book she'd been reading through the night, was wedged under her, jabbing at her ribs.

Freeing herself from the covers, Gwen sat up and lifted the book to her lap, positioning a pillow between her back and the headboard. She opened the book with a renewed sense of purpose; if it could explain Mordred's strange powers, it might yet hold the secret to defeating him and saving the Archive.

After a moment of searching, she found the part of the final chapter she'd been reading before sleep had claimed her, an account of the Knights' final years before they dissembled. Discovering nothing helpful in those pages, Gwen cursed the book for failing her. Then she saw the faded script on the inside of its back cover.

The swirling letters had melted into the soft velum glued to the stiff leather backing, but Gwen could still make out each faint character. She read the first two sentences aloud to herself: "The Oath of the Knights of Maren. Swear fealty and be called." The remaining three lines were written in another language; she guessed it was Old Ferencian. Slowly, carefully, she pronounced each word.

"Ca litera ede castere. Ca stiva ede rizer. Ca crisa ede essent."

Gwen had no idea what it meant. Frustrated, she slammed the book closed and tossed it on the foot of the bed, accepting the awful truth: The Archive was going to burn and she could do nothing to save it. The one thing she truly loved in the world—the one thing worth living for—would be taken from her, and all she could do was watch. For four years, she'd risked everything to visit the collection, fiercely protecting her dangerous secret. What would she do if she could no longer withdraw its treasures? How could she survive without reading? Feeling helpless, she sat on her bed and stared down at the book near her feet.

She noticed the tiny sword fastened to the tome's cover no longer pointed upward; it had rotated almost ninety degrees and was angled toward the binding. Wondering if she had loosened it when she slammed the book shut, Gwen rocked forward on her knees and probed the sword with a finger. It didn't budge. She grabbed the book and spun sideways on the bed, kicking her legs over the edge. Holding the tome in her lap, she pushed hard on the sword with her thumb, determined to straighten it. It still wouldn't move.

Until she lifted her hand.

It was then that the little sword came to life, slowly spinning around the brass stud that was its axis, making a quarter turn before coming to a stop.

Gwen stared down at the book, eyes wide in disbelief. *Did that just happen, or am I losing it? Maybe I'm still asleep.* But she knew that what she seeing was real, not imagination, not the product of a dream. She watched for more signs of life from the tiny sword. When nothing happened, her amazement surrendered to curiosity and experimentation. She turned the book in her lap and waited.

The sword answered her, revolving again.

Gwen repeated the exercise, carefully observing the result of each manipulation. She noticed that the sword always ended up pointing in the same direction—like a compass. But that begged the question: What was it pointing at?

She flipped open the book's back cover and read the faded words again. "The Oath of the Knights of Maren. Swear fealty and be called."

Gwen leapt from the bed, book in hand. "It's all true," she laughed, making the connection. "The knights still exist. They're out there somewhere, and it's showing me the way." The overwhelming anguish of a minute before was gone, and she felt like she'd been reborn. If she could find them in time, maybe they could stop the Archive from burning.

Gwen wrestled a clunky suitcase from her closet and clicked open its locks. She rifled through her dresser drawers, stuffing the suitcase with clothes, then she ran to the adjoining bathroom to retrieve her toiletries.

Lugging the suitcase down the hall and through the kitchen, she noticed the red message light on the refrigerator door was still flashing atop its vidscreen. Only now, a picture of Victor Herrat's chubby face competed for attention with that of Gwen's mother.

In a fit of anger, Gwen grabbed a tall brass peppermill from the kitchen counter and smashed the display; the distorted faces of her mother and the director smiled back at her through a web of shattered plastic. Then she turned around and brought the peppermill down on the vidlink she'd set on the granite counter top the night before. The satisfying CRUNCH! sent pieces of the device flying in all directions.

It was official: Gwen Degan was a decap, a fugitive. And though she knew breaking the law made her an Incendi target, she felt liberated. Never again would she be a tool of Morgan Fay's Corporation or a bargaining chip for her parents. No longer would she have to pretend to be something she wasn't just so she could do the one thing she truly loved. In her heart, she knew there was another way, and with the help of Guillaume de Lac's book, she was going to find it.

With the suitcase stashed in the trunk of the car, Gwen set *The Knights of Maren* on the front passenger seat, so she could keep her eye on the sword as she drove. The tiny blade realigned itself as she backed out of the driveway and continued to slowly turn as the car altered course. It was pointing south, and Gwen followed its lead through the eastern part of the city, the castle on the hill staring down at her, bearing witness to her escape.

It wasn't long before she found herself driving along the Coin Canal, competing for space with an ever-increasing flow of Corporation trucks heading in the same direction. The sword was pointing directly past her at the waterway, indicating her destination was somewhere on the other side, somewhere on the island.

Her childhood had been filled with frightening stories about Old Tintagel, the home of outlaws and crime and violence. As she approached the East Bridge, Gwen considered stopping and turning back, but she knew that was impossible. She glanced at the sword fastened to the book resting on the seat next to her.

"I hope you know what you're doing."

# CHAPTER 12

Arti didn't speak to Merl on the way back to the Camel Lot. Her anguish at leaving Gal to the mercy of Mordred had hardened into resentment so thick, Merl was afraid he might never break through it. As he backed the motorhome into the garage and shut off the engine, he pleaded with her.

"I'm sorry, Arti. I...I had to get you out of there." He leaned back in the seat, covered his face with his gloved hands, and rubbed his eyes. "I couldn't let you be taken."

"Why didn't you protect her?" screamed Arti. "Why didn't you use magic...the stuff you learned from the book? You studied it. You said so." Tears spilled down Arti's cheeks, and the words hiccupped from her throat. "You should have done *something*!"

She glared at Merl, wondering why she had put so much faith in a man she barely knew, afraid that her misplaced trust had cost her friend's life. Why hadn't she been more careful? Why hadn't she listened to Gal's warnings?

"It's not that easy," said Merl, wounded. "Spells take time and…concentration…and I need the book to focus them. *The Meditations* are very dangerous; if I'd tried using one of them against Mordred, I might have done more harm than good. He's not one to underestimate."

Arti's eyes narrowed, accusingly. "You know him?"

Merl sighed. "I know *of* him, yes. He's Morgan Fay's right hand, captain of her Incendi police, and cruel to the core." His expression darkened behind a curtain of shame. "And though I wish with all my heart it wasn't true, he's my son."

"What?" gasped Arti. "I mean…how? I mean…"

"I didn't find out about him until years after Morgan's betrayal, long after she left me for dead in the flames. I…I never knew about a child." Merl shook his head slowly. "She never told me."

"You mean…you were…"

"Close." Merl looked down at Arti, uncomfortably. "*Very* close."

"If she didn't tell you, then how did you find out? That Mordred was your son, I mean."

Merl turned in his seat and looked back at the motor-home's rear bench where the *Grail Tome* was stored.

"The book told me. Two years ago. I was having a difficult time with a passage called *The Eye*. It's a piece translated from an old dialect of South Verinese, containing wonderful allusions to time and memory." His icy blue eyes thawed a little. "Quite sublime, really.

"I was focusing my thoughts, concentrating on each phrase in isolation, careful not to allow the words to overwhelm me. Then it happened: a window opened in my mind revealing a truth that I was not prepared for.

"I saw an infant curled up in Morgan's arms, a tiny little creature squirming and crying with all its might. Then there was the image of a fair-haired child—a boy about eight or nine years old—dancing before a sparring pole, driving his feet and fists into the structure with unnatural force. The last thing I saw was a tall man, the boy grown, standing stiffly at attention. She was there again—Morgan, I mean—placing on his head a hat with the Incendi badge. I could hear her words: *Flames took your father, and with flames we will cleanse the world.*

"It was like a lightning bolt to my brain. I told myself it was just imagination, nothing rooted in reality. But it would not be denied, I knew it was true. I knew I had a son." The old librarian's face hardened. "And like his mother, he's become a monster."

Arti remembered the night Mordred attacked her on the bridge, how fast he moved and the strange language he used. "He knows *The Verses*, doesn't he? That's why he's so strong."

"Yes," said Merl. "Morgan trained him in the art of striking with words, and he's become a master of that discipline. And to answer your next question, I have neither the strength nor the skill to stand against him. The best fighters are those who study *The Verses* as children; it was something the Knights of Maren discovered when training their first pages. The power of words grows in unison with the mind and body. If a youngster is instructed properly, as an adult they will be far superior in combat to one who has come late to the Art. My abilities pale in comparison to those of Mordred; he would have easily beaten me—and captured you. Our quest would have ended today." Merl's face revealed just how difficult it had been for him to abandon Gal. "I couldn't let that happen."

Even though she understood his decision, Arti's heart refused to accept it. "Gal is my friend," she said fiercely, tears returning to her eyes. "We should have tried."

Bowing under the heaviness of grief, Arti looked down at Gal's bag cradled in her lap. Noticing the corner of a piece of cardboard poking up through its cinched mouth, she opened the bag to find the glossy ad from the records room, featuring the happy family. And below it, squeezed in next to the coins and cans of food, was the familiar mustard-yellow book with an embossed crown on its cover.

Tears streamed down Arti's cheeks as she lifted *The King's Errand* from the bag. The bookmark waited in place at the penultimate chapter; Gal would never know how the story ended. Arti hugged the book tightly against her chest and wept.

For the rest of that day and the night that followed, Arti refused to talk to Merl. She woke the next morning to see Merl sitting at the round table examining Excalibri and its well. The pen and sphere rested atop the closed *Grail Tome,* and he was staring at them through a thick magnifying glass, muttering appreciatively to himself. Leaning stacks of smaller books covered the rest of the table, paper marks protruding from pages containing notes from the old librarian's decades of research.

Merl had given Arti some herbal tea to help her sleep, making a bed for her on the cushioned rear bench after removing the *Grail Tome* from its hiding place there. Her rest had been fitful, and as much as she wanted to escape the traumatic events of the previous day, she couldn't. But being awake was even worse, and she wished she'd never opened her eyes.

"There's some bread and honey on the counter," said Merl, still peering through the thick lens at the ornate silver pen. "And I found another tin of Crentian Herb. Pour yourself a cup." He nodded toward the tea pot resting on the small cooktop.

"I'm not hungry," mumbled Arti, pulling up her blanket and turning away from him.

Merl lowered the magnifying glass and leaned out from the table to look back at her.

"I know how difficult yesterday was for you," he said, with more sternness than sympathy. "And it's clear you blame me for it. But let me remind you that it was *your* idea to go back to the school, and that I warned against it. I'm sorry about Gal—I mean that. But the threat facing us is bigger than her, or your parents, or you, or me. If Morgan Fay writes the final page of *The History*, no one will be safe, no one will be free.

"I never told you, Arti, but I used *The Meditations* to see the future Morgan will scribe if we don't stop her. It was only a fleeting glimpse of what could be, but the intensity of the evil I felt in that moment nearly killed me." Merl shivered, remembering the terrible vision the *Grail Tome* had shared with him of the world under Morgan Fay's spell. "Every scribe and reader was dead, and without the power of words for protection, what was left of humanity had surrendered its will, forced to worship a dark deity that had once been the woman I loved."

Merl looked hard into Arti's eyes. "We can't let Morgan write the future. The words must be *yours*."

He lifted his magnifying glass and returned his attention to Excalibri. "Now eat. You can't begin your training on an empty stomach. Today, you're going to familiarize yourself with Merrill's pen," said Merl. "Then we'll see if you can write something with it."

Arti grudgingly gave in to Merl's demands. She ate standing up, watching the old librarian grunt and groan and mumble to himself as he went back and forth from peering at the pen through the magnifying glass to leafing through the books piled around him. After taking her last sip of tea, Arti joined him in the U-shaped booth, shuffling into place behind the round table.

To start, Merl had Arti repeatedly pick up Excalibri, hold it in the "writing position," draw letters in the air, then set it down again. Although the pen fit Arti's hand perfectly, manipulating it was more difficult than she anticipated. The closest thing to writing she had ever done involved scratching letters on a chalk board when she was teaching Gal, but using such a precise instrument was much more demanding. Arti's hand was already cramped when Merl cleared away some of the books and pulled a piece of paper from a cabinet above the small refrigerator, pressing it down on the table in front of her.

"Don't do anything until I tell you." He rubbed his chin nervously, the palm of his leather glove making a bristling sound. "I don't know how this is going to work, so we may have to experiment. The one thing we can't do is waste ink; all we have is what's in the well. We might be able to get more from Vivian, but I'm not sure."

"What do you want me to write?" asked Arti.

"That's a good question." He wet his lips and searched the texts on the table, finally selecting a small dog-eared note-book. Flipping from one bookmarked page to the next, he muttered incoherently until he found what he was looking for.

"This is it." He checked the book's cover. "These are the notes I gathered in Parmell's Great Hall twenty years ago." He held the book up with one hand and aimed the magnifying glass at it with the other. "The collection it came from was to be purged, and I had to hurry to record it." Merl's icy blue eyes scanned the book's page.

"Yes, here we are: *On the Wielding of Excalibri, from the memoir of Merrill of Astenga.*" The old librarian cleared his throat. "*Forged together in truth, the pen and the will are one.*" He closed the book and set it on the table.

"*The pen and your will are one.* That's what Vivian said when she gave me Excalibri," recalled Arti."

"She did? Hmmm," mumbled Merl. "I wonder if she read Merrill's memoir. It's the only direct quotation from a *Grail* scribe that I've ever found. I'm sure the translation is accurate; all we have to do is figure out what it means."

Arti rolled her eyes. "Oh, great. So, what am I—" She stopped talking and squinted across the table at Merl. "Do you hear something?"

Merl jerked his head sideways and listened. "A car." He waved his hand at Arti. "Get down and don't make a sound."

Wiggling his way out from behind the round table, Merl crouched to look out through the windshield of the driver's compartment, just as a dark sedan came to a stop halfway between the garage and the Camel Lot's main building. The car's door opened, and a young woman with auburn hair tied back in a ponytail stepped from the vehicle. After looking around for a moment, she reached back into the car and removed something.

"It's a woman," hissed Merl. "She appears to be alone." He paused. "And she has a book!"

Arti started to speak, but Merl pressed a finger to his lips for quiet, continuing his surveillance. The young woman kicked the car door closed and stood next the vehicle, holding the book out in front of her. A moment later, she started walking toward the garage and the motorhome within.

"She...she's coming this way," stammered Merl. "I...I have to go out. I'll get rid of her." He looked frantically at the pen and ink well, and the pile of books on the table, and at Arti. There was no time to hide any of them. "Don't make a sound."

Arti sprawled on the seat and listened, her heart pounding like a drum. She watched Merl open the motorhome's narrow door and step outside; it closed with a 'click' behind him. Then she heard him address the stranger, impressed by his apparent calmness.

"Can I help you, young lady?"

After some hesitation, the stranger replied. She sounded quite nervous, if not a little frightened. "Um...I'm not sure. Who are you?"

Merl put on an air of authority. "I mean no offence, miss, but that was my question for you. And if you don't mind me asking, what is that you're holding behind your back?"

"None of your business." There was something eerily familiar in that assertive response. Arti was sure she'd heard the voice before. But where?

"There's no reason to get upset," said Merl. "It's just that it looks like a book, and I happen to know a thing or two about them." His voice softened, "You can trust me."

Arti cringed. What was Merl thinking? If the stranger was a Corporation spy, they were done for. Why not just tell her everything and hand Excalibri and the *Grail Tome* over while he was at it? A long pause followed before the young woman spoke again.

"Yes, it's a book and it...brought me here. I know it sounds crazy. I...I'm sorry for bothering you." The stranger's voice faded as if she was leaving.

"Please, may I look at it?" Merl was brimming with excitement, the same exhilaration Arti had sensed in him when he witnessed her pull the words from the tome. She strained to listen.

"Oh, my," said Merl. There was no hiding his ecstasy. "You are definitely in the right place, my dear. I'm Merl, and there's someone I want you to meet."

# CHAPTER 13

The motorhome's door opened and Merl looked up at Arti from the bottom step, a hand raised to signal everything was alright, that the visitor was not a threat. With her back wedged into the corner of the booth, Arti stared out warily from behind the round table and the fortress of books.

"It's alright," said Merl. "She's a friend." He arrived at the top of the landing and turned, waiting for his guest to enter.

Arti ignored the declaration, her eyes locked on the door, scrutinizing each of the stranger's features as she ascended the stairs: the auburn hair, the green eyes, the full lips. When the physical puzzle was complete and framed by memory, Arti screamed.

"It's her!" She gestured frantically at Merl, "Oh my god, it's her!"

Merl was confounded by Arti's panic. "Calm down," he demanded. "What are you talking about?" His face hardened, and he turned to the young woman. "What is she talking about?"

Arti didn't wait for the girl's answer. "She's the one from the vidads. She works for the Corporation. She's a spy!"

Merl's eyes flashed at the book in his hand, wondering if it had been a clever deception. He stepped away from the young woman and reached for a knife on the counter.

"Stop!" yelled Gwen, seeing Merl's gloved hand close on the weapon's handle. Keeping her eyes on the blade, she pleaded with Arti.

"I'm not who you think I am." She took a calming breath and lowered her voice. "Just...let me explain. Please." Stepping slowly past Merl, she eased herself into the booth, hands up in surrender.

"It's a long story."

For the next two hours, Gwen told Arti and Merl everything. How as a slave to her parents' ambition she had started modeling for the Corporation at the tender age of twelve. The day she entered the Archive and took the tiny book of letters. Her triumph in breaking its code, her re-birth as a reader—and the perilous lie she had lived to keep that secret.

As compelling as Gwen's story was, Arti was reluctant to believe it. How could she be sure the young woman was telling the truth? She *seemed* nothing like the person in the vidads, but it might just be a clever act. *A picture is worth a thousand words. Show, don't tell. You are the Corporation.* Arti could never forget that it was Gwen who spoke those awful words.

"When I found out they were going to burn the Archive, nothing else mattered," continued Gwen. "Those books are the only thing I've ever cared about." She nodded at *The*

*Knights of Maren*. "But *it* gave me hope and brought me here. I'm just not sure why."

Merl ran his finger over the tiny sword attached to the book's cover. "I've read about the Finding Swords, but I always considered them the stuff of legend." He held the book up for Arti and Gwen.

"It is said the Knights of Maren had them tacked to a vambrace, one of their forearm guards. Having sworn fealty to the Order, those seeking their liege lord would speak the oath, and the sword would guide them to their leader. It's how the knights came together in times of need."

"The oath? You mean the words I pulled from the tome?" asked Arti.

Merl nodded, "Indeed." He flipped open *The Knights of Maren*'s back cover. "*Swear fealty and be called*. And there's the oath below. When Gwen read it, she was brought here. *You* are her liege lord, Arti, and," he was beaming with delight, "she your knight."

"A knight?" Gwen scoffed. "I don't know anything about being a knight. What am I supposed to do?"

Arti beat Merl to the answer, knowing his explanation would go on forever.

"We have to take something from Morgan Fay. A very powerful book." She patted its tattered twin resting beneath Excalibri and the ink well.

"The *Grail Tome*," said Gwen.

"That's right," said Arti, wondering how she knew. "It's identical to this one, except it's got all its pages. Long story short, I have to write the last page and save the world." Seeing the skeptical look on Gwen's face, Arti added sarcastically, "Hey, a little sword brought you here. Don't judge."

Merl waved his hand in the air dismissively. "Gwen, you said that Fay was going to burn the Archive. When?"

"Corporation Night." Her brow wrinkled with worry. "They're planning a vidlink special. The CEO's going to perform the Lighting herself. The whole country will be watching."

"Hmmm, interesting." Merl bridged his gloved fingers and squinted in thought. "Why keep the Archive for twenty-five years? Then burn it?"

"I was told it was to celebrate the Corporation's twenty-fifth anniversary," said Gwen. "The dawn of a new era."

"*The dawn of a new era*?" grumbled Merl. "Sounds ominous. But what could it—"

"Timing," said Arti. "It's all about timing." Gwen and Merl looked at her, puzzled.

"Don't you see?" said Arti. "Fay doesn't want to wait. Every time a book is burned, *The History* gets closer to its final page, right? What if destroying the Archive is enough to take her right to the end?"

"Yes," said Merl. "A collection of the greatest books ever written. That could do it." Color drained from the old librarian's face. "That means the fate of the world will be written on Corporation Night." He sighed, "Just five days from now."

"Getting the book wouldn't be easy, no matter how much time we had," said Gwen. "I've worked at the castle for years; it's impossible to come and go without being seen. We'll have to pass right by Incendi headquarters to get up to Fay's office—that's if the book's even there. If we're caught," Mordred's image flashed in her mind, "we're dead."

"The book will be there; I'm sure of it," said Merl. "Morgan will be watching it closely, especially now that she knows the Challenger exists." He nodded at Arti. "I doubt she'd let anything draw her attention from it." The old librarian rubbed his chin, wondering if they'd ever have an opportunity to snatch the tome. Then it came to him.

"The Lighting. That will be our chance. Morgan won't burn the Archive inside the castle. She'll—"

"Do it outside," finished Gwen. "On the clifftop." Her eyes met his. "That's where it's going to happen."

"She'll have to leave the *Grail Tome* alone," concluded Arti, "and that's when we can take it."

Gwen frowned and shook her head. "It still won't be easy."

"No, it won't," agreed Merl. "It will have to be well thought out. And although I remember the castle well, I'm sure the interior has changed a great deal over the years. Do you think you can provide us with a detailed floor plan?"

"I think so," said Gwen. "But I'll need something to make it out of."

Arti placed her hand on one of Merl's notebooks. "Would these covers do?" She looked up at Merl to see if he would approve. "It's for a good cause."

"I guess so," said the old librarian. "It's what's *in* the books that's valuable. And while Gwen is working on that, *you* will be practicing with Excalibri.

"What's wrong?" asked Merl, noticing Gwen still wore her frown. "I know we're asking a lot of you. It will be dangerous, there's no denying it. If you don't feel—"

"It's not that," said Gwen. "I'll do whatever I can to help get the book from Fay. It's the Archive." She shook her head, "I can't let it burn. I won't."

"I have no intention of letting it burn," said Merl, his brow wrinkled in thought. "I just hope my idea works."

# CHAPTER 14

The man was far too thin for his height, and he wore layers of tattered clothing and a tired grey face much older than his years. He knew the shiny stack of coins on the desk would feed his family for a month, with a little extra left over for a night of whiskey and forgetting. He shuffled his feet anxiously, anticipating his reward.

Big Billy Johnson sat back in his squeaky leather chair and thumped his boots down hard on the worn desktop. He had the oak bureau's legs cut off to allow him to recline in such a fashion, refusing the limitations of a tiny stature. But no one dared call the undisputed King of Old Tintagel small. Not if they wished to see another sunrise.

In stark contrast to the concrete and metal of the arena, Big Billy's office atop the Cauldron was richly adorned with finely carved moldings, inlaid cabinetry, and plush furniture. The most prominent feature of the large room was also its most valuable—at least to Big Billy. His library covered one expansive wall, its burgeoning shelves of books filling the space from floor to ceiling.

Every business transaction that took place on the island had to first cross Big Billy's stunted desk and receive his approval. If money changed hands south of the Coin Canal, it was with Big Billy's blessing—and a fee for his "protective services." Any threats to his domain were met with quick and forceful rebuke. Having received a report of one such trespass, he was determined to answer it.

"Now listen, Rory, my boy. You only get paid if you answer all my questions. Little Donny here says you've news of a crossin' at the West Bridge."

Big Billy nodded at the giant of a man standing next to him. A thick red scar ran from Donnie's forehead to his chin, crossing one cloudy eye and a corner of his thin-lipped mouth. He was more like a son to Billy than an employee, intensely devoted and loyal.

"He says you told him it was a squad o' Flames." Billy's eyes narrowed. "Give me the goods, Rory. Everythin' you know."

Answering the command, words rushed from the thin man's mouth. "Yes, sir. It was yesterday, in the afternoon. I was near the West Bridge. A big black sedan crossed, turnin' east on Canal Street. They was drivin' fast, and I couldn't see through the dark glass, so I had my son track 'em. Runs like the wind, he does. As luck would have it, the car didn't go far. It parked on Market Street, and four Flames in their blacks got out. They went into the back of the old school, so my boy waited to see what they was up to." The man paused, afraid he had been too long-winded.

Intrigued, Big Billy pulled his legs off the desk. "Go ahead, Rory. What did the boy see?"

The man licked his lips, encouraged by Big Billy's interest. The stack of coins was almost in his pocket; he could taste the first sip of whiskey.

"A camper truck shows up, and two kids get out. My son said one was a local girl named Gal Hadd, maybe eleven or twelve, and another he didn't know, a bit older. They went into the school, too. A couple minutes later they come a runnin' out with a Flame hot on their heels. The older girl got to the truck, but the Flame caught the Hadd girl." The man was careful with his words. "My son says he hit her real hard, maybe even killed her. The truck pulled away before the Flame could get to the other one."

"Who was drivin' the truck?" asked Big Billy.

"My lad said it was an old man." He laughed, "But you know kids, they think anyone north of thirty's over the hill."

Big Billy looked up at the ceiling, trying to picture the scene in his mind. "A strange turn, to be sure. Is that it?"

"No, sir. It gets even stranger." The thin man's brow furrowed. "I'm only tellin' you what my son told me, and I know it sounds crazy, but—"

"It's okay, Rory. Just get to it."

"A white car, one of them sporty import deals, comes racin' down the street. Before it even comes to a stop, out flies a fella and kicks the Flame for a loop. My son said he would never have believed it 'less he saw it with his own eyes. And he ain't one to lie, sir, I swear. He said the fella took the Hadd girl and put her in the car, then drove away. And just as he's leavin', the Flame gets up like nothin' happened. No worse for the wear."

Big Billy leaned toward the thin man. "Did your son ever see the fella in the white car before?"

The thin man nodded slowly, convinced the reward was his. "Yes, sir. He said he saw him right here in the Cauldron. It was the fella from Ference, the one that fought The Mountain and won. The Poet."

The coins jingled in the thin man's pocket as he was escorted to the door. Crossing the threshold, he turned and bowed to Big Billy. "Thank you, sir."

Little Donny placed a huge hand on the man's shoulder and spun him around. "On your way, now," he grumbled, closing the door behind him.

Staring through the wide window at the dark arena below, Big Billy erupted, "Flames on my turf! In uniform, no less! And in broad daylight!" He slammed a fist down on the arm of his chair. "She's gone too far. It's disrespect."

Little Donny frowned and nodded his agreement. "Just to chase some kids? It don't make no sense, Boss."

Big Billy turned and winked at the huge man. "Good lad. That's the meat o' the potato. If the older girl's a decap, she must be somethin' special for Fay to send her Flames over." He shook his head. "But she promised she'd never do it. That she'd stay on her side. The kid must be worth a lot to her."

"What are you gonna do, Boss?"

"It's an insult, my boy, and I can't let it stand—it ain't good for business. I'm gonna make her pay for what she wants. Send word to every one o' my captains, from the Coin Canal to the Docks, from the Lookout to Island Park. I want the girl and old man that was drivin' the truck, and the other kid if she's still alive. And give all the boys fair warnin': The Poet may be with 'em, they should travel in numbers."

Gal tried to rise, but the eruption of pain in her head forced her back down. She closed her eyes, begging the world to stop spinning, but was answered by the sour taste in her throat promising another torturous bout of vomiting.

A hand lifted her head gently, and she heard a woman's quiet voice. "Lance, hand me the pail. She's going to be sick again."

There was something familiar about the woman's accent, but Gal was too ill to care. She heaved violently and spit into the pail, convinced she was slowly being turned inside out. With every beat of her heart, a drumming pain pounded at her temples making her wish she was dead.

Gal's forehead was wrapped in a cotton bandage, a spot of blood seeping through the material above her left eye. The whole side of her face was puffed out and bruised a deep purple, making it look like she was wearing a ghoulish mask. Her right arm was slung across her chest, fingers splinted and bound. Supported by Vivian's hand, she slowly collapsed back into the bed, wary of any sudden movements that would ignite another explosion of pain. Finding the pillow, Gal lost consciousness again, and Vivian dabbed her neck gently with a wet cloth to cool her, noticing a loop of twine tied to a silver key overlapping the gold chain and sapphire pendant she had given her.

"Will she make it?" asked the young man standing help-lessly next the bed.

"I've given her something for the pain and to reduce the swelling. The next few hours will tell." Vivian sighed, "If there's internal bleeding, we may lose her."

He lowered his head. "I should have been there sooner... before he could..."

Vivian put a hand on her nephew's arm. "It isn't your fault, Lance." She looked down at Gal. "I blame myself for not sending you with them. I pray it didn't cost this child her life."

"There is only one to blame," said Lance. "I will find the man who did this and avenge her." But his words carried a tinge of doubt. "He should not have survived that kick. He's been trained, I'm sure of it. And *very* well."

Together, Vivian and Lance kept vigil through the night, taking turns delicately ministering cool compresses to Gal's neck and face to reduce the swelling and allay her fever. It was shortly after sunrise when the girl stirred.

"Water," she mumbled. "Thirsty."

Lance could see the relief on his aunt's tired face. She tipped a cup to Gal's lips. "Just a little," she said. "You can have more, later."

Gal squinted up at Vivian with her good eye. "Arti? Is she okay?"

"Arti is fine," said Vivian. "Just rest. You'll be together soon."

Gal tilted her head slightly, noticing the young man standing behind Vivian. "I've seen you before. At the Cauldron." A stab of pain forced her eye closed, and she winced. "You're The Poet."

"Yes," said Lance. He could see how difficult it was for Gal to speak. "Try to rest. We can talk when you are well."

"But there ain't much time," said Gal, fighting the pain battering her skull. "If you're one of them knights, she'll need your help. The Flame, he's gonna kill her."

Lance moved to the edge of the bed and rested his hand on Gal's shoulder. "I will not let that happen." He leaned close to her, and his voice dropped to a whisper. "Paci et guarigne a coraggia." *Peace and healing to the brave.*

The words were like a delicate caress; Gal lied back and drifted to sleep.

# CHAPTER 15

Morgan Fay choked back her rage and fear, lips tightly pursed as if she was about to explode. Trembling, she rose unsteadily from her chair and turned to look out through the tower's narrow window. The island in the distance mocked her.

"I ask you to do one simple task, and you fail me!" she screamed.

Mordred stood in front of Fay's desk, head bowed, eyes averted. He slumped like he was carrying a tremendous weight, his knees about to buckle under the load.

"She had help," he croaked, knowing the explanation would fall short. "An old man. And another...trained in the Art."

Fay spun around as if she'd been slapped. "A knight? Are you certain?"

Mordred nodded feebly, hoping the information would temper her rage. "His kick had the strike of words. He... surprised me."

Fay looked down at the massive tome opened on her desk. The letters continued to appear, snaking their way across the page. With each passing day, they came faster, taking *The History* ever closer to its conclusion. She clenched her fists and sneered at Mordred.

"I want guards posted at the castle day and night; only Victor Herrat and his staff are permitted on the grounds. Is that clear?"

Mordred nodded again.

Fay looked hard at her son. "Before the Lighting, you will find the girl and kill her. Alone."

Mordred started to speak, but Fay cut him off. "No more words. Don't come back until it's done."

The Incendi captain straightened, gritting his teeth. For a brief moment, a flash of anger ignited in his eyes, and he had to fight his desire to strike out. His mother saw the look and thought it best to soften her tone. Mordred was a weapon— her weapon—but like a trained beast answering the whip, he had a wildness that could never be completely tamed. One too many lashes, and he might turn on her.

She smiled softly and took his hand. "Please do this for me, Son. I trust only you."

Surprised by her tenderness, Mordred's thin face brightened. "I will, Mother," he said. "I promise."

Threading his way down the spiraling stone staircase, Mordred arrived on the landing next the door with its bright flame insignia and noticed Victor Herrat hastily shuffling down the hall toward him, one pudgy hand holding his cap in place, the other wrestling with the scarf trailing in his wake.

"Captain! Captain!" shrieked Herrat, giving Mordred no option but to stop.

"I have an important matter to attend to, Director," said Mordred. "Please, make it quick."

Herrat huffed and puffed a moment before he managed to force the words out. "Miss Degan is missing!" he cried. "Gone! No one has seen her since yesterday, and her parents are in a panic."

"Miss Degan? Missing? Are you certain?"

"Yes," said Herrat. "A neighbor saw her leave. With a suitcase. They found her vidlink in pieces." He covered his face with his hands. "The Lighting. We planned on filming the ads for it tomorrow. I'm ruined!"

Mordred was stunned. Gwen Degan, a decap? He felt a sudden hollowness in his chest. The beautiful young woman he had believed in and admired was a lie. A work of fiction. How had he been fooled?

If her disappearance had come at any other time, Mordred would have gone after her, made her pay for her deceit, made her pay for his feelings. But the mission his mother had given him was more important; even Gwen Degan would have to wait.

"I'll put out a warrant," said Mordred, maintaining his composure. "I suggest you find someone else for the ads."

Gal drifted in and out of consciousness for another day and night, with Lance and Vivian taking turns watching over her. Her left eye was ringed by a deep shade of purple, but Vivian's careful checks on its pupil revealed no dilation, a good sign. It was under Lance's watch that Gal finally came out of her fretful sleep.

"I'm thirsty," she said, gently probing her bandaged brow with the fingers of her good hand.

A tired Lance nodded and poured a glass of water, lifting it slowly to her lips. She took it from him, with a painful frown. "I can do it."

"How are you feeling?" he asked. To Gal, the handsome young man's smile and accent seemed like remnants of a dream.

"I'm okay," she answered, swallowing the cool liquid, experiencing the strange sense of déjà vu. "Did I talk to you before?"

"Yes, you and Lance are already acquainted," said Vivian, stepping into the room. She looked relieved. "You were in quite a state. You look much better now, but you must take things slowly. It will be a while before you can exert yourself."

"The Flame. I remember," said Gal. "We were at the school. He chased us and...Arti!" She started to get up, but Lance gently restrained her.

"Your friend is well," he assured her. "I saw her get away."

"And I'm sure Merl is looking after her," added Vivian. "Do you know where they might be?"

"Yeah," said Gal, with a painful nod. "The Camel Lot, off Center Street and Cobden. He's been there for a while. He told us it was safe."

"He must be using the tome to hide from Fay," said Vivian. "Good."

Gal started to rise again. "I gotta go," she said. "I wanna see Arti." The sudden dizziness convinced her that it wasn't a good idea.

"You're not going anywhere," said Vivian. "Lance will take you to her when *I* say you're ready. Until then, you need to rest and get your strength back." Gal frowned at the old woman but didn't argue.

Between recurring headaches and dizziness, Gal managed to eat and drink a little. As the pain and nausea lessened and her condition improved, her inquisitiveness returned.

"Can I ask you a question?"

"I am at your disposal," came Lance's elegant reply. Gal thought he talked funny.

"At the Cauldron, Arti and me watched you beat The Mountain." She looked at him suspiciously. "How'd you do it?"

Lance's modesty made him reluctant to discuss the matter, but he knew Gal wouldn't be put off; the girl was nothing, if not stubborn.

"The de Lac family has trained in *The Verses* since they were first written. You know of what I speak, having seen one of the great books yourself. My ancestors were the first Knights of Maren, named after our island home. From a small child, I learned how to use the poems to give me strength and direct my will.

"The big Parmelese man—the one I faced in the ring— was strong in body but not in mind. I had the power of words to draw upon, and he only hate and anger." Lance couldn't hide his shame. "It was not a fair fight, and there was no honor in my victory. I don't know why, but Aunt Vivian thought that my appearance might draw the attention of the Challenger, the one who could wield Excalibri." He smiled. "She was right."

Gal found herself staring at Lance long after he finished speaking. She'd never met anyone like him. He was incredibly good looking, yes, but that was only part of his appeal; Lance's gentle manner and kindness were what Gal was most drawn to. As she studied his handsome face, she remembered his car, the sleek white Ferencian Charger.

"Are you rich?" she asked.

Lance smiled, shyly. "My family is the wealthiest in all of Ference."

Gal's infatuation was complete.

The arrival of Gwen Degan at the Camel Lot had put Arti on edge, but the young woman seemed to be nothing like her sexy vidad persona. Even so, Gal's words continued to echo in Arti's head: *Seems and is ain't the same thing.* Merl believed Gwen was an ally, magically escorted to them by a Finding Sword, but Arti wasn't so sure. It all seemed too convenient, too coincidental.

Gwen parked her parents' car in the end garage bay where it would be out of sight, then started constructing a model of the castle on the motorhome's floor while Merl and Arti dug into the old librarian's notebooks piled on the round table, searching through his reams of research, hoping to find more information on how to write with Merrill's pen, Excalibri. But their efforts produced nothing that could add to the cryptic description from the ancient Astengan's memoir: *Forged together in truth, the pen and the will are one.* Arti had no idea what it meant—if it meant anything.

"This is stupid," she said, pushing one of the notebooks aside. "Why can't I just dip it in the ink and write with it? How hard can it be?"

"There's a lot more to it than that," Merl grumbled, frustrated by Arti's impatience. He sat back and crossed his arms. "But I can see you don't believe me, so let's try it your way." He pushed a piece of paper in front of Arti, plunked the ink well down on the table above it, and nodded curtly at the pen, "Go ahead. Write something."

Gwen stood up to watch, wondering if her so-called liege lord could accomplish the task. Regretting her protest, but not willing to lose face, Arti picked up Excalibri and adjusted it in her hand, making sure it was in the proper writing position. She carefully flipped back the lid of the ink well and very slowly dipped the pen into the container, withdrawing it with the same level of care. She held the pen over the well for a moment, just in case the precious black fluid on the point dripped. The ink stayed on the nib, and Arti took a deep breath readying herself to write.

She lifted Excalibri over the paper, lowering it slowly until its blackened point met the clean white surface. Moving the pen in a straight line, she expected to see a trail of ink in its wake, but there was nothing there; the sheet remained blank.

"What's going on? The ink won't come off." Arti examined the nib, perplexed.

"I told you so," barked Merl. "Your will is not one with the pen."

"I don't even know what that means!" cried Arti. She tossed the pen onto the paper (an action that made Merl cringe) and leaned back in the booth, shaking her head.

Gwen sat down beside Arti. "You can't give up," she said. "This is too important." Arti just stared straight ahead, unwilling to accept her encouragement.

"I don't know if this will help," continued Gwen, "but when I read, I try to picture the characters—what they look and sound like. You probably think it's strange, but I like to dream that I'm with them, that I'm in the story. That the story is…about me." She smiled at Arti. "Do you ever do that?"

Arti glanced sideways at Gwen, "Yeah, sometimes." The memory of sitting with her parents in their secret library under the soft warm light of the reading lamp came back to her. *And they lived happily ever after.*

"Then what if you tried working backwards?" said Gwen. "You know, start at being *in* the story, at seeing it in your mind like it's real. Like it's true. Maybe the pen will work. That might be what that scribe meant."

"Yes," said Merl. "Very good, Gwen. That's just how Merrill described it: *Forged together in truth.*" He looked at Arti. "It's worth a try."

Arti leaned over the round table, taking Excalibri in her hand again, suspending it above the piece of paper. She closed her eyes, opening her mind, trying to bind her consciousness to the pen. But she couldn't sustain the effort. Too many thoughts hid in the shadows, breaking her concentration, shattering her will: distrust, resentment, fear. She tried to repel them, to silence their voices, to focus on a single image. After a minute of mental struggle, Arti surrendered.

"I can't do it," she said, bowing her head. "I just can't." She looked up at Merl and Gwen, defeated.

The old librarian slowly pulled the blank sheet of paper away and nodded at her. "We'll figure it out," he promised. "It'll just take some more practice, that's all."

Gwen placed her hand on Arti's shoulder. "Don't give up."

Arti couldn't understand why they had such faith in her, why they believed she was the one who could defeat Morgan Fay. It was impossible to think that the future would be entrusted to her. After all, she couldn't even save her own parents. She couldn't save Gal.

As Arti held the image of her young friend in her mind, she experienced a strange sensation. It was much like her escape from the burning library, when she thought she heard the books speak to her. She felt herself drifting away from her seat at the round table; there was no Merl, no Gwen, no moto-rhome, no Camel Lot. The world around her evaporated, and she was transported to another place and time, like stepping through a misty veil.

What she saw was impossible.

From the window of the motorhome, Arti watched her-self cross a grassy meadow and disappear into a forest, hood up, hands tucked in the bulging front pocket of her hoodie. It was near dark, and Merl stood in the clearing, watching her leave, glancing down at a glowing object in his gloved hands. A vidlink?

Next, she was staring down at a *Grail Tome* open on a desk. Unlike Merl's book, this one was pristine, none of its pages missing or burned. The image lasted for only a moment before another vision, more ominous and terrifying, replaced it.

Looking out from behind a pitch-black door, she could see herself standing with Gwen in a hallway, next to the body of a fallen trooper. The two of them were talking, and it was obvious that something was wrong, very wrong. Arti could see utter desperation in her own eyes, a look of doom and failure that made her shiver. That fear only deepened when she heard herself speak the ominous words: *"What hope do we have?"*

The gut-wrenching question burned in Arti's mind like a flaming hot ember, propelling her back to the present, returning her with a start to the confines of the motorhome, to Merl and Gwen.

"W...what happened?" asked Arti, trying to get her bearings. Having no recollection of the sudden and strange visions she'd just experienced, Arti was surprised to see Merl peering over Gwen's shoulder; he had been sitting across from her just a moment before. Gwen was still to Arti's left, but wearing an expression of shocked wonder.

"You did it," said Gwen. "You wrote something." She pointed at the edge of the round table near the center of the U-shaped booth.

There, in perfect swirling black script, were two words: *Siegea Perilisi.*

# CHAPTER 16

As Lance said goodbye to his aunt Vivian, Gal waited in the Charger, sitting back in the soft leather seat, admiring the sleek dashboard with its shiny glass dials. The left side of her face was still very swollen, so she had to turn her head sideways and look through her good eye to take everything in. Her head was still wrapped in bandages, and the fingers of her right hand remained splinted. Vivian said she could take the splints off in a couple weeks, but her fingers would take months to mend. The headaches and dizzy spells, she said, might last even longer. For the second time in a week, the girl and the old woman said their goodbyes, this time Gal returning the hug she was offered.

"Look after Gal and the others, Lance," said Vivian. "And yourself." She kissed her nephew's cheek. "Be true to your name and your oath. You are the last of your line trained in the Art, but eighty generations of the de Lac family are with you. A Knight of Maren is never alone."

Lance threw his leather jacket over his shoulder and grabbed his duffel bag. He smiled at her and nodded, finding strength in the words.

The trip from Lakeside Antiquities to the Camel Lot was not a good one for Gal. They were only halfway down Center Street when she leaned forward in her seat, eyes closed to combat a fiery stab of pain in her head.

"I will stop," said Lance. "This is too much for you."

"No," objected Gal, still hunched over. "Keep goin'."

Fighting her nausea, she managed to give Lance directions to the old car dealership, but the short journey seemed to last an eternity. She was relieved when they finally arrived, desperate for the car's motion to end.

"Go to the back," said Gal, squinting through her good eye. "There's a g'rage."

The Charger rumbled past the main building and, for a moment, Gal forgot how much pain she was in. She could see the motorhome's grill peeking out of the bay; Arti and Merl had made it back. But then she noticed a car parked in the last bay and wondered who it could belong to.

Inside the motorhome, the three occupants were discussing the meaning of the words Arti had written on the round table.

"As you'd expect, it's Old Ferencian," said Merl. "Translated, it means *Perilous...*" he hesitated, "...ah... *Siege.*"

"But what does *that* mean?" asked Arti. "Why would I...I mean the pen write it?"

"It's difficult to say," said Merl, rubbing his chin.

Arti hadn't known Merl for long, but she could already read him like a book. He was hiding something; she was sure of it.

"Maybe it has to do with the quest," offered Gwen. "*Siege* could refer to getting the book from the castle, and we know it's going to be dangerous. That could be the *perilous* part."

"Hmmm…yes," agreed Merl, happy to accept Gwen's explanation. "It will be a perilous siege. That must be it. The pen is warning us of what's ahead." He turned to Arti, "That makes sense, don't you think?"

"Could be," replied Arti, masking her suspicion.

The sound of a car approaching interrupted the discussion, and the three scrambled from their places around the table.

"Are you expecting someone?" whispered Gwen, gathering up the pieces of the model castle from the floor of the motorhome.

"No," answered Merl, "but we weren't expecting you either." For a moment, he wondered if their luck had finally run out.

"It's the car from the antique shop," gasped Arti, bending to look out through the motorhome's windshield. She waited for Merl to drop down beside her. "Isn't it?"

"There can't be more than one such vehicle on the island," said Merl, straining to see.

When the door opened and Lance stepped out, Arti couldn't believe her eyes. The slicked back hair, the handsome face, the leather jacket.

"It's The Poet!"

"The one you saw fight at the…what's it called?" Merl searched for the word.

"Cauldron," said Arti. "Yes, that's him. I'm sure."

Gwen joined Arti and Merl on the floor to get a look. "He's *way* too good looking to be a fighter," she said.

"He's opening the other door," said Merl. "What's he up to?"

When Lance lifted his passenger from the car, Arti shouted at the top of her lungs, "Gal!" The cry could easily be heard outside the motorhome.

"What was that?" asked Lance, carrying Gal gingerly toward the garage.

"Sounded like Arti," winced Gal. "Guess she's happy to see me."

It was the greatest of understatements. Arti was beside herself, overwhelmed by a mix of joy and relief that made her forget about everything else: the pen, the quest, the impossible mission still ahead of them. Gal was alive, and they were together again. It was a miracle made even more remarkable by the devotion shown her by the handsome young man cradling her in his arms.

Arti flew down the steps of the motorhome and threw open the door, with Merl and Gwen in tow.

"Are you okay?" she asked, alarmed by Gal's appearance: the bandaged head with its spot of blood, the bruised and swollen face, the splinted fingers.

"She will recover," said Lance. "She needs time to rest and heal."

Arti nodded, leading them toward the motorhome. "We'll make a bed for her." Her eyes pleaded with Merl.

"Yes, yes. I'll get a blanket and pillow." He directed Lance, "Take her to the back. She'll be comfortable there."

After delivering Gal carefully to the wide rear bench of the motorhome where he and Arti made sure she was comfortable, the young man introduced himself.

"My name is Lance," he said on bended knee, "and I swear fealty, my liege."

Arti stiffened, not knowing what she should say. Beside her, Gwen giggled.

"You are a Knight of Maren?" asked Merl, rescuing Arti.

"Yes," said Lance. "I was summoned by my Aunt Vivian. She believed *The History* would soon be written, and the Challenger to Morgan Fay would be found here in Tintagel. When Arti came for the pen, my aunt was filled with hope. But something still troubled her, so instead of having me accompany you, she thought it best that I watch from afar." Lance glanced back at Gal, solemnly. "It was a decision she deeply regrets. As do I." He looked at Arti and offered his pledge: "I will not fail you again."

"Thanks," was all Arti could think to say.

Lance nodded, then turned to Gwen, his mood more upbeat. "Are you also Arti's friend?"

Gwen glanced uncomfortably at Arti, knowing she didn't dare make such a claim. "Um...I..."

"Gwen is also a knight, Lance," said Merl, "but untrained in *The Verses*. She was guided here by a Finding Sword."

Lance couldn't hide his amazement. As a young page, he had been raised on tales of the ancient knights and their magic, the Finding Swords being an important part of that lore. It was said that the tiny objects were the knights' most cherished possessions because they could help them locate their liege lord no matter how far away he might be. One need only speak the oath they shared, and the sword would point the way. Lance recalled his family's motto, the words his

Aunt Vivian said to him when he and Gal departed Lakeside Antiquities: *A Knight of Maren is never alone.*

"Gwen knows the castle and will guide us on our quest," added Merl.

"Very well," said Lance. He hadn't taken his eyes off Gwen. "If you would like, I would be happy teach you some of the *farapenne de moets.*"

"Lance is trained in the 'strike of words,' Gwen," explained Merl. "It's a very special kind of martial art."

Gwen's face lit up. "Yes, I've read about it. I'd love to learn from you."

"It will be my honor." Lance bowed, amusing Gwen with the gallant gesture.

"Keep in mind, there's much work to be done," said Merl. "We must complete our mission on Corporation Night, and there's precious little time to prepare. I'll fill you in on the details, Lance."

In a flatbed truck parked at the corner of Waverly and Canal Streets, two passengers sat in the cab while a cargo of men with clubs and knives crouched behind them.

"Butch said he'd meet us here," mumbled the man behind the wheel. "Said he might know where The Poet's at."

The driver was over six feet tall, but sitting next to Little Donnie in the pick-up's box-like cab, he looked tiny. The long red scar crossing Donnie's cloudy eye made him even more intimidating.

"Well, if he ain't here soon, we're headin' down to Vinnie's on Market to see if he's seen anythin'. Big Billy's expectin' results; I ain't goin' back to him empty handed."

Little Donnie's patience was wearing thin when a trio of ragged looking men came shuffling down the street toward them. A hand signal from the one in front and the driver's relief confirmed the man's identity.

"That's Butch. I told you he'd make it."

Addressing Little Donnie at the open passenger window, Butch was wary of the big man whose reputation preceded him.

"You lookin' for that Ferencian fighter?"

"Yeah, The Poet. Seen him?"

"Been a fancy white import—one of them Chargers—parked down a dead end next a little shop by the lakeshore. Only been there a couple weeks."

"How do you know it's his?"

The man laughed. "Aren't many of them cars around. And the old lady that owns the shop's from Ference. What are the odds?"

Little Donnie chewed his lip. "Okay, we'll look into it. If you're right, there'll be a little somethin' for you at the Cauldron. Drop in and see me." The big man tapped the hood to go, but the order was ignored.

"Who's that?" said the driver, looking up the street. A long black Destrier sedan was cruising toward them.

"If that's Flames, they got a death wish," said Little Donnie.

Butch jumped back from the door as the big man leapt out of the truck. He snapped his chunky fingers at the men crouched on the flatbed and pointed at the approaching car. The throng of fighters jumped down to the pavement, clubs and knives at the ready.

"Don't do nothin' 'til I say," ordered Little Donnie. If they were Incendi, he expected they'd be armed with lighters, and things were going to get messy.

The Destrier came to a stop only a few yards in front of the truck, its smoky glass making it impossible to see the sedan's occupants. Little Donnie and his men formed a line in front of the pick-up, preparing for battle. This was one turf war they were determined to win.

The driver's door opened, and Mordred stepped out, the hard soles of his shiny leather boots making a scraping sound on the pebbled asphalt. Expecting other Flames to emerge from the car, Little Donnie and his men waited and watched.

But Mordred was alone and carried no weapon. He walked slowly toward Little Donnie's line, showing no concern for the group of armed thugs standing before him.

"I'm looking for someone," said Mordred. "A girl from Main named Penderhagen." He removed his black fedora and brushed it nonchalantly with his fingers. "Apparently, she has some friends on this dirty little island of yours." He looked up, studying the men's faces, watching for a reaction. "An old man with a motorhome." Mordred paused. "No? How about a younger one, drives a white sports car?" He arched his brow, pretending to be impressed. "It's r-e-a-l nice, I doubt you'd forget it."

He saw what he was looking for: a slight frown from one of the men, the one who'd been standing beside the truck when he arrived.

"So you *can* help me," said Mordred. "Good, because I'm in a bit of a hurry."

In a blur of motion, he was on them, words spilling from his lips, barely audible above the thuds and cracks of muscle and bone. Mordred spun along the line of men, arms and legs striking at all angles, evading the feeble thrusts of clubs and blades directed at him. One after another, the men fell, bleeding and broken.

Little Donnie crawled toward the truck, a shattered leg trailing behind him, blood seeping from his nose and ears. Mordred delivered a spinning kick to the big man's throat, and he went down in a heap.

Only one islander was still conscious. Butch was sitting with his back against the Destrier's front wheel, cradling an arm dislocated at the elbow. He couldn't feel his legs, and the rest of his body quivered convulsively. Terrified eyes looked up at Mordred as he crouched beside him.

"The man with the white car," said Mordred. "Where?"

Butch looked at the bodies strewn around him and burped out an answer, "The sh...shop. L...Lakeside. D...dead end."

"Dead end," repeated Mordred. He stood up and straightened his uniform.

Butch heard the strange words but didn't see the kick coming.

# CHAPTER 17

The white paneled door flew off its hinges in an explosion of splinters. Passing the stairs and the tall clock wedged in the corner, Mordred stalked into the main room through its archway, the soles of his boots clicking on the hardwood floor between islands of area rugs. He weaved his way between the tables covered with merchandise, but none of the items were of interest to him. The Incendi captain wasn't hunting bargains; he was hunting people.

"Judging by your entrance, I doubt you care that we're closed," said Vivian, from behind the counter. The old woman showed no hint of fear. "Who are you? What do you want?"

"I think you know," replied Mordred. "The one who drives the white car and those he's helping."

"Oh, so you've met my nephew, Lance?"

"Yes, but he ran away," said Mordred. "It's what cowards do."

"Oh, Lance is no coward," said Vivian. "He's a true Knight of Maren." Her green eyes locked on the Incendi captain's, "Not a heretic like you."

Rage ignited in Mordred's eyes. Muttering a string of words, he leapt across the counter and clenched his hand around Vivian's throat, lifting her off the floor. He held her in his vise-like grip, taking pleasure in her futile gasps for air.

"You'll tell me what I want to know," said Mordred. Sneering at her, he mouthed another verse…

With the *Grail Tome* resting on the round table under the soft glow of the dome light overhead, Merl took his seat in the motorhome's U-shaped booth and directed the others to join him.

"Arti," he said, pointing a gloved finger, "take your place, as before." He looked up at Gwen. "And you, Gwen, next to Arti, please." Finally, with a nod, he invited Lance to sit, "Young knight, if you will."

Merl seemed content with everyone's position. An empty space remained where Arti had written the cryptic phrase *Siegea Perilisi* on the edge of the round table, and she was sure Merl planned it that way.

"This is the first meeting of the new Knights of Maren," announced Merl, formally. "Like the book knights of old, each of us has a seat, and no place at this table has prominence over another. We are equals here." He glanced at Arti, and she saw the message in his eyes: *Gwen deserves your respect.*

The old librarian intertwined his gloved fingers and straightened in his seat, adding weight to his words. "Together we share one goal: to take the undamaged *Grail Tome* from Morgan Fay, so Arti may write its final page. Our chance will come on Corporation Night when Fay is to perform the Lighting. And although we are one in this quest, each of us has a very important role to play.

"Gwen, you know best the layout of the castle—save for Morgan Fay's suite. My memory of the upper tower should help with that. It will be your job to provide us with a detailed plan, the best route to get inside and retrieve the tome." Merl glanced at the floor where Gwen's model of the ancient building was taking shape. "I like what you've done so far. Just remember, no detail is too small. When you've finished the model, we'll use it to plan the mission. And on Corporation Night, *you* will act as guide.

"As the only one trained in *The Verses*, it will be your job, Lance, to protect Arti and Gwen from any...resistance." Merl turned toward the young man, worry etched on his face. "Security will be very tight. Morgan won't like leaving the book alone, so I expect you'll be greeted by a significant number of Incendi guards. They'll be armed with lighters. On their highest settings, a touch from one can kill.

"And there's someone who poses an even greater threat. You know of whom I speak."

"The man in black," said Lance.

"Yes. Mordred would enjoy nothing more than killing you, and Arti, and Gwen, and me." As the old librarian spoke, Arti wondered what Lance and Gwen would think if they knew Merl was talking about his own son.

"On my honor, I will do all I can to keep you safe," vowed Lance, looking around the table at his quest mates. He was so passionate and sincere that Arti found herself staring at him after he spoke. When he noticed her attention, she quickly looked away, red-faced.

159

"You already know *your* task, Arti," said Merl, irritated by her inattention. "We will continue your training with Excalibri. You must be prepared to write the final page of *The History* under very difficult circumstances. When Gwen and Lance get you into Fay's office, the rest will be up to you. You must be ready."

"I wrote with it," said Arti, glancing down at the small wooden box holding the pen, "but I don't know how I did it." Her eyes pleaded with the old librarian, "I don't know if I can do it again."

"You must find a way," said Merl, "for all of us." He reached over the round table and rested his gloved hand on the *Grail Tome's* singed cover.

"Place your hands on the book, young knights. We will say the oath, together."

Lance offered his hand first, his expression solemn and determined. Gwen smiled and extended her own hand, resting it next to Lance's. All three turned to Arti, waiting for her to join them in the ritual.

Arti took a deep breath, feeling crushed under the incredible weight of responsibility. "I hope I don't let you down," she said, before adding her hand to theirs.

"You won't," said Merl, less than convincingly. He began to speak the oath, and the others joined in.

*"The book is my shield.*
*The pen is my sword.*
*The ink is my blood."*

And though she appeared to be asleep on the cushioned bench in back of the motorhome, Arti was sure she could hear Gal mouthing the words along with them.

160

Now that they knew their roles, each of the quest mates began preparing for the mission in earnest. Merl insisted that he and Arti have privacy in the motorhome. Gal was allowed to stay, needing the comfort of the vehicle's rear bench to recover from her injury, but Merl wanted nothing to interfere with Arti's practice with Excalibri. Arti noticed how Lance looked at Gwen and the eagerness he displayed in accompanying her to the adjacent bay where his Charger was parked. She hoped that whatever was going on between them wouldn't distract them from the mission.

"Just don't leave the Camel Lot for any reason," Merl told them. "We're safe here."

The garage's tall open door allowed in ample light, and even with Lance's car dominating the space, there was more than enough room left over on the oil-stained concrete floor for Gwen to work on the castle model while Lance ran through his "exercises" next to her.

They were a strange combination of slow motion movements—kicks and spins and punches—accompanied by a string of slow chant-like whispers, Lance's eyes remaining closed as he uttered them. He was barefoot and shirtless as he ran through the routines, and before long his lean body was slick with sweat, adding a golden sheen to his sculpted muscles and the intricate grail tattoo covering his back. Gwen found she was paying more attention to him than her work.

"If I am interfering, I can go elsewhere," said Lance politely, looking up at Gwen from a handstand.

"Um...no...it's okay," said Gwen, brushing a strand of hair from her face. "I...I was just wondering if..."

"Yes?" replied Lance, nimbly flipping his feet under him. "What is it?"

Gwen set down the pair of scissors Merl had given her to cut the notebook covers. "Well, I'd like to take you up on your offer. I'd like to learn how to strike with words—if you wouldn't mind giving me a lesson. After I'm done this, of course." She pointed at the model.

"It would be my pleasure," said Lance. He retrieved his t-shirt from the Charger's hood and pulled it over his head. "If you would like my assistance to finish your task, I am yours. Then I can teach."

"Sure," she said. "I could use the help."

With Lance's aid, Gwen was able to complete construction of the mini castle by the middle of the afternoon. The model was quite ingenious, requiring no tape, glue, or adhesive of any kind. Each piece joined the other by way of tabs and slots, one fitting snuggly into the next. Sections of the building could be removed, leaving the others intact, and there were tiny pencil drawings on the walls and floors indicating important features. Relying on her incredible memory, Gwen even identified locations in the building that offered hiding places that might prove useful in avoiding Incendi guards.

"It is very good," complimented Lance, examining the finished product. "So much detail."

"Thanks, you were a big help," said Gwen. She leaned in close beside him. "I just hope I didn't forget anything."

"I doubt it," replied Lance. "You strike me as one who forgets very little."

"Speaking of 'striking'," said Gwen, playfully, "you made a promise."

"Ah, yes, *farapenne de moets*. You wish to learn the strike of words. What do you know of the Art?"

"I just finished a book that talked about it, a translation of *The Knights of Maren*, by Guillaume de Lac. It was the book with the tiny sword on its cover, the one that led me here."

Lance's face lit up. "I am also a de Lac. Guillaume was my ancestor. My aunt Vivian often spoke of his writings. I would love to see this book."

"It's in the motorhome. I can show it to you later." Gwen glanced at the adjacent garage. "I don't want to interrupt Arti and Merl."

"Of course," said Lance, following Gwen's eyes. "Arti has a very difficult task ahead of her. I hope the librarian can help her find her words."

"Me too," said Gwen. She turned to Lance, her face brightening, "Now for that lesson."

Lance offered Gwen his hand and helped her to her feet. "Very well," he said. "But I must tell you the strike of words is very difficult to learn and takes many years to master. Do not be disappointed if it eludes you.

"You may think it strange but I have never seen *The Verses*; they are an oral tradition in my family. The only written record of them is in the *Grail Tomes*. Merl has offered to show them to me tonight." He couldn't hide his excitement. "It is the greatest of honors.

"But before we speak more of the poems," said Lance, resuming the role of teacher, "you must know how to center yourself. Only the knight who is centered can direct his will and fight with words."

"Okay," said Gwen. "How do I do that?"

"You need to focus your breathing." Lance took Gwen's hand and pressed it against his chest. "Here," he said, inhaling deeply.

Gwen felt his muscles tighten beneath his shirt. "I...I see," she said, slowly pulling her hand away.

"Now close your eyes and concentrate," said Lance. "Find your center. This is the place of power within you. Feel each breath begin and end there."

Gwen obeyed, slowly inhaling and exhaling. One long, deep breath in and out. Then another. And another.

"Very good," said Lance, studying each rise and fall of her chest. "You breathe well."

"Um...thanks. Done it all my life," she quipped. "Keeps me alive."

"But it is probably the first time you thought about it, controlled it," countered Lance. "If you cannot find your center and the place where your will resides, words have little power."

"You mean *The Verses*. I remember reading that there are one hundred and twelve of them."

"That is true. And as my master taught me, the power behind every one of them comes from here." Lance tapped his chest again. "From the heart. From the will."

"Your master? Who was that?" asked Gwen.

"His name was Jean de Lac, *The Bard of Lucinne*," said Lance, his eyes sparkling with reverence. "He was my uncle, an honored knight, and a great fighter. My father died when I was a child, and before his passing, my uncle promised him he would continue my training. I am the last of the de Lacs to learn the Art."

"I'm sorry," said Gwen. "About your father, I mean."

"Thank you." Lance looked down at his hands, rubbing them together. "My earliest memory is of my father teaching me *Ca Castere Chevallero*, the first of *The Verses*." He laughed, "I stumbled over the words—and my feet. But my will was strong, and I practiced until I was successful. I still remember how proud my father was."

"I can tell you miss him," said Gwen. "You must have been close."

"Yes," said Lance. "Very close. Do...do you have family?"

"No," she said abruptly.

There was an awkward silence that made Lance regret he'd asked. "I'm sorry, I did not mean to—"

Gwen brushed it aside. "It's alright, you were being polite. It's just something I'd rather not talk about. Not...not now."

Lance nodded. "Very well." He smiled to raise Gwen's spirits. "My student, it is time for you to learn the first verse."

"The one your father taught you?"

"Yes, *Ca Castere Chevallero*. It means 'The Knight's Shield'. It is the simplest of *The Verses*—and the most important."

"Oh yes, 'castere' is Old Ferencian for 'shield,'" said Gwen. "I remember it from the Knight's Oath. But I don't understand the connection between *The Verses* and fighting. What happens when you say the words?"

"*The Verses*...how do you say...bind to one's will, amplifying it, adding strength and speed to the body. When a knight speaks a verse, he does so from instinct, relying on the words that will best serve his will at that moment. A few verses need only be spoken once in combat, so long does their power last. That is the case with *Ca Castere Chevallero*. As the name suggests, it is a verse of protection."

Lance moved behind Gwen. He reached down and lifted her arms, bending them at the elbows and crossing them in front of her at neck height.

"This is the blocking form," he said, his cheek brushing hers, his chest hugging her back, "the position taken to turn away a kick or punch. If the strike comes low, your arms move down and away. If it comes high, your arms move up." Like a puppeteer, he guided Gwen through the blocking motions.

"With *Ca Castere Chevallero*," said Lance, stepping around Gwen to face her again, "the blocking form is used to repel an attack and throw your enemy off balance, so *you* can strike back. Your footwork is very important. Good fighters move their feet well, and as my uncle used to say, the best fighters *dance*."

"What are the words in the verse, and when do you say them?" asked Gwen, intrigued.

"The words can be spoken well before the block," said Lance, "and the power of *The Knight's Shield* will linger. Do you want to try?"

Gwen took a deep breath. "Why not?"

"Why not, indeed," smiled Lance. "I will say the verse slowly. Repeat after me: *Ca farapenne esta rizer, pe mi esta castere*."

Gwen said the words, careful to pronounce them just as Lance had. Every accent was perfect, every inflection precise. *The strike is the sword, but I am the shield.*

"Well done," said Lance. "You have a skill with words to match your memory. Now, try it again, only this time I want you to assume the blocking form and center yourself before you speak. Reach into that place where your will resides, draw upon its strength. I will strike but not harm you. I promise."

"I trust you," said Gwen.

"Good. Now try to turn the strike away."

Gwen assumed the blocking position, feet apart, arms raised. She breathed deeply, focusing.

"Concentrate," said Lance. "Find your center. Speak the words and become the shield. Feel the power of your will."

Gwen took a few deep breaths, then recited the verse again: "Ca farapenne esta rizer, pe mi esta castere."

The words flowed from her lips with a melodic ring, and as soon as she uttered them she felt a tingling sensation in her chest. It spread out, enveloping her body like a warm second skin.

Lance smiled, sensing the change, impressed that she had managed it on the first attempt.

"Well done, Gwen." He raised a fist in front of her crossed arms. "Now feel the power of the Knight's Shield and turn the strike away."

Lance drove his fist toward Gwen's face, and she was shocked by her body's reaction. Her arms drove the attack to the side with such speed and force that she nearly fell over. She regained her balance, and the expression on her face was one of elation.

"That was incredible!" she laughed, staring at her arms as if they were strangers. "I...I can't believe I just did that!"

"Believe it," said Lance, impressed. "Your will is strong."

"Can...can we do it again?" asked Gwen, barely able to contain her excitement.

Lance nodded. "Of course." He waited for Gwen to ready herself. "But this time I will strike faster."

"Okay," replied Gwen, wondering how much faster he could be.

Lance smiled a little too deviously for Gwen's liking. "Ready?" he asked.

"Ready," said Gwen.

Gwen concentrated on her breathing, trying to focus the power she would need to repel the attack. Feeling the steady cadence of the Knights Shield return, she couldn't help but giggle with delight. Then she saw Lance's lips move and knew she was in trouble.

Lance struck out, allowing Gwen to turn his fist away just as she had the first time. But as the momentum of the block twisted Gwen's body, with blinding speed Lance spun in the opposite direction, around and behind her. Before she knew what was happening, she was wrapped tightly in his powerful arms, unable to move.

Gwen struggled, before finally giving up. With a playful sigh, she ended her resistance, feeling Lance's iron hold weaken but not release her. She turned in his arms, wondering if this was still part of the lesson.

With her chest pressed against his, Gwen could feel the hard contours of Lance's muscles. A mix of excitement and fear washed over her, amplified by the intimacy of the young man's embrace. Her heart was racing, and she looked up at him, wondering if he could feel its fluttering beat. Their eyes met, and time seemed to melt in the lingering alchemy of the words they had uttered. For that moment, they were together, joined, their energies pulsing as one. It was as if they had known each other all their lives, sharing a bond as ancient and powerful as *The Verses* themselves.

"I yield," whispered Gwen.

Lance looked from her eyes to her lips, then back again. "As do I," he said.

# CHAPTER 18

Morgan Fay held the pen up, so the shaft of light from the setting sun streaming through the tower's narrow west window could ignite the intricate designs spiraling down its golden "blade". Fay marveled at how close she was to the goal she had labored decades for, the moment when Wyzera's shining sword would grant her the power to command the future.

Twenty-five years ago, that achievement seemed impossibly distant, out of reach, unattainable. But like the swirling characters magically appearing on the *Grail Tome's* pages, each passing hour brought the CEO ever closer to her crowning glory, the moment she would scribe the destiny of the world.

Preparations for the Lighting were well underway. The sounds of construction echoed off the castle walls from the clifftop, as the Corporation Night ceremony's stage neared completion. The pomp and pageantry was a decorative smoke screen, a distraction for the masses. They were oblivious to the fact that the burning of the Archive was the means by which

Fay would forever steal their freedom. And as much as she despised Victor Herrat, the puffed up little director deserved credit for pulling it all together on such short notice. Especially with his star, Gwen Degan, nowhere to be found. Fay mused over the sudden disappearance of the pretty young actress, so adored by her fans. Why would one so privileged choose to decap? And why now?

She returned to her desk, leaving the questions behind. They didn't matter. The world was going to change, and no one—not Gwen Degan or Victor Herrat or the countless people staring into their vidlinks—would see it coming.

Fay slid open the desk's top drawer and removed a pristine sheet of paper, repeating an exercise she had done countless times before. In the beginning, she had relied on *The Mediations* to guide her thoughts and form words on the page, but that was no longer necessary. Practice and discipline had eliminated the writer's block that had once stemmed the flow of ink from Wyzera's pen, Fay's relentless edits suffusing her will into a final passage that was nearing completion.

She dipped the golden pen into its well and lowered it to the paper, reciting the sentences as they flowed from her hand. It was a narrative rife with hatred and anger, spite and malice, a riveting prophecy, a sublime description of a dreadful future. When the pen stopped moving, there was still a narrow ribbon of white at the bottom of the page. Fay still had one line left to craft, a last sentence that would forever echo through the ages.

Waiting for the words to come, her tired mind wandered, carrying her back to the day she arrived at Tintagel, the first time she entered the castle, the moment she set eyes on the *Grail Tomes*. They were together in the center of the round tower room, reclining on their marble pedestals, two perfect twins, the most wonderful books ever written. She remembered wanting nothing more than to lose herself in them, to surrender to the power radiating from their pages. But Merl would not allow it.

*There are rules. The books are dangerous.*

She had scoffed at his short sightedness, his fear. *The Meditations* offered her something he couldn't. That his love couldn't. For a fleeting moment, the fog of resentment lifted, and she saw Merl's face. The tenderness. The pain.

She drove the image away, extinguishing the last ember of guilt still smoldering in her soul. "I will not be denied what is mine," she hissed.

The bitterness and loathing in those words ignited a dark and ominous vision, a revelation of a world in which the hopes of others held no merit. In this new realm, Morgan Fay was an icon, worshipped and revered by all. Her will was their bondage, her aspirations the shackles and chains of their enslavement. Humanity existed only to serve her, having relinquished the last vestige of its freedom. She alone would possess the power of words, holding court as the sole arbiter of destiny, immortal and omnipotent.

A goddess.

Fay's hand started to move again, the pen gliding across the page, giving birth to the last line of the future she would command...

*Morgania Fayus, Magia di Moets, periri touda lectera dal tierri.*

*Morgan Fay, Sorceress of Words, shall perish all the readers from the earth.*

Billy Johnson stared through the window at the dark warehouse below, his favorite book, *The Shoreman*, open in his lap. Only now did he understand what Riley Moncrest, the main character in the story, felt when he lost his child.

*I drowned along with him, my soul sinking to depths of despair no anchor could reach. And every day, I stand on the shore, waiting for the tide of sorrow to wash over me.*

Little Donnie had been like a son to Billy, and so much more. A cherished friend, a confidant, the right hand that he would be crippled without.

Billy's four captains stood in solemn silence on the other side of their boss's desk, waiting to be addressed, respectful of his loss. A day after the terrible news had reached the Cauldron, they had been summoned. Each man shared Billy's North Verinese heritage, having the same strong roots in the Old Country. It was a bond that deepened the vow they had made to their leader, earning them territory and trust. Billy turned in his chair and set the book on the desk, his eyes meeting each of his captains, in turn.

"Ridley York o' the lake shore. Docker Mike Burnaby. Tully Smith o' the Lookout. And Foley Irwin, down from the canal. My thanks to all o' you for comin'.

"You know why I've called you here," continued Billy. "Little Donnie's dead, along with seven other boys, includin' one o' Ridley's." He looked again at the man standing to his left. "My condolences to you and the lad's family." The East End captain nodded soberly, in reply.

"It ain't exactly clear what happened," said Big Billy. "I've heard say that it was a squad o' Flames that done it; a black Destrier was seen rollin' about." He rubbed his chin. "It ain't the first such report of Incendi on this side o' the bridge o' late."

Billy stood, his tiny frame looming over the men. "But let me make it clear, my boys: if Morgan Fay wants a war, it's a war she'll be gettin'.

"I don't speak lightly," said Billy, "and I know it sounds dauntin', to say the least. But if we don't take the Witch on the Hill down now, we stand to lose the island. It ain't gonna happen under my watch."

Foley Irwin, Billy's tall, wiry captain from the north of the island closest to Main asked the question the others were thinking: "What about the Incendi?"

"They got lighters," added Tulley Smith. "Not to mention that captain o' their's." Dark bags hung under The Lookout leader's bright blue eyes. "Mordred's his name. I've heard some say he did yesterday's killin' alone."

"That's dock slop and you know it," barked Mike Burnaby. "Ain't no man could take down Donnie and a boat load of Cauldron boys."

"Butch wasn't killed by no lighter, he was beaten," said Ridley York. "I've heard things 'bout that Mordred, too, and I'm startin' to believe 'em."

"And so you should," said Billy. The statement stunned the group into silence. "I've reliable reports that he's unnatural strong and fast. Strength like that be the stuff o' tall tales, but such tales often carry a grain o' truth." He tilted his head back in thought. "We'll have to deal with Mordred; ain't no way around it."

"No disrespect, Boss," said Foley Irwin, "but you ain't said how. We ain't got no weapons, the Deal don't allow it."

Big Billy's lip curled into a sly smile. "I've got a little tip for you, boys. When you make a deal with someone you can't trust, *don't* trust 'em." He spun around and took a few small steps to the window. He gestured for his captains to join him and tapped on the glass. A moment later, light filled the warehouse below.

There, next to the ring platform in the middle of the cavernous arena, were two pallets stacked high with electro-shock batons. Lighters.

"Well I'll be beached!" blurted Tulley Smith. "How'd you get those?" Big Billy nodded at Burnaby to explain.

"I know the driver that takes ship cargo to the Corporation factory that makes 'em." He combed a hand through his bushy beard and winked under his wool watch cap. "Made a deal with him to slip one in every now and then for the return trip. Took a while to get 'em all."

"There's enough to arm two hundred men," said Big Billy. "You'll split 'em even amongst you. Put 'em in the hands o' your best, and make sure they know how to use 'em."

"Sounds like you got a plan," said Ridley York, eager for revenge. "When are we crossin'?"

Big Billy continued to stare down at the ring. "The Witch is plannin' a Lightin' for Souls Eve—what the Main-siders call 'Corporation Night.' She likes burnin' books." The little man turned and looked across the room at his library, his face red with rage. "But we're gonna burn her."

# CHAPTER 19

Merl couldn't hide his frustration. "Two days," he grumbled to himself. "We only have two days."

Arti sat across from the old librarian, leaning over the round table, exhausted by her efforts to get the pen to write again. The page Merl had given her to prepare her draft remained blank, and no matter how hard Arti tried, she couldn't force a drop of ink from Excalibri.

"I can't do it," she said, defeated. "It just won't work. I'll never write a whole page; I can't even make a mark."

Her lament made Merl feel guilty. "I'm sorry for getting upset, Arti. I...I wish I knew how to help you." He nodded at the words *Siegea Perilisi* written on the table's edge. "Just remember that you *have* written with it; the pen has answered you. Take a break, and clear your head." Squeezing out from behind the table, he added, "I'll go see how Gwen's model is coming along."

*Gwen.* Arti still wasn't sure she could ever trust some-one who had worked for the Corporation. And even if she could, the way Gwen looked at Lance made Arti wonder if she'd be able to stay focused on the mission. She was going to be their guide, after all.

Still holding Excalibri in her hand, Arti pulled her hood up and lay her head down on the table, wishing the world away. She hadn't realized just how tired she was, having barely slept for two days. She'd been riding an emotional roller coaster—the terrible pain and guilt at losing Gal, followed by the euphoria that accompanied her young friend's miraculous return. It had taken a toll on her, and combined with the incredible weight of responsibility she now bore, Arti could feel her body shutting down. She was asleep just seconds after closing her eyes, and a dream began streaming like a vid in her mind...

She was sitting at the round table, Excalibri in hand. The dome light above the booth was off, the motorhome was dark, and she could barely see the page in front of her.

"I can't do it," she said, the words echoing through the cabin, driving away what little light remained. The black shroud of fear grew thicker and heavier.

Arti knew the others were depending on her, and she was sure she was going to let them down. Even if they managed to take the *Grail Tome* from Morgan Fay, it was up to her to write the final page of *The History*. The thought that Excalibri would refuse to work for her again was terrifying. If that happened, she would fail her quest mates, just as she had failed her parents. Morgan Fay would win, and the fear that cast its shadow over the Corporation would smother the whole world.

Arti never felt so alone, so helpless. "It's over," she said, her eyes filling with tears. "I can't do it."

But the pen disagreed.

Excalibri's nib started to glow. At first, its tip was a tiny ember, barely noticeable, a warm point of light piercing the inky gloom. But it got brighter and brighter until a halo of gold spread out from it, illuminating the round table and U-shaped bench like an arena.

Arti held the pen at arm's length, alarmed by its transformation, watching as the light from it continued to expand, devouring more of the darkness around her, filling the cabin with a warm glow, pushing back the shadows, driving away the fear.

It was then that Arti noticed Merl sitting across from her, the fingers of his gloved hands forming a pyramid under his chin. Gone were the doubt and worry he had worn like a mask, his icy blue eyes revealing a depth of knowledge and confidence that was comforting.

Lance appeared next to the old librarian. The handsome young man smiled and nodded, his expression exuding dedication and discipline. He was her fearless champion and would protect her with his life, a life that would not be given easily.

Sensing someone else at her side, Arti turned, and Gwen was there. The young woman's beauty was matched by a righteous ferocity, driving away all doubt. She possessed a singular will, powerful and inspiring, something Arti knew she could draw upon to hold the darkness back.

There was one person missing from the dream. Arti held the pen high, searching for Gal, looking to the place Excalibri told her she should be. Gal wasn't there, but Arti could hear her friend's voice. It sounded distant and hollow.

"Arti," she called. "Arti." Her voice grew louder. "Arti!"

Arti awoke with a start. She lifted her head, suddenly aware that she was alone at the table. The weak dome light on the ceiling above her was on, and she felt a hand on her shoulder. She turned to see Gal squinting curiously at her.

"Who were you talkin' to? And whadya write on the table?"

Arti didn't remember saying or writing anything. She could only recall looking at the others sitting with her in the glow of Excalibri's light.

But Gal was right; where Merl and Gwen and Lance had been, there were swirling black words inscribed on the edge of the round table. Puzzled, Arti looked at the sword-shaped pen in her hand, wondering how it had acted, again, without her knowledge.

The door to the motorhome flipped open, and Merl ascended the stairs. He could tell by the look on Arti's face that something had happened.

"What's wrong?" he asked, fearing the worst. Surprised to see Gal standing, he added, "Why are you up?"

"She wrote somethin' on the table," said Gal, propping herself against the narrow counter, opposite the booth.

In what was more a leap than a step, Merl crossed from the top of the stairs to the round table and bent low, his lips moving silently as he read what was inscribed there. Gwen and Lance had entered the motorhome and were now standing in back of him, trying to see what had the old librarian so entranced.

Merl was beaming. "Incredible!" he said. "Just incredible!"

"What is it?" demanded Arti, looking down at the inscriptions on the round table. "What do they say?"

Merl read each pair of words slowly, working his way around the circle: "*Merlini Sagia. Lancea Coraggia. Gweneath Justea.*" And just inches from Arti's heart, "*Artia Bendi.*"

178

"Our names," said Gwen, looking past Merl at the elegant characters. "I see Merl, Lance, Gwen, and Arti."

"Yes. It is Old Ferencian, the language of my ancestors," added Lance, "the language of the *Grail Tomes.* I think I can read it."

"You are correct, young knight," said Merl. He stepped back from the table, and with a sweep of his hand, invited Lance to translate.

Lance pointed to each title in turn, his hand tracing the curving edge of the table. "*Merl the Wise. Gwen the Just.* And *Arti*...hmmm...how do you say...*the Blessed.*"

"You forgot *your* name," said Gwen. "What does it call you?"

Lance lowered his eyes, too modest to answer, so Merl read it for him.

"It says: *Lance the Brave.*" The old librarian chuckled. "It appears the pen has named us."

A long discussion ensued about the titles, but no one was sure why the pen had produced the words.

"It confirms our allegiance in this quest," said Merl, finally. "That is enough." His brow wrinkled. "More importantly, your bond with Excalibri has strengthened, Arti. It should give you confidence that the words will come."

Arti sat next to Gal on the rear bench, considering Merl's conclusion, hoping he was right. What bothered her was the lack of control she felt in wielding the pen. It was as if Excalibri was the scribe and she the tool. If she was to write the final page of *The History* that would determine everyone's future, including her own, Arti wanted to make sure it was *her* voice, *her* will that flowed from the pen. But what was her will? Not knowing that bothered her even more.

"It's been a long day," said Merl. "Gwen, Lance, get the garage cleaned up. I'm going for some air, then I'll get supper started. A good meal will do us wonders. After we eat, we'll study the model. We have a lot of planning to do."

Merl followed Gwen and Lance out of the motorhome, and Arti remained with Gal, sitting on the edge of her bed. The injured girl had suffered more dizzy spells and a severe headache after witnessing Arti's strange dream-writing epi-sode. Her face was pale, and she looked exhausted.

"How are you feeling?" asked Arti.

Gal just shook her head, regretting the motion when a wave of pain followed it.

Arti could tell that more than a headache was bothering her friend. "What is it? What's wrong?"

Gal frowned and pressed her cheek against the pillow. "Nothin'."

"I know you too well," said Arti. "Something's both-ering you. Tell me."

Gal puffed out a breath and looked up at Arti. "Why didn't you write my name on the table?" she sulked. "Why can't I be a knight like you guys?"

Arti smiled. "So that's it; you feel left out?"

Gal was in a full pout now. "It's just that...I thought I was your best friend. Why wouldn't you 'clude me?"

Arti leaned close to Gal. "You *are* my best friend. Never doubt that. And you're as wise, brave, just, and blessed as all of us put together. In fact," she smiled, teasingly, "you are such a handful, I doubt Excalibri could come up with a word for you."

Gal stubbornly turned away. "But I ain't no knight. Merl even said so."

"Merl says a lot of things," barked Arti, "but he doesn't decide who *my* knights are." She glanced at the narrow wooden box on the round table, hoping what she was about to say was true. "That's up to me and Excalibri."

Wishing to put Gal at ease, Arti added, "I'll make you a promise. When you get better, I'll write your name on the round table. And you'll have the *best* of all titles."

"Really?" said Gal. "You'd do that for me?"

"Of course I would," said Arti. "You saved my life—more than once. I owe you 'big time,' remember?"

"'Kay," said Gal, appeased. She rested her head on the pillow, finding comfort in Arti's vow. "Thanks."

"But you have to get better, first," insisted Arti. "That's the deal." She winked. "Take it or leave it."

Gal smiled against the pain and closed her eyes. "Deal."

# CHAPTER 20

Arti couldn't remember a meal tasting so good. After months of canned soup and stale bread, the stew and biscuits were exotic delicacies that sent her taste buds dancing. The stew was Merl's concoction, beef and vegetables and who knows what else mingling together in a rich broth. Lance had provided the biscuits, fresh from his Aunt Vivian's oven. She'd even included butter wrapped in foil that Arti applied in generous amounts to the tops of the warm, flaky pastries. The scents filling the motorhome elicited memories of her family's kitchen on cold winter evenings, of laughter and warmth and love. Morgan Fay and her Incendi had taken that away from Arti, but in less than twenty-four hours, she would get her chance to strike back.

While the others washed their dishes using the hose in back of the garage—a convenient source of water Merl discovered when he first arrived at the Camel Lot—Arti made sure Gal was looked after, spoon-feeding her a bowl of the stew's warm broth.

Arti pretended to be upbeat, trying to convince her friend that she'd be better in no time, her old self again. But the recurring chills and severe headaches were proof Gal still had a long road to recovery. Managing to keep down a few mouthfuls of the broth and a nibble of biscuit, she frowned and waved away any more.

Setting the bowl and spoon aside, Arti reached into the pocket of her hoodie and pulled out Gal's tattered old wedge-shaped cap.

"Lance forgot to give you this," said Arti. "I'll put it here. You can wear it again when the bandage comes off." She placed the cap on the shelf behind Gal's bed, next to her other precious belongings: the glossy ad of the happy family, and *The King's Errand*.

"My lucky cap. Thanks," said Gal, wincing as she lied back. "Musta fallen off when the Flame hit me. The last thing I remember was my fingers gettin' smacked. Then everthin' went black."

"I don't even want to think about it," said Arti, shivering at the memory of Gal facing down Mordred in the street. "I'm just glad Lance got there when he did."

Before the planning session began, Merl honored his promise to Lance, setting the *Grail Tome* down on the round table, carefully opening it to the chapter containing *The Verses*, reminding everyone that this was a very special privilege, and that the book should never be opened by anyone but him.

The young Ferencian couldn't contain his excitement. His whole life, he had recited the words on the pages, training in the *strike of words*, perfecting his technique. But the artistry of the poems left him speechless, each verse beautifully decorated, elegant and rich with color. Arti and Gwen looked on, sharing in Lance's appreciation of the ancient text.

"It is wonderful to see them with my own eyes," said Lance, finding his voice. "Thank you."

"The honor is mine," said Merl. "The de Lacs and *The Verses* have been apart for a very long time. I'm glad to witness the reunion."

After allowing Lance to leaf gently through the collection of poems, under his watchful eye, Merl closed the tome and lifted it to the counter. He knew the young knight could have lost himself in its pages for days, but time was a luxury they didn't have.

"Let's get that model together, Gwen. We need to start planning."

With the others sitting at their places, Gwen erected the miniature castle, carefully connecting one section to another. At just over a foot high at its tower end and more than three times that long, it barely fit on the round table. As an added touch, Gwen included a border depicting the ancient building's grounds. The flat pieces, drawn with contour lines to indicate the slope of the earth, were wedged into place under the miniature castle's outer walls. Once the model was assembled, Gwen squeezed in next to Arti, sitting at the place where her name was inscribed.

"I call to order the second meeting of the Book Knights," announced Merl. "Those named by Excalibri at this table have but one quest: to seek the *Grail Tome*. Tomorrow night we must succeed in that task." His expression darkened. "Failure is not an option."

He nodded at the model. "What are we facing, Gwen?"

Gwen brushed a strand of hair from her face. "Okay, um...let's start here." She pointed at a square located on the model's border next to two curving parallel lines.

"This is the outer checkpoint, a few hundred yards from the castle at the base of the hill. Everyone coming in has to stop here, first, so their identifications can be checked. Most days, there are two guards on duty, regular Incendi, but I'm guessing there will be more on Corporation Night."

Her finger traced its way along the curving road crossing the sweeping contours of the slope, stopping at another square, the same size as the first.

"Checkpoint number two," she said. "More Incendi and a heavy steel gate that connects to a ten-foot-high fence that surrounds the castle." Gwen pointed at the dark line weaving its way across the cardboard.

"The road comes right up to the building and runs along its southern wall, then it goes under a covered parkway. Here." Gwen gently rotated the model, table and all, so everyone could see, reaching out and gently tapping the structure.

"The main entrance is under it, the one the studio staff and execs use." She removed the gabled parkway, revealing a set of double doors on the castle's lower wall. She pushed on the doors with her finger, and they swung open on tiny tabbed hinges.

"You can get to the tower this way, but you have to go up the main stairs or take the elevator. I'll show you."

Gwen removed the roof of the main building. At intervals along the second-floor hallway, small doors opened into a series of divided compartments: the wide studio, the narrow Archive, the elevator across from it, and at the far end, Incendi headquarters with a flame inscribed on its miniature door. In a corner, next to the police office where the main building abutted the curving tower, there was a narrow passageway.

"The tower stairs are through here," she said, wedging her finger into the gap. "And this is where the stairs are accessed from outside." She pointed to the tower's round base, at an opening in the shape of a gothic arch.

"That's where the Incendi enter and leave the building. It's the quickest way in and out of their headquarters. No one else is permitted to use the tower stairs. I was told they lead down to an old dungeon, the place where the Incendi keep their prisoners: decaps, readers, and in the deepest cells, scribes." She immediately regretted sharing the information, knowing that Arti's parents had likely been held there for interrogation—or worse. "I'm sorry," she said, turning to Arti. "I—"

"It's okay," said Arti, frowning down at the model. "We need to know everything." She took a deep breath, "Go ahead."

Reluctantly, Gwen continued, "I...I'm pretty sure the stairs go all the way up to Fay's office at the top of the tower."

"They do," confirmed Merl. "The stairs are original to the castle. I've used them countless times. We stored the rarest and most valuable books up there." In his memory, he could see the *Grail Tomes* resting on their marble pedestals in the center of the room. "The steps spiral all the way up from the ground to the tower suite. There's a platform at the top leading to a heavy iron door, its hinges secured deep within the stone." He glanced at Lance. "It is impenetrable to even the most determined assault. If it's locked, there's no getting through it."

"Then how are we going to get the book?" asked Arti. "When Fay leaves the tower to perform the Lighting, she's going to lock the door."

Gwen shook her head. "I didn't know about the door. Arti's right; what's the point, if we can't get into Fay's office? All of this," she waived her hand at the model sprawled on the table, "was for nothing."

"Oh, but we can get in," said Merl, slyly.

Lance grinned at the old librarian. "Merl the Wise, I think you are keeping something from us."

"Very perceptive, young knight. In fact, I've kept *it* for twenty-five years."

From below the table Merl produced a rusty black key half the length of his forearm. The ancient tool was made of iron with an open bow at one end of its hammered shaft and an intricately shaped bit at the other, containing a complicated pattern of wards and teeth.

"This key opens the door," said Merl. "There were only two made. Morgan has one," he reached across the table, "and this one I'm giving to you, Gwen. Arti will have enough to worry about carrying Excalibri and its well. And Lance will have his hands full dealing with the guards."

"Then we can do it," said Arti, relieved. "We just have to get to that door."

"And that won't be easy," added Merl, soberly. "Here's what I propose…"

The old librarian stood, reaching across the model, pointing at a cluster of trees drawn on the perimeter of the grounds just outside the first checkpoint. "Gwen, will this forest provide enough cover to hide the motorhome and Lance's car?"

"I think so. It's pretty thick in there. Even with most of the leaves down, they should be well hidden."

"Good," said Merl. "That's where we'll park." He traced his finger along one of the contour lines running outside the fence and stopped where the barrier started to climb the cliff edge below the castle. "At dusk, you'll leave the trees and make your way here. You'll cut through the fence—I have bolt cutters—and climb the slope to the castle. I'm hoping that with all the activity on the clifftop, the three of you should be able to make it up the hill, without being spotted."

Merl pointed his gloved hand at the main doors on the castle model. "The tower entrance will be swarming with Incendi, so your best bet is to enter here. You'll make your way up the main stairs to the second level and go to the end of the hall, accessing the tower stairs through the passage next to Incendi headquarters." His finger traced the route, ending at the narrow slit beside the door with the tiny flame insignia.

"I expect you'll run into some guards; there's no way around it." He nibbled nervously on his lower lip. "Lance, you'll have to deal with them. When you get to Fay's door at the top of the stairs, Gwen will use the key to open it."

Merl's eyes met Arti's, and he suddenly looked worried. As difficult as it was going to be to get inside Fay's office, it all came down to her ability to wield Excalibri.

"Get the book, and get back here as fast as you can," said Merl. "*The History* may have already arrived at its final page, or we may have to wait until it does. And if for some reason you can't make it back, as soon as the page is ready, you'll have to write it, no matter where you are. That's why you're taking Excalibri and its well with you."

"Aren't you coming with us?" asked Gwen, realizing Merl had not included himself in the mission.

"I am too old to fight like young Lance here," he said. "Your memory and youth makes you a much better guide,

Gwen. And Arti is the only one who can wield the pen. We must play to our strengths, and mine is knowledge."

Merl sat back and bridged his gloved fingers. "While you complete your quest for the book, I will lay siege in my own way: through *The Meditations*.

"Morgan's power has been unchallenged, her control unrivalled," he explained. "The last thing she'll welcome, on the eve of reaching her ultimate goal, is uncertainty." A mischievous smile curled his lips. "Revealing my existence through the second *Grail Tome* should get her attention."

Arti's eyes lit up. "When she realizes the other tome survived, she'll think there's another *History*. Another final page."

"Yes," said Merl. "She won't know that it was burned away in the fire. It will be her worst fear come true: that the other great book has survived, it's in the hands of the Challenger, and someone else is stealing her prize while she's playing to the cameras. It should draw her attention from her tome in the tower. And from you."

"A bluff," said Arti.

"A bluff," nodded Merl.

The old librarian looked across the round table at Gwen. "And if I can convince Fay the final page is being written before she lights the pyre, I might also be able to save the Archive." He sighed. "I will try."

The planning session ended close to midnight, after Merl was confident everyone had memorized their roles. The old librarian had divided the mission into four stages: forest to fence, fence to castle entrance, castle entrance to Fay's door, and Fay's door to the tome. Gwen would carry the key and act as guide, deciding how and when to move; Lance would cut through the fence and deal with any guards who might get in their way; and Arti would make it all worthwhile, once they got the book. That last bit terrified her, and as she lie next to Gal's bed, sleep seemed impossible.

Merl had laid out the booth's cushions for Arti and Gwen on the floor of the motorhome, he and Lance taking up residence for the night next to Lance's Charger in the adjacent garage. None of them would sleep well, knowing how difficult their task would be. Even so, Merl's last words, before calling the second meeting of the Book Knights to an end, impressed upon them the importance of being ready: "We only get one chance at this."

"Are you awake?" whispered Gwen.

Arti delayed in answering, "Yes."

"I can't sleep," said Gwen.

"Me neither," admitted Arti, envious of Gal's long, deep breaths emanating from the bench above her.

"Let's talk a while; maybe it'll help."

Arti stared up through the darkness at the motorhome's ceiling. "What do you want to talk about?"

"Anything but tomorrow night," Gwen laughed. A nervous silence followed. "I...I'd like to know more about you."

"Really?" said Arti. "Why?"

"You love books," said Gwen. "I never thought I'd ever meet someone who was like me."

*Like you?* This time Arti wanted to laugh.

"Tell me about your library," said Gwen.

"It was hidden in our house," said Arti, picturing the little room with its shelves full of books, wrapped around the two soft leather chairs warmed by a tall reading lamp. She didn't know why she was sharing something so personal with Gwen; the words just started to flow from her.

"The room wasn't very big, but it had a lot of books. When I was small, my mom and dad would read them with me before I went to bed." Arti remembered her parents' faces in the soft light, the warmth of their touch. It was the first time in weeks that she'd been able to see them so clearly in her mind.

"I really miss them," said Arti. Her lip quivered, and she was glad Gwen couldn't see her face in the darkness.

Gwen sensed the sadness in Arti's voice. "Sorry, I'm doing it again. I know it hurts you to think about them. I can tell you really cared for each other."

"Care!" blurted Arti, loud enough that Gal stirred above her. "They're still alive and I'm going to save them."

"Okay, okay," said Gwen. "I didn't mean it that way. It's just that I envy you."

"You envy *me*?"

"Yes. Your parents...love you. Mine only care about themselves, their careers. They don't even know me. All my life, I've had to pretend to be something I'm not—for them. So they could have what *they* want. My life's been one big lie."

"So you just left? Your home and your job with the Corporation?"

"Best thing I ever did," said Gwen. "I hated every minute of it."

"But everyone knows who you are. You're famous."

"So? It means nothing when you're alone. The Archive is the only thing that ever made me happy, that gave my life meaning." She sighed, "Those books are all I have."

"Not anymore," said Arti. "You have us now—Lance and Gal and Merl and me."

There was a long silence, and Arti thought she heard a sniffle from Gwen.

"Are...are you alright?" asked Arti.

"Yeah," said Gwen. "It's just that...that's the nicest thing anyone's ever said to me."

From that moment on, despite the four years that separated them in age, Arti and Gwen were like friends at a sleepover, whispering stories well into the night. They talked about their favorite books, the fantastic worlds they explored, the heroes they loved, and the villains they despised.

"Now we're characters in our own story," said Gwen, yawning. "I wonder how it will end."

"I don't know," said Arti. "At least, we'll find out together." Pulling the blanket up, she rolled onto her side and closed her eyes.

Morning seemed to arrive early, the bright light of the rising sun pouring in through the windshield of the motorhome. Gwen was already up when Arti stirred, but Gal remained quiet on the bench above her, wound up tightly in her blanket as if she'd fallen prey to a huge constricting snake. Arti could hear Merl and Lance talking outside, above the hollow noise of a kettle being filled at the back of the garage. They sounded sober and subdued, aware of how important the coming evening would be.

Manners at breakfast were just as restrained, each member of the quest ignoring the fact that the oatmeal needed salt and the tea was too weak. Barely a word was spoken, the silence finally ending with Merl's address.

"Tonight's the night," he said, stating the obvious. "We'll leave here half an hour before sunset." He checked the clock hanging on the end of the overhead cupboard. "Nine hours from now. The model of the castle is in the garage behind Lance's car, should anyone need to look at it or review the plan. If you've forgotten anything from last night, or if you have any questions, ask me *before* we leave. Once we depart the Camel Lot, we won't have time for deliberation or to amend our strategy. Things will happen fast, and everyone needs to be ready."

Arti felt the oatmeal curdle in her stomach at the finality of the old librarian's words. If she was this nervous now, she couldn't imagine how she was going the feel when darkness fell and the mission began.

"Arti will continue her practice with me, here." Merl nodded at Lance, "You can use the garage, again, to exercise. Don't overdo it; you'll need all your energy for this evening. Gwen, you can join Lance, if you wish. Go over the plan, and see if we've forgotten any details. Use that memory of yours to make sure we've accounted for every possibility."

Lance smiled at Gwen. He welcomed the chance to spend more time with her but couldn't hide his worry. She and Arti would be under his protection, tonight. He could handle a few dozen Incendi bearing lighters, but the thought of facing Mordred was something else, entirely. He couldn't guarantee the outcome.

Gwen sensed Lance's unease. "We'll be ready," she said.

The next few hours passed like the day before. Arti sat with Merl at the round table, staring down at a blank sheet of paper, Excalibri in hand. He asked her questions in a low voice, trying to get her to focus her thoughts through the pen, to write something, anything. It was a useless exercise.

*Forged together in truth, the pen and the will are one.* If Arti heard Merl say those words one more time, she was going to scream. She wondered why someone as smart as Merrill of Astenga didn't leave better instructions.

Arti looked closely at Excalibri, at the shining silver pen with its intricate engraving, the tiny pommel, hilt and guard. At least the pen had survived the centuries, she thought. *But it's no good if I can't control it.* She pictured the ancient Astengan holding it two thousand years ago, just as she was now.

Merl sighed deeply, bringing Arti out of her daydream. "It's midday," he said. "I can see you need a break." He rubbed his eyes. "So do I." He edged his way out from behind the table and walked stiffly to the door. "Grab something to eat. I'll be back shortly."

Arti set Excalibri down on the piece of paper and turned to see Gal sitting up, a mound of blankets and a pillow at her back.

"Any luck?" asked Gal.

"No, nothing. I can't figure it out," said Arti. "And I'm running out of time. What if I can't do it, Gal? What will happen to everyone?"

"You'll do it," said Gal, tight lipped and serious, half of her face still one big purple bruise. "Just like Ward Weatherin'ton did."

"Ward Weatherington?" Arti looked at *The King's Errand* sitting on the shelf behind Gal's bed. Although the bookmark was in the same place Arti had left it a few nights before, she suspected another Gal deception. "You read the last two chapters, didn't you? When?"

"The mornin' after we watched the fights at the Cauldron," confessed Gal. "Before we came here. You were still sleepin'." She frowned. "Sorry, I couldn't wait. I had to know how it ended."

Arti smiled. "It's alright. I should have known you'd be sneaky," she chided. "Well, what'd you think?"

"It was the best," beamed Gal. "You weren't kiddin' about it bein' a surprise. Just when it looked like Ward was dead meat, he fooled everyone. I think he kept goin' because of his little brother, Petey; he didn't want to let him down. The way he used the gem to get the map and trick the wizard was so cool." She paused, looking deep into Arti's eyes. "That's why I know you're gonna write the final page. Because you're just like Ward: you never give up."

Gal's unwavering support reminded Arti of just how special her young friend was and how much she had come to depend on her. Maybe Merl, Lance, and Gwen deserved their descriptions etched by Excalibri on the round table. But as wise and courageous and just as they were, Gal eclipsed them all. And if Arti was truly blessed, as the pen had named her, she knew Gal's friendship was a big part of it.

"I'll keep trying," Arti promised. She lifted Excalibri from the paper and examined it in her hand.

"You heard her," she said. "Work!"

# CHAPTER 21

Fay turned the tome's broad pages until she found the verse, then carefully averted her eyes. Staring directly at the last *Meditation* for too long was extremely dangerous. Even with her decades of disciplined training, there was no guarantee she would have the fortitude to withstand it. She was entering uncharted territory, delving into language that only Wyzera and Merrill, the original scribes of the *Grail Tomes*, had the skill to explore.

It was desperation, plain and simple. With only hours to go before the Lighting, all the preparations had been made. The stage was set, the lights and cameras in place around the temporary arena. The Network feed had been tested and the Archive, Fay's collection of the most dangerous books ever written, had been transplanted to its place on the ceremonial pyre, ready to be sacrificed. At nightfall, the reclusive CEO would reveal herself to the world and light the match that would summon a new era. But there was still someone who could prevent her from crafting that future.

*From the flames to the Isle of Avalon, the Challenger has come.*

And though coincidence made Arti Penderhagen the best candidate, Fay had dismissed her fear of the girl countless times, knowing a helpless decap had no chance of breaking into her fortress. No chance of getting anywhere near the *Grail Tome* hidden behind stone walls, an iron door, and hundreds of armed Incendi police. But she also knew *The History* did not lie. For her plan to be assured of success, Fay needed to deal with her nemesis. The girl had to be found and eliminated—at all cost.

Mordred had yet to return or facelook Fay with news of the girl's discovery and demise which meant he was still searching for her on the island. As dangerous as Mordred was, she feared her son was too blunt an instrument for such a delicate operation. Without a clue to point him in the direction of the girl, he might well destroy all of Isle and never find her. He certainly wasn't going to get any tips from the locals. They were off the Network grid and under the strict rule of Billy Johnson and his syndicate, petty thieves and cutthroats who Fay tolerated to achieve her ends. She expected Mordred's efforts would ruffle Big Billy's feathers, but she didn't care. Her "deal" with the little man, like everything else she suffered to arrive at this day, was coming to an end.

Fay had used the potency of *The Maze* to locate the Penderhagen girl once before but had faced a great deal of resistance, what she knew to be magic. Powerful magic. Who or what had been its source, she couldn't say; but it had required all her effort to overcome, to push it back, to pierce its veil. And though she tried numerous times to repeat that success, the only products of those labors were frustration

197

and exhaustion. Wyzera's pen would not write, and the girl's whereabouts remained a mystery.

Fay required an even stronger spell, a *Meditation* that could not be blocked, that could shatter the most formidable shield of concealment. *The Mind's Eye* was Wyzera's greatest achievement, a passage that could transport its reader to any time and place. It could find the answer to any question, and drive all but the most strong-willed mad.

Slowly, warily, Morgan Fay looked down at the page, holding Wyzera's golden pen over a blank sheet of paper next the great book. She gathered herself, summoning her will, focusing it with all her might on the passage's title. The moment her eyes locked on the words, her mind was gripped by invisible hands, cold and strong and pitiless. She gasped as her consciousness was severed and torn, pulled into the passage, mingling in tiny fragments among each swirling character. Fay was not just reading the words, she was part of them, existing above, below, and between them. She could hear her own hollow voice utter the ancient language:

"Guardero Intera,
Vedio Desira,
Occhio Essera,
Fiammo Feuira."
*Look Within,*
*See Desire,*
*Eye of Being,*
*Flame of Fire.*

Fay fought to hold on to her reason, to remember who and where she was. The fragments of her mind were scattering, dissipating, seeping into the words on the page. She knew that if she remained in the purgatory of *The Mind's*

*Eye* too long, she would never escape it, forever to wander its tormented landscape.

Drawing on all her strength, she managed to anchor herself against the powerful meditation's relentless tide long enough to form the question. It was torturous and slow, and she couldn't be sure its formulation made sense. But with a will worthy of the ancient scribe whose pen she wielded, Morgan Fay spoke the words.

"Where...is...she?"

Holding its bloody ink, the sharp point of Wyzera's blade descended to the virgin white paper and slowly carved its path, dragging Fay's hand along with it. A thin line of shimmering black formed the letters of three distinct words. When the message was complete, *The Mind's Eye* released Fay from its grip, and she was thrown back in her chair, the pen still clenched tightly in her hand. Her head whiplashed violently, and she blacked out. It was in that limbo between wakefulness and sleep, a place where the mind wandered, that she felt the presence of her son, Mordred, at the same time far away and beside her.

Fay felt as if her lungs were full of water. She convulsed violently and coughed, desperately trying to draw in some air. Choking, she fought to regain her equilibrium as constellations of stars swam before her eyes. Managing to draw in a few shallow breaths, her vision gradually cleared, and she found the strength to sit up. Leaning over the desk, she gazed down at the words she had written, knowing her son had heard them.

The shop owner's will was strong, stronger than any of his victims before. Maybe that was why Mordred couldn't get the old woman out of his mind. *A librarian, a protector, an Elder in the Order,* she said. Is that why she'd been willing to die? Vivian de Lac's last gasping words promised him defeat at the hands of her nephew, and the end of Morgan Fay's reign. *Your mother's time has come.* How did she know he was the CEO's son? What other secrets had he strangled with her?

Mordred spent the night tearing the old woman's house apart, searching for a clue to the Penderhagen girl's whereabouts. He found nothing. After resting through the last hours of darkness, he rose with the sun and departed Lakeside Antiquities, determined to use whatever force was necessary to capture his prey. It was Corporation Day, the Archive would burn at nightfall, and he had sworn to find and kill the girl before then. *I will, Mother. I promise.*

Driven by his murderous vow, the Incendi captain left a trail of destruction in his wake as he travelled west across the island. Four left for dead on Park Avenue. A brutal melee on Bay Street. A saloon leveled on Waverly. None had produced any useful leads, and by the time he arrived at the Docks, word of the Flame's bloody inquisition had preceded him. It was eerily quiet next the shore. No pedestrians. No traffic. No boats. Isle was as silent as the setting sun.

The black Destrier rumbled down Water Street unopposed, passing locked doors and shuttered windows. If the girl was here, there was no way of knowing. Mordred needed help, the kind only his mother could offer.

He had been witness to it before, the ancient tome open on her desk next a word carved through paper: *DRAGONS*. It had led to the school where the Penderhagen girl and her young friend had been hiding. But he had failed to take her. Failed his mother. He longed for another chance, another clue.

As the plea faded in his thoughts, he could hear his mother's voice. It was distant and hollow, as if she was calling to him through a long tunnel. The words were labored and weak.

"West," she moaned. "Camel...Lot."

Mordred slammed his foot down on the Destrier's accelerator.

Cobden Street was as far west on the island as he could go, and Mordred was starting to doubt himself. Doubt that he'd heard his mother's message. With the needle on the Destrier's fuel gauge almost on empty and the sun barely peeking above the horizon, he was running out of time.

Passing Johnson Avenue, he noticed a building in the distance with a high pointed roof stabbing at the sky. In front of the odd-looking structure, there was a sign featuring a creature with a long neck and undulating back. Mordred's eyes were drawn to the words emerging from the cartoon character's mouth, ignoring the larger script above: *Buy at the Humps, Save at the Pumps*. He was almost past the entrance when the faded name above the slogan registered.

The Camel Lot.

Mordred slammed on the brakes and skidded to a stop. He spun the sedan around and entered the driveway leading into the abandoned dealership. In the fading light, the main building looked empty. Large display windows were devoid of glass, strands of wire and cable hanging like vines within. A few old cars stripped of their wheels, headlights, doors, and hoods sat in a line next the building, the paint on their roofs and fenders faded by decades of weather. Mordred slowed the Destrier, looking for any sign of life or habitation. There was none.

He continued to the back of the lot and noticed a garage with three large open bays. The first was empty, as was the second, save for a discarded box in the shadows. But as he continued to drive by, he was surprised to see the nose of a black Corporation sedan peeking out of the last bay. When he looked at the executive plates, he could barely contain his excitement. The car belonged to Gwen Degan's parents.

Mordred made a quick inspection of the vehicle, a thousand questions running through his mind. If both the Penderhagen girl and Gwen Degan had been here, what was their connection? And even more important: Where had they gone? He knew that if he couldn't answer that question soon, he'd never be able to face his mother again.

A puddle of water at the mouth of the first bay told him someone had been there recently; it hadn't rained in days. But the "box" in back of the middle bay was even more remarkable. Even from thirty feet away, hiding from the waning light, Mordred recognized the shape: a long rectangular box connected to a tall cylinder standing on end. He remembered the intensity of his mother's fear, the terror of losing what she treasured most in the world.

Mordred turned the car around and sped away.

# CHAPTER 22

Lance's white Charger hugged the asphalt as it headed north. Arti stared out from the cumbersome motorhome as it trailed the sleek white sports car, wondering if the world might be different tomorrow, if the future could be stolen from Morgan Fay.

If that was going to happen, they'd first have to take Fay's book from the heavily guarded castle tower. As dangerous as the mission would be, the true test for Arti would come after, when she would have to write *The History's* final page. The thought of it terrified her.

The car and motorhome left Canal Street and slowly traversed the West Bridge's arching steel span from which Arti had narrowly escaped Mordred two months before. It seemed a lifetime ago. Arti glanced back at Gal propped up on the rear bench of motorhome, remembering that harrowing night and how her young friend had rescued her. The memory was cut short when she looked ahead and saw two black sedans blocking their way.

"Don't panic," whispered Merl. "We expected this. Lance will handle it." The old librarian's shaking hands betrayed his confidence; he had yet to witness the young knight in action.

The Charger came to a stop a few feet from the blockade, the motorhome easing up behind. Arti felt her heart thumping in her chest and wondered if their hopes were going to be dashed before they even left the island. From the passenger seat, she held her breath and watched as Lance casually stepped from his car, shrugging on his black leather jacket and walking down the sloping platform toward the line of troopers.

There were six of them, all armed with lighters. One, a heavy-set man with a dark complexion, spoke to Lance, looking past him at the car and motorhome. The trooper scowled and waved a hand at Gwen, a command to step out of the Charger, then he turned to give directions to his men. They started jogging toward the car and motorhome, lighters raised.

They didn't get far.

One moment Lance was standing with his arms in his jacket pockets, smiling at the officer. The next he was a blur of motion, spinning, kicking, dancing around the Incendi. Had Arti blinked, she would have missed it. The six Incendi were down, five of the electroshock batons in pieces on the ground beside them. Lance scooped up the remaining one along with a vidlink that had been clipped to the lead trooper's shoulder, handing them through his car's passenger window to Gwen. Then he walked to the two Destriers blocking the bridge. They were parked on an angle, noses meeting at the center line of the span. Lance's lips moved, and he jumped at the first car, releasing a kick that sent the vehicle spinning across the deck into the steel railing, shattering its windows. As Arti and the others watched in awe, he turned and did the same to other car. The gap between them was now wide enough for their vehicles to pass.

"Knight of Maren, indeed!" gasped Merl. He laughed and put the motorhome in gear.

With the sun almost at the horizon, they passed block after block of Corporation factories, heading east toward the castle and nightfall. The streets were nearly as deserted as those on the island. The few people they did pass were scurrying home to watch the biggest spectacle in Corporation history, heads down, eyes glued to their vidlinks and the pre-Lighting Netcast featuring a who's who of vidstars walking the red carpet under the castle's parkway.

At the outskirts of the city, the Charger and the motorhome joined a line of other vehicles, the last of the dignitaries with invitations to the exclusive event. Lance's white Charger seemed at home among the sleek sports cars and limousines threading their way east toward the grand spectacle on the hill, but Merl's motorhome, rumbling and rocking and burping blue smoke, looked oddly out of place. Many of the luxury vehicles passed the motorhome as it labored up the winding slope, chauffeurs blasting horns and directing angry gestures at the old man behind the wheel.

"At least we don't stand out," said Arti. Merl's brow furrowed at her sarcasm.

Rounding a long sweeping corner, Arti saw the castle looming high above them, getting ever larger, bathed in the light of the setting sun. Powerful searchlights flashed on its rooftop, their spinning yellow shafts not yet visible against the sunset sky. Beyond the tall castle tower at the cliff's edge, another stand of lights burned like bonfires. Arti guessed it was where the Lighting would take place, where the Archive would be ignited for all to see.

Gwen indicated to Lance a narrow dirt road covered in dead weeds that split from the highway, leading to a forested area at the base of the escarpment. After a few hundred feet, the road ended at a small meadow surrounded by a mix of nearly naked maple, birch, and ash. The grassy brown clearing was just large enough for them to turn the vehicles around and face back toward the road. Arti looked over her shoulder at the clock hanging from motorhome's cupboard. They had twenty minutes before the mission would begin.

With the last light of day waning, Merl stood with Gwen and Lance in the clearing. Lance held the bolt cutters, and Gwen was busy tying the iron door's key to her belt, having set the trooper's lighter on the ground next to her. She had given Merl the stolen vidlink, so he could monitor the Netcast and better time his efforts to announce himself to Fay through the *Grail Tome*. It was a daring diversion, one that the old librarian hoped would convince Fay the Challenger was far away from the castle with the second book in hand, primed to write its final page and steal her glory.

Inside the motorhome, Arti sat next to Gal on her bed. "We...we have to go." She tried to keep a brave face but failed miserably.

"I know," said Gal.

Arti looked at the round table where the pen and the ink well sat atop the ragged *Grail Tome*. "Do you think it will work?" she asked.

"It hasta," said Gal.

Arti brought her hands to her face and closed her eyes. "I'm scared, Gal. I'm really scared."

Gal clenched her jaw to keep her own emotions at bay, the deep bruise around her eye darkening with the effort. She reached out and gently touched Arti's arm.

"Do you remember 'The Rule'? If things go to crap and we get split up?"

Arti rubbed tears from her eyes and nodded. She remembered her blunder at The Sea Dog, a rickety old saloon down by the Docks. It was Arti's second week on the island and just the second time she had partnered with Gal on a pickpocketing run. She had jumped Gal's signal and mistakenly bumped a big docker who guessed right away that her clumsiness was by design. It was only by luck that she managed to break free of him. That and Gal's well-placed kick between the big man's legs. It wasn't until Gal arrived back at the records room after an hour of agonized waiting that Arti knew her friend was safe. That she hadn't lost her.

"I remember," said Arti. "Get away, and get home."

Gal pointed her splinted fingers at the floor. "This is home, now. No matter what, get back here." Her lip quivered. "You promised to make me a knight."

"I will." Arti leaned over and hugged Gal, another tide of tears coming as they held each other.

Arti stood and wiped her eyes with the back of her sleeve. Crossing to the round table, she lifted Excalibri and its well, carefully slipping them into the front pocket of her hoodie. Then she looked down at the old *Grail Tome*, singed and torn, hoping with all her heart that she might soon look upon its twin. As she descended the steps to leave, with her hand pressed against the motorhome's thin door, she looked back at Gal.

"Steal or starve," she said.

"It's almost dark, and the last guests are arriving," said Merl, studying the images flashing across the vidlink screen. "The Lighting ceremony should be starting soon. Go to the edge of the trees, and when it's safe, head for the fence. When Fay makes her appearance on that stage, you make your move. It's your call, Gwen."

Gwen gave the old librarian a reluctant nod, hoping he could keep the Archive from burning. The books had changed her life, had given it meaning, and her heart ached knowing they would perish if he failed. She thought of the little book of letters and how it had opened up another world to her. She could feel its crisp pages in her fingers, smell its colored paper, hear its letters speak. *Apple. Ball. Cat.* How could anyone destroy something so precious, so innocent?

"Do you have them?" asked Merl, turning to Arti as she joined them in the clearing.

Arti patted her pocket and nodded. "The pen *and* the well. I'm ready."

"Good," said Merl, glancing down nervously at the vidlink. "Then I suppose you should get going." He sighed. "All I can wish you is good luck...and my thanks on behalf of the Order. Farewell, young Book Knights. Be safe."

"Here goes nothing," said Gwen, shouldering the electroshock baton. The iron key to Fay's door dangled from her belt as she turned and started toward the trees.

Cradling the bolt cutters, Lance smiled and bowed at Merl. "Au revia," he said in his native tongue, before following Gwen.

"You better get moving," said Merl, seeing Arti's hesitation.

She looked past him at the motorhome's window, hoping

Gal would be alright, that she'd be able to keep the promise she'd made to her.

Merl's words brought her back. "*The History* unfolds in mysterious ways," he said, smiling at Arti. "I look forward to reading the final page."

Gripped by fear, Arti's only reply was a nervous nod. She lifted her hood, then stuffed her hands into her pocket, holding tight to Excalibri and its well as she jogged after Lance and Gwen.

Returning to the motorhome, Merl sat down at the round table and brushed his gloved hand across the *Grail Tome's* charred cover. "I am going to consult *The Meditations* and announce myself to Fay," he said, looking back at Gal sprawled on the rear bench. "It will not be easy." He flipped a swath of pages until he found what he was looking for.

"Ah, here it is," he said. "Yes, this should work." He glanced up at Gal again and cleared his throat. "But before I begin, I must first enter a trance. It should last a minute or two." His icy blue eyes exaggerated the point. "No matter what, *don't* disturb me."

"'Kay," pledged Gal, understanding the seriousness of the situation.

Gal pulled the gold chain of her sapphire pendant from under her shirt and began to roll the sparkling blue stone between her fingers, watching intently as Merl bowed over the book with eyes closed, humming. The old librarian's strange behavior continued for a while before his eyes suddenly opened, and he stared, unblinking, at the page. He didn't move a muscle and made no sound. If Gal hadn't known better, she would have thought he was dead.

Merl remained frozen until he heard the gentle click of the door closing next to him. The long bandage spotted with dried blood lay in a twisted pile at the foot of Gal's bed, and both she and her lucky cap were gone. The old librarian smiled when he looked down at the title of the verse he had randomly selected. *The Hidden Hand*. It was an amazing coincidence, in light of his theory.

"*Siegea Perilisi,*" he whispered, before turning back to *The Meditations* and getting down to work.

As dusk settled, Fisherman's Wharf should have been bustling with activity. But the boats were moored, the market closed, the captains, mates, and crews nowhere to be found. They'd been paid for their obedience, and no questions were asked, no objections made; the order had come down from the top.

Only the largest of the harbor's covered boathouses showed signs of life. Light peeked out through gaps in its painted shiplap walls, and there was movement and the sound of muffled voices beneath its high metal roof.

The big scow in the slip sat low in the water, loaded down by the mass of men and material. The cargo of passengers, dressed in dark clothing, sat shoulder to shoulder in lines spanning the ship's wide flat deck. Each man was armed with an electroshock baton, some at the stern also shouldering ropes and grappling hooks. The last of them had found a place to sit, just as Big Billy Johnson started to speak.

"This is a night to remember, my boys," he said. "One you'll be sharing with your grandkids." The little man paced alongside the boat as it lifted and fell gently on its watery bed.

"You all know what we're facin'. In little more than an hour, Captain York'll be droppin' us at Castle Point. We got a date with the Witch on the Hill."

Big Billy looked from one man to the next, making each feel as if the message was for him alone.

"It'll be a tough climb, but the old stone stairs are still passable, and Tulley Smith and his boys from The Lookout have pegged the rock face to give us holds. When you make it topside, find your captains, form up and fight like hellions." He sneered, "Until every Flame be out."

The men roared and waved their lighters above their heads. "But the Witch," yelled Big Billy above the din, "the Witch is mine!"

He crossed his stubby arms, waiting for the men to quiet. "I won't mince words with you. We do this to avenge Little Donny and the boys we lost. We do this so Fay can take no more from us. We do this for friends, for family, and future!" He was screaming now, "We do this for Isle!"

# CHAPTER 23

Winding their way through the thick web of bare saplings and branches, they arrived at the edge of the forest. The fall evening air was cool, and Arti shivered under her hood as she looked out from the trees, inhaling the damp, musty odor of wet leaves. The sun had dipped below the horizon leaving an aurora of pinks and golds in its wake, the smooth shimmer of Lake Ogden in the distance mirroring the effect. Soon the steep slope ahead of them would be shrouded in darkness, and they could begin their climb.

The beams of the huge flood lights placed high atop the castle walls were aimed at the sky and spun topsy-turvy, spiraling up, widening until they disappeared into the noth-ingness of space. The elaborate clifftop set was a stone's throw from the castle's tall curving tower and was surrounded by camera platforms overlooking an elevated stage supporting a table upon which there was a small mountain of books—the Archive. Heat lamps were aimed down at the sloping stands wrapped around the sacrificial pyre, warming a boisterous assembly of the rich and famous dressed in their designer suits and gowns with high end vidlinks sewn into the material, flaunting their wealth and privilege in a broadcast spectacle the likes of which had never been seen.

"To the fence," whispered Gwen. "Stay with me."

She crouched with the lighter in her hand and started up the slope, Lance and Arti in tow. They pressed themselves against the wire mesh, and immediately, Lance went to work with the bolt cutters. Mouthing a verse under his breath, in no time he had snipped an opening in the barrier large enough for them to slip through. But Gwen didn't move.

"Fay hasn't made her appearance yet," she explained, looking up the hill at the glowing theater. "We'll wait until we're sure she's left the castle."

As if on cue, there was a surge of music and an eruption of applause. A spotlight from an overhead boom targeted the stage, and a voice rang out from the public-address system, "Ladies and gentlemen, honored guests, citizens of the Corporation, please welcome the CEO of Fay Industries, Morgan Fay!"

Through the fence's chain links, Arti followed the spotlight as it moved across the raised platform, illuminating a single figure with long black hair, wearing an ebony gown. The applause grew louder as Morgan Fay arrived at center stage. *The Witch on the Hill*, thought Arti. *It's her!*

"Now," said Gwen. "To the top."

Lance pushed back the section of fence for Gwen and Arti, then crept up the slope after them. To their left, under the lights of the second checkpoint closest the castle, a squad of Incendi stood guard at the gate. Facing down the road, they were oblivious to the trespassers. Arti moved as quietly as she could, knowing a noisy stumble would spell doom for the mission.

Gwen stopped again at the crest of the hill and lied flat on the ground, making a shushing sound. Lance and Arti followed her example, hugging the earth, heads down. The car park at the center of the castle's main building was just above them, across a paved driveway. Illuminated by lights on the gable's ceiling, two Incendi officers stood at attention next the castle's main doors, electroshock batons clipped to their belts. Turning her head ever so slowly, Arti's eyes registered many more guards at the far end of the castle next the base of the tower and at intervals along the pathway leading from it to the stage. Backlit by the bleeding glow of the set, they appeared as faceless shadows.

Gwen reached down the slope and tugged at Lance. He slid along the ground and moved up next to her. Arti couldn't make out the words she whispered in his ear but could see him nod and mouth a reply before edging slowly back down to her.

"Stay here," he whispered.

Arti wanted an explanation, but Gwen and Lance were already on their feet, heading across the driveway. The troopers guarding the doors perked up, seeing bodies emerge from the darkness.

"Halt!" demanded one of the men, drawing his lighter. "I need to see your invitations and ID's."

"I'm sorry I'm late," said Gwen haughtily, combing a hand through her hair as she stepped into the light. "The limo had a flat. Needless to say, I've fired my driver. It's so hard to get good help these days."

When the guard saw Gwen's face, the recognition was immediate. "You...you're...but...I thought—"

"Yes, I know," answered Gwen. "There's been a misunderstanding. I have my invitation right here." She reached back and withdrew the lighter from her belt, jabbing its point into the trooper's chest. A white bolt flashed, and he collapsed. Before his partner could react, Lance murmured something and chopped him in the neck, catching him as he fell.

Arti was amazed at how fast it all happened. She looked down to where the other guards were stationed, to make sure none of them had noticed the assault. There were no sudden movements, no shouts of alarm.

Answering Gwen's signal, Arti scurried across the driveway while Lance dragged away the unconscious troopers. Returning quickly, Lance tested the door to see if it was unlocked. It was. He opened the heavy oak slab a sliver and listened for anyone who might be on the other side, prepared to silence them before they could vidlink for backup. Hearing nothing, he led Gwen and Arti inside, closing the door behind them.

They entered a foyer of shining granite, beyond which a massive ramp of stone steps bordered by ornately carved balustrades curved its way up to a second-floor landing. Hung high on a wall above the stairs was a life-sized portrait of Morgan Fay. Long black hair cascaded past a bare shoulder the same porcelain white as that of her perfect young face with its penetrating blue eyes. She looked so regal and beautiful that Arti understood why Merl had fallen for her.

"Let's go," said Gwen, heading for the stairs. "I expected more of a greeting. We've been lucky."

Arriving at the second-floor landing, Gwen hugged the wall and peeked around the corner. To her relief, the hall was also empty. She raised a finger to her lips for quiet, holding the lighter firmly in her other hand. If they were going to get to the tower, they would have to travel the length of the corridor undetected. Suddenly, a place that had been so familiar to her for so long seemed foreign and threatening.

Arti knew what was behind each door, having memorized Gwen's model. The studio where Gwen worked. The now empty Archive stamped with the Incendi symbol. The elevator across from it. And at the far end of the hall, looming ever nearer, Incendi Headquarters.

Arti's heart leapt into her throat. At any moment, she feared Mordred might step out from behind the jet-black door with its shining yellow flame. The image of the tall man's chiseled face was burned into her memory, always lurking, ready to strike. But the door remained closed, and the Incendi captain did not appear. No one did. It all seemed too easy.

Then she heard the loud clomping sound of many boots on the stairs behind them.

They had almost made it to the end of the hall when the troopers rounded the corner. The squad approached with caution, forming into lines three men wide and four deep. They weren't sure what they were facing yet, but two of their officers were down, and they weren't taking any chances. Behind a wall of shields, lighters were set to kill.

"Get behind me," said Lance.

Arti obeyed, but Gwen remained at his side, lighter raised, unwilling to have him face the troopers alone.

Voices cracked over a vidlink carried by the squad commander in the back row, a big bearded man with a slash for a mouth. The flood of messages streaming over the device clipped to his chest pocket were muffled and disjointed. In the flashing jumble of alarm calls, Arti heard the words "under attack!", "fall back!", and "lighters!" The sudden change in the troopers' faces told her that they were rattled by the reports. It sounded like a riot was happening outside.

Lance kept his eyes on the approaching Incendi. "Go," he told Gwen, calmly. "Open the door for Arti. Get the book."

"There's too many," objected Gwen.

"I count only twelve," said Lance.

"Only twelve!"

"Gwen, we have to go," begged Arti. "Trust him, he can do this. If I don't get the tome, nothing else matters. Remember?"

Arriving at the halfway point of the hall, in unison the troopers began banging their shields with the butts of their electroshock batons. The hard clacking echoed down the stone corridor like peals of thunder.

"You must go," repeated Lance.

Gwen finally relented. As Lance stared down the troopers, she placed her hand against his cheek, kissing him softly on the lips. Lance smiled, then began mouthing the verse Gwen recognized as *The Knight's Shield*. She said the words along with him as she hurriedly led Arti into the narrow opening past the buttress of stone.

The passage led to a column of spiraling stairs boring its way up one side of the tower. Light sconces covered in rusty wire mesh protruded from the stones overhead, throwing just enough light to illuminate the tight, winding path. Arti knew Fay's suite containing the *Grail Tome* was to be found on the floor above them, but she couldn't help but cast her eyes downward, remembering what Gwen had said about the ancient stairs: "*...they lead down to an old dungeon, the place where the Incendi keep their prisoners; decaps, readers, and in the deepest cells, scribes.*"

Arti wondered if her parents were somewhere down there at this very moment begging to be rescued, and she hoped they'd understand why her feet were carrying her away from them. As if to remind herself, her hand went to the small box and ink well bundled in her pocket.

The stairs emerged through a floor near the top of the tower, at one end of a crescent-shaped platform surrounding a curving inner wall, the far end of which arched away into darkness. The tall iron door was only a few feet from the stairs, just as Merl described: a thick, heavy pitted mass with hinges set deep in the stone and a rough hammered handle fastened with wide rusty rivets above a narrow key hole. Light escaped through a gap at the foot of the door, warming the rippled granite at Arti and Gwen's feet.

Gwen reached down and untied the key from her belt. "Cross your fingers," she said, aiming its tip at the opening in the door.

Before Gwen could insert the key, Arti heard a hiss of words behind her. A dark phantom leapt from the shadows, ripping the key from Gwen's hand, knocking both her and Arti to the cold stone floor.

Arti struggled to get to her feet, stars dancing in her eyes. Gwen was already up but stood frozen in fear. Standing before them was the Incendi captain, Mordred.

"I didn't want to believe it," he said, grinding his teeth at Gwen in disgust. "A decap. A traitor. The Corporation gave you everything you ever wanted, and this is how you show your appreciation?"

Mordred turned his glare to Arti. "And you, reader. There's no escaping this time."

The Incendi captain dropped the key on the stone floor and kicked it through the gap under the iron door. A verse rumbled from his lips, and he crossed the space between them. Gwen stepped in front of Arti, raising her arms defiantly.

Scoffing at the gesture, Mordred struck out at Gwen with blinding speed, but her arms miraculously answered the attack, driving his fist away. *The strike is the sword, but I am the shield.*

Mordred stepped back, astonished. "Who taught you that?"

"I did." Lance was standing on the platform at the edge of the stairs. Without taking his eyes off Mordred, he waved Gwen and Arti away.

"Ah, the young man with the fancy white car." Mordred brought his finger to his pursed lips, then pointed it at him as the name came, "Lance." He casually crossed his arms, as if he was making small talk. "Your aunt told me all about you. But she wouldn't tell me where you were hiding." Cold blue eyes looked up at Lance from under the fedora. "Too bad, I might have let her live."

The words hit Lance like a hammer blow. He tried to quell his rage, remembering his master's words: *Anger does not serve the Just.* "I will avenge her," he said, eyes locked on the Incendi captain as he shrugged off his leather jacket.

Mordred tossed his fedora to the floor. "We shall see," he growled.

# CHAPTER 24

"Ladies and gentlemen, honored guests, citizens of the Corporation, please welcome the CEO of Fay Industries, Morgan Fay!"

The grand spectacle's Master of Ceremony, vidlink star Barry Briton, stepped away from the podium's microphone, burying his dimpled chin into the ruffled shirt of a ridiculous red tuxedo, bowing his way into the wings as the spotlight found Morgan Fay and followed her across the stage.

An audible gasp arose from the audience at the sight of their enigmatic leader. Save for a few of Fay's top executives seated in the front row, it was the first time most of them had laid eyes on her. She looked so young, so impossibly young. Vidlinks popped up like periscopes from a sea of silk and satin, adding a deluge of streaming images to the event's flood of coverage. It didn't matter how or from where she was being watched, the spell she cast was the same, one of adoration and awe.

Fay eased up to the podium, a dark angel basking in a halo of light. She looked out at her audience and smiled, knowing this was the moment she had waited a quarter century for. Every face, every set of eyes surrendered to her. The cameras that ringed the stage were a tool of that unquestioned authority, the far-reaching reins with which she steered a nation. The exhilaration she felt made her wonder why she had ever doubted herself.

Her fear of the Challenger had come to naught, and even if such a person did exist, it was too late to stop what she had put in motion. Although an unlikely candidate, Fay believed the Penderhagen girl was the one named in *The History*. The girl had been hiding somewhere on the island and was likely already dead if Mordred understood the clue Fay had offered him through *The Meditations*. But even if the girl was still alive, no one had ever passed *The Test*, and no one ever would—not with the only surviving *Grail Tome* safely out of reach behind impenetrable walls of stone and iron. Fay smiled, knowing she would return to the book tonight after the Archive was a pile of smoldering ash. The final page would be waiting for her, ready to receive Wyzera's pen. Ready to receive her words.

Waves of applause and cheering washed against the stage for over a minute before Fay raised a hand for silence. The hush was immediate, and the CEO let it hang in the air for what seemed an eternity before offering the gift of her voice.

"Praise the Corporation," she intoned into the microphone, and the crowd chanted the words back to her in a deep, enveloping echo.

"Tonight we arrive at a milestone, a great moment in our history," said Fay, her ivory face framed by a close-up that flashed across countless screens. The audience stared into their devices to better regard the beauty and depth of her expression, conditioned as they were to abandon flawed reality for virtual perfection.

Fay raised her arms in a solemn gesture, the sleeves of her shimmering black dress hanging like wings below her upturned hands. "It has been twenty-five years, and we have come so far together. Our righteous journey to overcome the legacy of those who would dictate our existence—who would inscribe our lives and bind us with words—has not been easy.

"But your courage and strength have vanquished the literate, and your children are free, at last, to live in a world of unbridled vision." She smiled into the camera and was answered with a chorus of delighted gasps.

"Such an achievement demands a worthy sacrifice," said Fay, looking across the stage at the mound of books on the pyre, "a ceremony to rid us of the past, a ritual to finally achieve our true potential."

She took a deep breath and declared royally, "It is time for the Archive to burn!"

A roar of approval shook the stands, and thousands of vidlinks were thrust high into the air, aimed at the pile of books on the platform, eager to record its destruction. A chant crept through the audience like a hungry flame, starting low and growing, reaching out, demanding to be fed.

"Burn! Burn! Burn!"

Fay closed her eyes in ecstasy as the mantra reverberated through her. She leaned toward the microphone and spoke her slogan above the steady drone, "A picture is worth a thousand words. *Show*, don't tell. *You* are the Corporation."

Another cheer went up, and the chant continued, louder than before, "Burn! Burn! Burn!"

Fay lifted a long match from the podium and held it up in front of her with both hands for the audience to see, a religious relic, a symbol of their communion. Keeping it raised at arm's length, she gracefully approached the pyre of books in long, slow, sweeping steps, the silky fabric of her gown floating along with her. The chant reached a fever pitch, her followers voicing their delicious ignorance, their sumptuous need to submit.

"Burn! Burn! Burn!"

From overhead, a tall boom camera followed her across the stage like a great serpent tracking its prey, preparing to strike. A flaming torch stood next the platform upon which the books were piled, and Fay came to a stop, standing solemnly beside it. Another microphone was lowered until it was close enough to amplify her words. Staring into a monitor off stage, a puffy, red-faced Victor Herrat let out a deep sigh, seeing the CEO had found her mark. Everything was perfect, everything in place. It would be his directorial masterpiece.

Fay thrust a hand toward the audience, palm out, demanding silence again. The chant suddenly ended, and a thousand vidlinks hung in the air, mirroring her gesture. She smiled, acknowledging the absolute obedience of her people, then returned her attention to the match in her hand. She carefully pushed its dark red tip into the blazing torch and watched it hiss to life, throwing sizzling sparks as it ignited. Every set of eyes was focused on its tiny flame. Watching. Waiting.

Looking directly at the main camera, Fay said the words she had waited two and a half decades to utter: "With this flame, I bring light. With this heat, I cleanse."

The CEO moved her hand toward the pyre slowly, aiming the burning match at a piece of paper near the base of

223

the mound of books. She let the tiny flame hover there, teasing the audience, heightening expectation. The moment was even more intoxicating than she imagined.

"You're too late, Morgan. It's over."

The voice was blunt and heavy, and Fay staggered back from the pyre as if she'd been struck. It sounded as if the words had been uttered directly into her ear by someone standing next to her. But she was alone on the stage, no one else there. Her heart raced, and a bead of sweat formed on her perfect brow. The elation was suddenly doused, replaced by confusion and terror.

"Yes, I'm still here," said the voice. "Surprised?"

Fay gasped as she recognized the man she betrayed so many years ago. "Merl? It can't be!"

The microphone carried her words out to the audience, and the chanting became muddled and disjointed before finally dissolving. Was this part of the ceremony? Some new element added to entertain them? Off stage, Victor Herrat was in a panic, knowing it wasn't part of the script. What was the CEO doing?

"Oh, but it is me," said Merl, his words pounding in Fay's mind. Fear distorted her face, and she stared out at the audience, paralyzed. "I'm very much alive, as is the *Grail Tome* I rescued from your madness. How else would I be speaking to you now?

Fay could feel the magic bristling in the words and knew that what he said was true. It was Merl! He lived! And so did the second *Grail Tome!* He was using *The Meditations* to speak to her, and that required a great deal of skill and control. Once, he had been afraid of the books, unwilling to tap into their potency, but now he commanded that power with apparent ease.

"You failed, Morgan. Arti Penderhagen wields Excalibri. The final page is hers."

Just then, a scream went up from the rear of the auditorium, and the crackling sound of lighters filled the air. In a desperate attempt to flee the ensuing violence, rows of spectators cascaded down from their seats, pushing into those ahead of them until wave after wave of bodies washed against the stage.

Fay stood like a statue next the pyre, suddenly old, as if the years she had cheated caught up to her at once. She couldn't help but think the chaos unfolding in front of her was a product of Merl's ominous pronouncement, that he commanded it. The horrible realization smothered her hopes; it was over, her dynasty was at its end, the legacy she had labored so hard for had been stolen. *The final page is hers.*

A squad of Incendi guards ran to the CEO, surrounding her, shielding her from the violent stampede. Fay forgot about the match she was holding until it burned her hand, and she flinched, casting it away. It landed softly on a crumpled page at the pyre's edge, its tiny flame surviving the wind of flight and fleeing bodies. It rested there, tasting the paper beneath it, before unfolding like the yellowy blossoms of a flower.

The fire crept to the outermost books on the pyre, their dry covers quickly surrendering to it. A four-hundred-year old Astengan treatise, *The Cost of Liberty,* bubbled away into memory; a collection of Parmellese epic poems dissolved, their heroes' feats to be forgotten. One great work unwillingly betrayed another, delivering death to its neighbor.

The troopers closed their protective ring around Fay and hurriedly whisked her away, narrowly escaping the tall boom camera as it crashed to the stage. The auditorium lights flickered once, twice, then finally went out.

His bond with the book was suddenly broken, and Merl lurched back in his seat, his gloved hands sliding from the *Grail Tome* open on the round table. It took a moment for him to gather himself, for each fragment of memory to fall into place. The spell had sapped his strength, and he breathed deeply, eyes blinking, waiting for the cobwebs shrouding his mind to clear.

From what he could tell, *The Looking Glass* had worked as intended, transporting his consciousness into Morgan Fay's. He had been there with her, a part of her, seeing and hearing everything she did: the faces, the voices, a thousand hovering screens.

Merl had been watching the vidlink, waiting for Morgan Fay to make her appearance. When she stepped onto the stage, a shiver ran down his spine; she hadn't aged a day in a quarter century. The image stirred up a painful mix of emotions in him, as if he was still looking at her through the flames, still trying to understand why she had answered his devotion with treachery. It surprised him that his feelings were still there, still raw after so many years. And even more surprising was the fact that, for a brief moment after announcing himself, he sensed the same regret, the same loss, in her.

He had delivered his message; he was sure of it. Morgan Fay knew he was alive and that he possessed the second *Grail Tome*. But the connection had not lasted long enough for him to weigh Fay's reaction to his bluff about the final page being written by Arti. Something happened that pulled her away, severing the link between them. There was screaming and panic and the distinct sound of lighters snapping the air, and the last thing he felt was Morgan Fay's utter dread at the thought that he was the cause of the violence, that he controlled it.

Then Merl remembered the burning match.

It had been in Fay's hand, and he felt the sting of its tiny flame along with her. She had been standing next the pyre when she dropped it, just as the Incendi were rushing to her aid. But where did it land?

Merl reached for the vidlink he'd placed next the book, just in time to see a squad of Incendi guards hastily escort Fay away. The streaming images went in and out of focus, shaking with the motion of the fleeing spectators. Bodies were everywhere, a battle line was forming between Incendi guards in riot gear and a rabble of armed men.

The last thing Merl saw before the vidlink went black made his heart sink. The bottom of the pyre was smoking, and a small flame appeared.

# CHAPTER 25

Within the narrow confines of the tower platform, Lance and Mordred faced off, circling one another, trading places on the floor's polished stone grid like two chess pieces in a deadly end game. Neither had faced as skilled a foe, and both knew that a misstep would be answered without mercy. For two combatants so expertly trained in *the strike of words*, the outcome was anything but predictable.

Mordred was privileged to have studied *The Verses* from the source, from the very pages of the *Grail Tome* itself. That direct connection had infused the power of the poems into his mind and body, each potent phrase forging memory and movement into a single entity, arming his will with an arsenal of terrible weapons.

And though Lance had learned *The Verses* indirectly through the oral tradition of his family, he was not without his own advantage. He could call upon the lessons of his Uncle Jean, *The Bard of Lucinne*, the great master and teacher who instilled in his nephew a true appreciation of the Art. The fighting poems were more than tools to the young Ferencian, more than rote devices to be employed in battle. To Lance, they represented the power of words in its purest form, something to be revered and respected. In return for his veneration, they answered his will, not as servants but allies.

Standing at the top of the narrow staircase, away from the gladiators battling in their stone arena, Arti and Gwen watched the dizzying flurry of strikes and blocks with awe, finding it hard to discern one man from the other in the violent blur of fists and feet. The steady hum of words reverberated through the space, a continuous cadence spilling from the combatants' lips as they spun and kicked and punched at each other. *The Cobra*, *The Falling Sky*, *The Dagger's Edge*; they recited one ancient poem after another to amplify their actions and shape their attacks. And each time those efforts were negated by an equally potent defense; *The Mongoose*, *The Storm Breaker*, *The Shattered Blade*. In harmony with their words, auras enveloped each man, shrouds of energy pulsing under the weak glow of the wall sconces.

Both fighters were marvels of speed and power, but their methods could not have been more different. Where Mordred was machine-like, structured, and precise, Lance had an elegant, flowing style. A dancer's style. As dissimilar as their techniques were, each countered the other perfectly, wills conversing and colliding with equal force. Frustrated by the stalemate, Mordred backed away from Lance, employing a different strategy, drawing upon his cruelty to shift the balance.

"She died well," he said, catching his breath, observing the subtle change in his young opponent's face, a flicker of emotion.

Gwen called out from the stairs, "Don't listen to him, Lance!"

Mordred started to circle again, studying Lance with a vulture's eyes. "I remember her final breath. The last beat of her heart."

Lance squared himself to his opponent, turning with him. From somewhere in his memory among the countless hours of training and practice, his uncle shouted a warning: *An unshielded mind is the knight's bane; the most dangerous strike comes from within.*

"She called you a Knight of Maren," growled Mordred, "but you left her alone and defenseless."

The accusation stabbed at Lance's conscience; his beloved Aunt Vivian was dead because he hadn't been there to protect her. When Mordred saw the flash of guilt in his opponent's eyes, the sudden inward look of self-doubt, he knew the young Ferencian's mental armor had been pierced. In the split-second Lance's guard was down, Mordred pounced, humming a rapid stream of words, lashing out with his right hand, grasping Lance's right wrist, spinning him violently toward the iron door. From behind, Mordred hooked his left arm under Lance's, wrapping his palm around the back of his neck, slamming him against the barrier. Still gripping Lance's other arm, Mordred wrenched it behind his back, driving it up into his shoulder blade. There was a sickening pop, and Lance grimaced at the explosion of pain as his shoulder dislocated.

Unable to free his arms, Lance desperately tried to wrap his legs around Mordred's, to gain purchase and break the hold. Mordred anticipated the effort, throwing Lance face down on the floor, straddling his back, making escape impossible.

"Knight of Maren," mocked Mordred. "You're nothing!"

He leaned close and whispered venomously in Lance's ear, "De la flamma, sombral." *From flame, shadow.*

Mordred slammed Lance's head into the granite floor, shattering his nose and opening a wide gash above his cheek. Arti screamed as blood poured from Lance's battered face, pooling on the stone slab beneath him. Gwen ran to Lance's aid, jabbing at Mordred with the electroshock baton. The Incendi captain mumbled a verse, and the white bolt from the lighter climbed up his back and leapt across to the iron door, repelled by the words. He let go of Lance's lame arm, grabbing the weapon from Gwen, shattering it against the floor before driving his fist into her stomach, propelling her backward into the wall. She thudded off the stone, curling into a ball, gasping for air.

With his head pressed against the blood slicked floor, Lance looked over at Gwen. The sight made him want to scream. He'd failed her just like he'd failed his Aunt Vivian. Like he'd failed Arti and his oath. Despite all his training, the countless lessons his Uncle Jean had taught him, Mordred had won, and it sickened Lance to think what he would do to Gwen and Arti. No matter how hard Lance struggled, he couldn't shake the Incendi captain from his back.

Mordred answered Lance's efforts by driving his face into the floor again. Still on his knees, he straddled Lance's back, wrapping an arm around his neck. Uttering another string of words, he began to strangle him.

Arti knew she must do something or watch Lance die. But what could she do? Gwen had tried to stop Mordred with the lighter, and all it got her was a fist in the stomach.

*I don't even have a weapon.*

Then Arti remembered Excalibri. Fumbling in her pocket, she withdrew the wooden case and flipped open its lid. Raising the pen above her head, point down like a dagger, she launched herself at Mordred, stabbing it with all her strength at his exposed back. He noticed her coming just in time to utter a verse—the same one he had used against Gwen and the lighter—but this time the words failed him.

Immune to Mordred's defense, the pen sank deep between his shoulder blades. With a roar, he released Lance from the chokehold, reaching back with both hands, clawing at Excalibri's tiny silver pommel.

Coughing for air, Lance rolled out from beneath Mordred, a poem flowing from his lips. He focused the power of *The Battering Ram* on Mordred's chest, delivering a crushing kick that sent the Incendi captain hurtling back into the iron door. Mordred staggered on his knees, trying to rise, but his legs would not obey him. He opened his mouth and uttered a last slurred phrase, a string of disjointed words that Lance didn't recognize, then he swayed for a moment and collapsed face down on the bloodstained floor.

Finding his feet, Lance warily approached Mordred's body. He reached down and touched the Incendi captain's neck but felt no pulse. "From flame, shadow," he whispered.

Lance turned to see Gwen standing. Her legs were a bit shaky, but she raised a hand to put him at ease. "I'm okay. Just got the wind knocked out of me. And my back hurts." She rubbed it and winced, "Can't wait to see the bruise." Lance's eyes softened beneath the mask of blood. "But you don't look so good," she said. "Your face. Your arm."

"I am fine," said Lance, delicately lifting the injured limb across his chest. It had popped back into place, and the pain had eased. He leaned down and pulled Excalibri from Mordred's back, noting the strange absence of blood on its inscribed silver blade. Relieved that the pen was undamaged, he handed it to Arti. "A Knight of Maren is never alone. You saved my life, and I am in your debt."

"Same goes for me," said Gwen, staring down with contempt at Mordred's lifeless form. Her eyes narrowed. "But how did you do it? The bolt from the lighter just bounced off him."

Arti studied the pen in her hand. "Excalibri wrote *The Verses,* so maybe that's why the words couldn't stop it." She shrugged, "I was lucky, I didn't know it would work."

"You were brave to try," added Lance. "Now let's get you inside; the book is waiting." He turned to Gwen, expectantly. "Where is the key?"

Arti answered for her, "Mordred kicked it under the door." Her expression darkened as the awful truth sank in. "We can't get the book. We...failed."

Refusing to accept the dreadful verdict, Lance bent down and stuck his fingers through the gap, hoping he might be able to reach the key. He felt only air.

"There must be a way," he growled, standing again, gauging the door's strength, searching for a weak point.

"It's no use," said Gwen. "Merl was right; the door's too solid—even for you. And we don't have the tools or time to try anything else. Judging by what we heard over the trooper's vidlink, something's happened outside. It sounded like a fight, as if they were being attacked. I'm surprised this place isn't swarming with Incendi, but I'm sure it soon will be." She scooped Lance's leather jacket from the floor, holding it so he could slip his injured arm through its sleeve. "We have to get Arti and the pen back to Merl before they lock the castle down—and just hope we get another chance at the tome before Fay finishes it."

Gwen and Lance started toward the stairs, but Arti hesitated, staring at the iron door. To be so close to the tome and not complete the mission was devastating. She looked down at Mordred's body, trying to find some solace in the knowledge that he'd no longer be hunting her.

There was little comfort in the thought. Morgan Fay was still going to win, and the future she would write would be too horrific to imagine. Merl's ominous words echoed in Arti's mind: *When she writes the final page, she'll have the means to find every scribe and reader in existence. No one anywhere will be safe. She'll burn every book...and kill us all.*

Lance's firm grip on Arti's arm pulled her from those morbid thoughts, and with Gwen close behind, he led her down the spiraling stairs, arriving at the landing on the second floor. A black boot stuck out from behind the buttress of stone and the hallway beyond, belonging to one of the troopers Lance had dealt with earlier. Lance went ahead to check the corridor and make sure there weren't any more Incendi waiting in ambush. When he whistled that the coast was clear, Gwen nodded for Arti to go.

"I'm not leaving," said Arti, defying the order. "If my parents are here, I have to find them." She turned back to the stairs, but Gwen blocked her way.

"You're going back to Merl," said Gwen, looking hard into Arti's eyes. "This isn't over. Not yet. If the final page is still blank, then there's still hope. You're the only one who can write it, so I'm not going to let you risk your life for anything. Or *anyone.*"

"What hope do we have?" asked Arti, fighting back tears. "I can't get the book from Fay. Not without the key. But if my parents are still alive, I have to free them. We could be together, even if it's only for a little while." Her eyes pleaded with Gwen, "I can't just leave them to die!"

"Who said anything about leaving them?" said Gwen. "Lance will take you back to Merl. I'll look for your parents."

Wondering what the hold up was, Lance returned just in time to hear the end of the exchange—and voice his objection. "It is too dangerous, Gwen. You said it yourself: the Incendi will be coming. They will—"

"It's the only way," said Gwen. "Arti has to get back to Merl—which means you need to be with her. Even with one good arm, you're her best bet at getting out of here. And if there are prisoners down there, someone has to release them. That leaves me."

"You don't have to do this," said Arti. "They're my parents, not yours."

"I'm doing it," said Gwen, "and we don't' have time to argue the point. Get going."

*Gweneath Justea.* Gwen the Just. The pen had named her well, thought Arti. "Thank you," she said, giving her a hug. "I won't forget this."

The thought of letting Gwen go terrified Lance, but he knew by the look in her eyes she wouldn't be talked out of it; her will was too strong. "You have to come back," he said. "Promise me."

"I promise," said Gwen. "You have more lessons to teach me, remember?" She smiled mischievously. "We'll pick up where we left off."

"I...I—" Lance stammered.

"I know," replied Gwen, already descending the chiseled tower steps.

The worry she saw on Lance's battered face made Arti feel guilty for letting Gwen go. Lance and Gwen had only known each other for a few days, but Arti knew love when she saw it. How awful it would be if something so beautiful died before it had a chance to grow.

*The least I can do is keep trying*, thought Arti, searching for some of the hope Gwen had invested in her. *I owe them that much.*

With Lance leading the way, Arti stepped over the bodies strewn along the castle's long second floor hallway. After witnessing Lance's battle with Mordred, she almost felt sorry for the troopers. Against the young Ferencian, they hadn't a chance.

The vidlink attached to the fallen squad commander's chest pocket was still spewing voices: "To the CEO!", "Hold them back at the stage!" As urgent as the orders were, the Incendi sounded less alarmed than before, as if they'd gained some level of control over the situation. But it still begged the question: who was attacking them?

Right now, that didn't matter. Arti and Lance cared only about getting out of the castle, back to the motorhome and Merl. To regroup and consider their options—if they had any. Arriving at to the top of the wide staircase curving down into the main foyer, they saw a handful of troopers attending to injured comrades sprawled on the floor. Their uniforms looked singed and torn, there was the smell of burning flesh and a lot of moaning.

"Stay behind me," said Lance, but Arti didn't need to be told.

The first shout went up when Lance and Arti were halfway down the stairs. The same trooper screamed into his vidlink, announcing the presence of intruders inside the castle. The alert meant there would be more guards on the way; they had to act quickly.

A verse hummed from Lance's lips, and he leapt the last twenty feet from the stairs to the lower floor, planting his feet into the chests of two troopers scrambling toward him with their lighters raised. They were flung backward, collapsing on the wounded sprawled next the castle's main entrance. Landing like a cat, with his good arm Lance punched and chopped a path to the door, snapping lighters and limbs with surgical precision, glancing behind him to make sure Arti was still close.

One trooper stood between Lance and the open door, feebly pointing his lighter at the young Ferencian's chest. Lance shook his head, and the Flame dropped the weapon at his feet. He moved clear of the threshold, falling back against the wall and collapsing to the floor with his hands raised.

"A wise decision," said Lance.

Lance looked out at the lit car park to make sure their escape route was clear. From behind him Arti could hear the chaos outside, a lot of yelling and screaming.

"The spectators are fleeing," said Lance. "We can hide among them until we make it to the hill. Hold on to my jacket, and don't let go."

Towed by Lance, Arti weaved her way through the panicked crowd, a river of terrified people dressed in their finest, many of the women running barefoot over the cold asphalt in their sparkling gowns. No one gave Arti and Lance a second look, so concerned were they with escaping the violence at the far end of the castle.

Having threaded their way across the driveway, Lance and Arti crested the hill. As she stumbled down the grassy slope shrouded in darkness, Arti looked back up at the clifftop stage. She could see a battle raging around the raised platform where Morgan Fay had addressed her audience. There were flashes of white from hundreds of lighters emerging from both sides of a battle line. Lance came to a stop on the hill, also looking back. He said nothing, but Arti could tell what he was thinking. The fight looked like it was moving toward the tower.

Toward Gwen.

# CHAPTER 26

A few minutes ago, it looked as if his men would win the day, but the tables had turned and the Incendi were gaining the upper hand. Standing on the stage with his back to the pyre, Billy Johnson knew he'd made a terrible mistake.

He thought he had planned well. The landing at Castle Point had been perfect, Captain York masterfully maneuvering the big scow into place next a thick ramp of concrete angling up from the depths toward the rocky shore like a beached whale. Lake Ogden was uncharacteristically calm, and Billy's men disembarked without incident, finding enough space on the rocky shore to gather until they could begin the ascent. In preparing the route, Tulley Smith and his Lookout boys had outdone themselves. Sturdy iron pegs stuck out from the rock face at regular intervals, offering hand and footholds that even the weakest climbers could navigate with ease. Those carrying the ropes and grappling hooks never even bothered to shrug them from their shoulders.

The islanders managed to arrive at the clifftop without being noticed. A hundred feet from the precipice, they faced a thirty-foot-high latticework of scaffolding upon which the Lighting's audience was seated, cheering and chanting with no inkling that an invasion force was approaching from below.

The ceremony was reaching its zenith, and a voice from the public-address system echoed above the din: "A picture is worth a thousand words. *Show*, don't tell. *You* are the Corporation." Big Billy recognized the speaker as Morgan Fay.

Billy had only met her once but would never forget the CEO's voice. It carried with it a timbre of power and purpose that was at the same time seductive and threatening. He last heard it at a clandestine meeting held in Fay's tower suite twenty years before, the night they made their "deal". Billy and his syndicate would control the island without interference from the Corporation, provided he kept Fay Industries' supplies flowing from the Docks into Main. One entrepreneur helping another, Fay had said. *More like a deal with the Devil*, thought Billy.

"With this flame, I bring light. With this heat, I cleanse."

Understanding the meaning of those ominous words, Billy raised his stubby arm and gave the signal to his four captains, bellowing above the roaring crowd, "Up you go! Hurry, my boys!"

Two hundred men, lighters in hand, scrambled up the scaffolding. At first, the audience members sitting in the back row smiled dumbly as the islanders appeared behind them, assuming they were production crew there to add a last dramatic element to the spectacle's climax. But when they saw the electroshock batons spark to life, it became clear that the intruders were not part of the show, and panic set in.

One row of terrified spectators pushed into the next until utter chaos enveloped the stands. The first Incendi guards who responded to the bedlam barely had enough time to draw their weapons before the islanders were upon them, bolts of white death crackling the air.

Accepting the meaty hand of Docker Mike Burnaby, Big Billy found his footing on the amphitheater's wide rear railing, a red cylinder clinging to his back, fastened by a shoulder strap. Below, the battle was raging, and he was pleased by the quick progress his men were making. People were running everywhere, the stands emptying. Billy took pleasure in seeing the rich mainlanders scrambling for their lives in designer suits and dresses, abandoning any dignity they pretended to possess.

But he wasn't after them.

Looking to the stage, he saw a woman in a long black gown standing beside a tall smoking torch next a platform covered in books. The spotlight illuminating Morgan Fay suddenly moved away, revealing a tiny pinpoint of light in her hand—a burning match. Billy watched as a squad of Incendi troopers rushed onto the stage, forming a protective ring around their CEO. His eyes followed the match as it flew from her hand, falling onto the edge of the platform where the books were piled.

"Get me to the stage!" yelled Big Billy. "As fast as you can!"

Docker Mike shouted orders to a few of his men, and together they plowed their way down the steps with Big Billy in their wake, fighting through the throng of fleeing spectators. Ahead of them, a tall camera boom fell, landing with a crash where Morgan Fay had stood just a moment before.

Its long arm snapped in the middle, throwing sparks from a severed wire. The stadium lights flickered for a moment, then went out.

The stage rose before Big Billy like a pier thrust out into a dark sea of churning humanity, and Docker Mike hoisted the little man onto it like cargo. Billy removed the cylinder strapped to his back and waddled quickly across the stage toward the pyre, relieved to see that he hadn't arrived too late. So far, only the books at its base had been turned to cinders, pulses of orange flickering out between layers of tightly bound charcoal pages. But the fire was gaining strength, its heat intensifying, and soon the whole collection would be alight.

In haste, Billy aimed the extinguisher at the advancing flames where they licked at a small book with letters and pictures on its cover: an "A" beside an apple, a "B" for a striped ball, a "C" next a fluffy cat. He remembered the book from his childhood when as a small, stunted boy, he had used the tiny tome to learn the alphabet and decode his first words. That knowledge had made him feel as big as a giant.

Billy squeezed the handle, propelling a cloud of thick white dust toward the pyre, shuffling around the platform, blasting quick pulses until every hint of fire was gone. Satisfied the books were safe from further ruin, he turned to locate Morgan Fay just as the lights above the stage came back on. In the darkness, he hadn't seen the black-clad trooper approach.

The Incendi looked down inquisitively at the extinguisher in the strange little man's puffy hands before thrusting the tip of his lighter at his head, releasing a stream of electricity that hissed through the air like a demented snake. Billy ducked and rolled away, avoiding the blast, ending up on the floor of the stage with his back pressed against the base of the smoking

242

pyre. As the trooper closed in to finish him, a bolt of white light snapped around the Incendi's neck like a noose, sending him to the floor in a crumpled heap. Ridley York smiled down at his boss, smoke rising from the tip of the weapon in his callused hands.

"Well done, Ridley," said Big Billy. "Thought I was a gonner." He accepted his captain's hand and regained his feet, just as the dead trooper's vidlink chirped out a string of commands.

"To the CEO!", "Hold them back at the stage!"

Wave after wave of Incendi reinforcements started to arrive, bolts of electricity leaping toward the thinning line of islanders. The troopers seemed to be coming from everywhere at once. Bodies fell amid the smoke and smell of burning flesh.

Facing overwhelming odds, Billy called his men back to the stage. It was the only high ground available, the only real estate their inferior numbers could defend. A moment ago, victory had been within reach, and now it was unlikely any of them would escape with their lives. Two of his captains were dead, and less than fifty of his men who made the voyage from the Docks still drew breath.

"I'm sorry, my boys," wailed Big Billy. "I'm sorry."

The hill was covered in a thin blanket of dew, and Arti struggled to keep from slipping, cradling the pen and inkwell in the pouch pocket of her hoodie. She wondered if the effort to protect them was worth it, having failed to get the *Grail Tome*. Without its final page, the pen and ink were useless; she'd never be able write her version of the future.

It would belong to Morgan Fay.

But even if she had the book and could get Excalibri to work, Arti had no idea what the future *should* be, let alone how to write it. The only instruction came two thousand years ago from Merrill of Astenga, Excalibri's original owner and one of the *Grail Tomes'* scribes: *Forged together in truth, the pen and the will are one.* Arti was sure it would take another two thousand years for her to figure out what he meant.

In the darkness, it took some searching to locate the hole Lance had cut in the fence, and all the while they could hear the fighting and the screaming and the chaos enveloping the tower on the clifftop behind them.

"Who do you think is attacking them?" asked Arti. "Who would do that?"

"I don't know," answered Lance, pulling back the sliced section of chain link, "but they are well armed. And it is clear they knew, as we did, that tonight was their best opportunity to strike."

Arti crouched and stepped through the opening. "Could they be after the tome, too?"

"It is possible," said Lance, "but I doubt it. Aunt Vivian said there were few who knew of its existence. It is more likely that those who strike tonight do so for their own reasons."

Hearing Lance speak of his aunt made Arti's heart sink. He had only just found out that she was gone, that Mordred had murdered her.

"I'm sorry," said Arti. "About your aunt, I mean. She was very nice."

"Yes, she was," said Lance. He slipped through the fence and joined Arti on the other side. "Uncle Jean taught me how to fight, but Aunt Vivian taught me...so much more. She was the wisest and kindest person I've ever known." His throat tightened, "I will miss her dearly."

The dark band of forest was disorienting, and they emerged from the trees on the road a short distance away from the clearing where the motorhome and Charger were parked. Merl was waiting there, the beam from the flashlight in his hand locating Arti and Lance as they approached. The light bounced from one to the other, probing, searching. When it finally settled on Lance's bloody face, the questions came.

"The book? Gwen?"

Lance shook his head, and Merl knew right away the mission had failed. And judging by the young man's appearance, quite badly. "Oh, no," he groaned, "Come inside, and tell me everything."

Arti climbed the stairs and looked back at where she expected Gal to be. The bed was empty, except for the blanket and the blood-spotted bandage strewn across it. She spun around at Merl. "Where's Gal?"

Merl lowered his head, knowing the explanation would be difficult. "She left," he said. "And I let her. I'll tell you why after you tell me what happened at the castle. Sit down."

Arti objected, firing a number of angry questions at him, but the old librarian cut her off. "Sit down! Now!"

Lance took his place in the booth beneath the weak dome light, keeping his injured arm crossed at his chest. Swallowing back her anger and worry, Arti also found her seat, removing the pen and inkwell from her pocket, plunking them down on the *Grail Tome* dominating the round table between them. She stared at the book, thinking about how close she had been to its twin tonight—to the final page. Then her eyes went to the name inscribed on the table in front of her: *Artia Bendi*. Arti the Blessed. *Excalibri couldn't have been more wrong.*

245

As requested by Merl, Lance provided a detailed description of the night's events, ending with a concise summation: "Without the key, we could not get the book. Gwen insisted on staying to free any prisoners in the dungeon." He glanced at Arti, knowing it was her parents who inspired the rescue, and she could see the deep worry in his eyes. "I agreed to get Arti out, and we fled while the castle was under attack."

Merl nodded soberly. "So Mordred is ...dead?'

"Yes," said Lance, seeing something in the old man's eyes that resembled regret.

Arti understood what Lance didn't. As awful as the Incendi captain had been, Mordred was Merl's child, his flesh and blood. Morgan Fay had stolen much more than a book from the old librarian.

"He deserved no better," said Merl. Water pooled in his blue eyes. "I'm sorry for your loss, Lance. I will grieve for Vivian." He studied the young Ferencian's bloody face, the broken nose, the deep gash on his cheek, more concerned with the injury he couldn't see. "Are you alright?"

"I will heal," said Lance, waving away his concern. "Those who attacked the castle tonight, do you know who they are?"

"No," answered Merl, "but from what I saw on the vidlink before it went black, there was a lot of them, and they were armed with lighters." He leaned back and covered his face in his gloved hands. "Why did they have to do this tonight, of all nights?"

"I believe it is for the same reason we tried for the tome," offered Lance. "They knew Morgan Fay would be outside the castle, that she would be vulnerable."

"But there's no way to know what's happened," said Merl, rubbing his eyes wearily. "She may have escaped, or they may have caught her. The final page of *The History* may still be empty, or she may be writing it now." He bowed his head. "And the Archive is burning. Oh, I've made a terrible mess of this."

Arti had waited long enough. "Why did Gal leave?" she asked, sternly.

Before Merl could answer, the motorhome door flipped open, and the familiar wedge-shaped cap appeared on the stairs. Slowly climbing the steps, Gal looked even more ill than before, half of her face a deep purpley black. Arti lunged from the booth, just in time to catch her as she collapsed.

"Cuz I needed to," she moaned, surrendering to Arti's arms. "'Case you screwed up." Gal swayed for a moment before she noticed Lance's face. "You look like crap."

"Let's get you back to bed," said Arti. She scowled at Merl for allowing Gal to leave in such condition, "What were you thinking?"

"Apparently, my theory was wrong," he said. "I...I shouldn't have let her go. I'm sorry."

"I ain't goin' back to bed," objected Gal. "I'm gonna sit at the table." She pulled away from Arti and plopped herself down on the edge of the booth's cushioned seat, flopping sideways until she was in the place marked with the cryptic words *Siegea Perilisi*. Drained by the effort, she leaned her head back and closed her eyes.

Arti gave up, taking her own seat again, shaking her head at her stubborn friend. *Why did she have to be so difficult? Wasn't tonight bad enough?* It was then she noticed the queer look on Merl's face. His eyes went from Gal to the table, then back again, his brow knitted in thought.

"What…theory?" asked Arti.

Gal squinted through the fog of another piercing headache, watching as Merl pointed at the script on the table in front of her. "I've read those words before," he said, "from an ancient edict that first mentioned the Finding Swords. Like the one that led Gwen to us. Do you remember?"

"Yes," said Arti. "You thought the swords were a myth. That someone made it up."

"But I was wrong," said Merl. "Gwen's arrival at the Camel Lot proved it. And it made me wonder if the legend I read about *those* words could also be true. Why else would Excalibri write them?

"*Siegea Perilisi* does not mean what you think, Arti. It does not mean 'perilous siege.' I had to let you and Gwen believe that. I had to wait and see." He shook his head, "But I'm afraid my theory was wrong. It…it can't be true."

"What can't be true?" demanded Arti. "I'm sick of your secrets! What do the words mean? Just tell us!"

Lance interrupted, "I wondered why they were written there." He looked at Arti, innocently. "I could have translated them for you. Like the words in the book, it is Old Ferencian. It means *perilous seat*."

"Yes," said Merl. "It is a term whose origin comes from the earliest days of the Order of Librarians, when they first enlisted the Knights of Maren. It was a secret, even then, and whereas the legend of the Finding Swords has survived, the true meaning of the *perilous seat* has long since been forgotten."

"So, what's its *true* meaning?" begged Arti.

"The Order believed the *perilous seat* belonged to the one knight who could complete the quest for the *Grail Tome* and deliver its final page to the wielder of a great pen. It was silly of me to think it was true. But the Finding Sword was real, so I had to take a chance." His eyes pleaded with Arti. "I had to hope Gal could do it."

"Gal? What does she have to do with it?" Arti looked across at her friend who, despite the pain in her head, was listening intently.

Merl sat back with a huff. "It doesn't matter. She's returned empty handed, so I've been proven wrong. Again." He sighed, "Morgan is going to write the final page, and there's nothing we can do to stop her."

# CHAPTER 27

Morgan Fay arrived at the castle tower's arching door, oblivious to the violence and chaos around her, unaware of the troopers escorting her to safety. She was in a state of shock, of utter disbelief. The goal for which she had dedicated most of her life had just been ripped away. Stolen.

*You failed, Morgan.*

Merl was alive, and he had rescued the second *Grail Tome* from the fire she set so long ago, its final page written by another. The future Fay had envisioned, the destiny that had taken her a thousand drafts to craft into words, would never be realized. The fighting on the clifftop was proof of her downfall, irrefutable evidence that Merl had prevailed, that she was paying the ultimate price for ignoring the warnings he gave her so many years before.

*There are rules. The books are dangerous.*

As Fay climbed the tower stairs, guards in front and back, she tried to decide how she would end her life. The fate prescribed by the Penderhagen girl would certainly include her punishment, but she would not allow herself to be treated like a common criminal, preferring death to disgrace. Her impending mortality made her think of her son, Mordred. She wished he was with her now, that she could share her last moments with him. That she could say good-bye.

Mordred's absence spoke volumes. He had failed to find the Challenger in time. He had failed in his promise. But where was he, she wondered? How close had he come?

Her questions were answered at the top of the stairs.

Looking past the lead troopers, Fay's heart skipped a beat at the sight of the black fedora resting at the foot of the iron door. There were dark red smears on the stone floor around it, hand and foot prints stamped on its wet surface. *Blood!*

"He was here!" Fay shouted. "Mordred was here!"

Her eyes went from her son's fedora to the iron door, then back again. *But why? He'd been hunting the Penderhagen girl and promised not to return until he found her. He would never have given up.*

The sudden understanding made Fay hysterical. "Get out of the way!" she screamed. "I need to open the door!" The confused troopers scrambled to let her by.

"Post two of your men on the stairs," Fay ordered her lieutenant. "No one is to pass. No one, do you hear me? And I want you to lead a search of the castle grounds with as many men as you can muster. You're looking for a fourteen-year-old girl. She could not have gotten far. Find her!"

The lead trooper bowed obediently, wondering what had inspired the strange orders. He kept the question to himself, curtly repeating the instructions to his men.

Ignoring the blood at her feet, Fay frantically lifted her gown and removed the key strapped to her leg. Her hands were shaking as she inserted it into the narrow slot above the iron door's handle. She prayed that her hunch was right.

Mordred had been on the Penderhagen girl's trail when Fay had spoken to him through *The Mind's Eye*, giving him the information he needed to find her. The only thing that would bring him back to the castle would be his prey.

*The girl was here!*

Fay's mind raced as she tried to make sense of it all. As she turned the key and pulled the heavy door open, the pieces of the puzzle fell into place. If what Merl had told her was true, that the Penderhagen girl had already written the final page, she'd have no reason to come anywhere near the castle. The fact that Merl had spoken to Fay through *The Meditations* had fooled her into thinking she'd been beaten, that the Challenger had already stolen her glory.

"He was lying!" hissed Fay. She remembered the last time she saw Merl alive, the devastation on his face, the look of betrayal as he stared back at her through the flames. It was a miracle he had survived the savage fire, but he could not have escaped unscathed. Nor, she guessed, could the *Grail Tome* he rescued. *He has it, but it must be damaged. He sent her for mine.*

When Fay saw the key resting on the stone floor a few feet past the threshold, it confirmed her theory. *Merl's key. The girl tried to get in, but Mordred stopped her.* She remembered her son's report after his quarry eluded him at the school: *She had help. An old man. And another...trained in the Art.*

Tears welled in Fay's eyes when she saw her *Grail Tome* still open on the desk where she left it. The words on *The*

*History's* penultimate page were coming faster than ever before. An hour ago, they had just started to appear on the top of the cream-colored sheet, and now they had almost filled it. She could see the long edge of *The History's* final page beneath it, peeking out, waiting patiently for her hand.

Collapsing into her chair, Fay watched the last word form in the bottom right corner of the page and realized it completed a sentence, the only one to appear since the book had first warned her of the Challenger's arrival on the island.

*A pagea ultime estam oblige.* To the final page we are bound.

Fay's breath was ragged, and her heart pounded in her chest. Reaching for the small box next the tome, she removed Wyzera's golden pen, smiling as the weak light of the wall sconces played upon its beautifully etched surface, igniting the swirling lines like flaming serpents. With her free hand, she reached for the matching inkwell, delicately opening its ornate lid. She carefully lowered the tip of the pen's blade into the vessel, watching as the dark ink adhered to the nib like congealing blood. She focused her thoughts, remembering the words. They were there, ready to answer her will.

Fay took a deep breath and turned the page.

Merl shook his head at Gal, "I should have known it was impossible. You could never have carried away a book that size—not in your condition. Even if you could get to it without being seen."

"You never said it had to be the whole book," protested Gal. She reached into her jacket and removed a folded sheet of creamy white paper. "The final page is all you said

Arti needed, so that's all I got." She slapped it down on the round table next to the inkwell and the wooden case holding Excalibri.

There was stunned silence.

"But...but how?" gasped Arti. "How did you get to the tome? The door was locked...and Mordred was there...and the guards...and we never saw you."

Gal peeked up at Arti from under her cap. "I watched you leave, then I followed you. I wanted to make sure you got into the Witch's room. I knew you wouldn't let me go with you, so I snuck out when he was in the trance, mumblin' and stuff." Gal looked suspiciously at Merl. "But you were fakin', wurncha?"

"I had to make you think you were getting away without me noticing," said Merl, lifting the folded sheet of paper, scowling at the state of it.

Arti was incredulous. "So you were behind us on the hill? And when we entered the castle?"

"I just kept far 'nuff away so you wouldn't notice," said Gal. "Then I hid for a bit when the troopers came, and I heard Lance beat the crap outa them. I wish I coulda seen it.

"By the time I got to the tower, you were comin' back down. I didn't know the Flame was up there." Gal smiled admiringly at Lance, "But you beat him, too. I knew you would."

"I had help," said Lance, with a nod to Arti. "But you have not explained how you entered Morgan Fay's room, how you got to the book without a key."

"Well, when I heard you comin' back down, I had to hide again." She frowned at Arti, "I knew you'd be pissed that I followed you. The only door nearby was the black one with the flame on it—and it wasn't locked." She looked pleased with herself. "If there's one thing I've learned from scroungin' buildins, it's that rooms can be connected in ways you wouldn't 'spect."

Arti looked back at the cardboard ad featuring the happy family, leaning on the shelf above Gal's bed with *The King's Errand* pressed against it. She remembered that Gal had kept it in the records room at the school, wedged into the tines of a large air vent. A light bulb went on in Arti's mind, and she immediately knew how her young friend had done it, how she had found a way into Fay's tower suite. It was the same way she had discovered a way into the records room.

*You never asked me how I got in here with the door locked.*

"A vent," said Arti. "You found a vent connecting Incendi Headquarters to Fay's office."

"Yep," said Gal, proudly. "It was a tight fit and a hard climb—'specially with my fingers messed up—but it led right up to it. The book was sittin' on a big desk, opened to the second last page. Words were formin' on it real fast. It wasn't quite full, but I bet it is by now."

"So you tore this page out," said Merl, appalled. He had unfolded the sheet and was examining its blank canvas. "What did you think we could do with it?"

"It's the final page," explained Gal, as if the old librarian was simple. "Arti can write on it, and all this crap's over." Seeing that Merl wasn't satisfied, she added, "Don't worry, I tore 'nother page out from the middle of the Witch's book and stuck it in the back to fool her." Gal grinned, "Boy, is she gonna be pissed when she turns to it."

Merl pressed the broad page down on the back of the damaged *Grail Tome* where the original sheet would have been. "It was a clever ruse, but it won't work. The final page is useless if it's not connected to the book." He sighed, knowing she only did what she thought was right. Gal sank back into her seat, confused and deflated.

"At least Fay doesn't have it," he added. "I cringe at the thought of the future she planned to write." The old librarian smiled weakly, "You denied her that, Gal, and it's a victory worth celebrating. But she's going to be very, very angry."

The vidlink propped on the counter came back to life, flashing three times before the picture and sound were restored. There was a view of the clifftop from overhead, floodlights bathing the stage and the grounds surrounding it. Even a wide swath of the hill was illuminated.

"We apologize for the technical difficulties," said the newsflash reporter. "We are back, and we are live! There has been an attempt by a criminal mob to disrupt our Corporation Night's Lighting. As you can see, our heroes in black have the terrorists surrounded. Rest assured, they will answer for their crimes."

The camera zoomed in on a group of men standing on the stage in front of the pyre. They were holding electroshock batons, aiming them out at converging squads of Incendi. In the center of the group stood a short, stocky man yelling orders to those around him. The base of the platform at his back was smoldering, but most of the books piled there were still undamaged.

"That's Big Billy!" shouted Gal, pointing her splinted fingers at the vidlink.

"Who?" asked Merl, leaning closer to the tiny screen, surprised to see the Archive was still intact.

"Billy Johnson," answered Arti. "The owner of the Cauldron. He runs the island, the docks, the saloons, everything."

"The one Aunt Vivian sent me to see," said Lance. "He arranged my fight with the big man. Now we know who was behind the attack on the castle."

"Musta had enough of the Flames on his turf and decided to fight back," said Gal. A finger of white light reached out from the Incendi line, and one of Big Billy's men collapsed to the stage.

"The Incendi are too many," said Lance, wishing he was on that stage fighting alongside the little man from Isle. "It is a battle he cannot win."

Merl turned away from the carnage on the screen. "And when he falls, the Archive will be lost. Morgan promised a Lighting, and she's going to deliver. But it won't stop there. When she finds out the final page has been taken, her vengeance will be swift and terrible."

"So what do we do now?" asked Arti.

"The only thing we can do," replied Merl. "We get away while there's still time, and we keep running—for the rest of our lives."

The voice on the vidlink was triumphant: "Your beloved CEO is safe and sound, praise the Corporation, and a search of the area is underway for any other insurgents involved in this evening's attack. Don't miss a moment as the spectacle unfolds. A picture is worth a thousand words. *Show*, don't tell. *You* are the Corporation!"

# CHAPTER 28

"Gwen is still up there," said Lance. "I must go back for her."

"She went to look for *my* parents," added Arti. "I'm going with him."

"And wherever Arti goes, I go," said Gal. "That's the deal."

Merl blew out a long breath, watching the action streaming across the vidlink screen. The violent stand-off was still underway on the hilltop stage. A dozen men with lighters stood shoulder to shoulder, fighting off wave after wave of armed troopers. Another of the defenders fell, and the protective ring around the Archive weakened. More Incendi were arriving, and lines of them were forming on the crest of the hill.

Merl knew this might be their only chance to get away, their best hope of evading capture. It was a big world, and they could hide from Morgan Fay and her henchman. But how could he argue with such bravery, such honor? The youngsters had sworn an oath with Gwen and would not abandon her or those she risked her life to save.

Neither would he.

"Then let's go get her," he said, slamming his gloved hand down on the severed page resting atop the *Grail Tome*, waiting for them to join him in the oath.

Gal was first to reach across the round table, adding her splinted fingers to his. This time Merl approved, smiling at the intrepid twelve-year-old. "The book is *our* shield," he said, including her in the pledge.

Lance placed his hand gently atop Gal's. "The pen is *our* sword."

As before, Arti added her hand last, but this time there was no reluctance, no doubt.

"The ink is *our* blood."

The moment Arti spoke the words, a sphere of amber light enveloped their stacked hands, binding them to the torn page and the damaged tome beneath it. The glowing ball's hold was so strong that it locked their arms together making it impossible to pull away. At the same time, Arti noticed a sliver of light peeking out of the wooden box containing Excalibri. As suddenly as it began, the golden aura collapsed, releasing them.

"What was that?" asked Lance, rubbing his tingling fingers.

"I have no idea," said Merl, dumbfounded. He was studying his own hand, "It was some form of energy."

"It was like before," said Arti, "when I wrote the names on the table. The light, I mean. The pen was glowing, too. I think the oath triggered it."

While Arti was offering her theory, Gal was squinting down at where their hands had been, at the sheet of paper she had torn from the back of Morgan Fay's book. "Holy crap!" she yelled. "Look!"

It was nothing short of a miracle. The page was no longer separate from the *Grail Tome* below it. It was connected to the charred book's binding, perfectly melded as if they had always been together.

"Amazing," said Merl, gently tugging at its edge. "It's joined. It's *actually* joined." He rubbed a gloved finger along the newly formed seam, mumbling to himself.

Then, as if a pail of cold water had been thrown on him, the old librarian frantically waved for Lance to rise, scrambling out of the booth behind him. He looked fretfully at the vidlink still showing the action on the castle grounds. The coverage was now being broadcast in split screen. On one side, another of Big Billy's men collapsed on the stage in front of the Archive's pyre. On the other, illuminated by the powerful spotlights aimed down from the castle walls, an overhead shot showed Incendi troopers advancing down the hill toward the chain link fence and the forest of naked trees beyond it. The chomping sound of a helicopter could be heard in the distance.

"Change of plans," barked Merl. "The tome has given us a chance to end this—here and now. You must wield Excalibri, Arti, before the Incendi get to us. The final page," he nodded at the book in front of her, "is waiting."

"But I still don't know what to write," protested Arti, eyes darting from Merl to the vidlink to the newly restored page.

"*Forged together in truth, the pen and the will are one,*" said Merl. "I don't know what that 'truth' is, but for some reason the book chose you. It's time to find out why."

Lance shrugged off his leather jacket, ignoring the stab of pain in his shoulder. "I'll do everything I can to stop them, Arti. To give you time." Before following Merl outside, he added, "Do this for your family. For Gwen."

Arti's heart was racing, and her mouth was dry. She reached for the restored page, gently turning it over, relieved that the magical bond held. Lifting Excalibri, Arti assumed the writing position, gingerly flipping back the well's ornate lid. Dipping the pen in the ink, she held it over the sphere, her hand shaking.

Her eyes were drawn back to the vidlink on the counter. Flashing across its screen was a shot of two vehicles parked in a forest clearing. As she watched the camera pan across the scene, light streamed in through the motorhome's windows, and the buzzing sound of the helicopter grew louder. "An insurgent camp has been located," said the voice on the vidlink. "The Incendi forces are closing in on it..."

"That's us!" shouted Gal. She leaned over the table and peered up through the window across from them, searching for the chopper.

The picture switched again, tracking three people at the bottom of the grassy slope running toward the forest. One of them fell and was helped up by the other two. "There are suspects fleeing the castle grounds," announced the voice. "They won't get far." The camera zoomed in on them, capturing their desperate attempt to escape.

Arti almost fell off the bench. "Mom and Dad!" she cried. "And Gwen!"

The shot widened, revealing a tall trooper in pursuit. He moved with an uneven gait, as if laboring to stay on his feet. Even so, he was gaining on them.

261

"Mordred!" hissed Gal. "He ain't dead!" She looked down at the tome's blank page and pleaded with Arti, "You gotta hurry up and write it before he catches them!"

Fighting a tide of panic, Arti clenched her jaw, gripping Excalibri tight in her fist, trying to make it come to life, knowing she held the fate of her family and friends in her hand. Mordred and the Incendi were coming, every second counted; if she couldn't do her part now, they were doomed. She begged the pen to obey, but it ignored her plea.

Arti glowered at Excalibri, tortured by its refusal to answer her. "Why won't you work?" she yelled. "You knew Gal would bring me the page, so let me write it!"

The thought rose like an island out of a sea of despair.

Arti glanced at the first cryptic words Excalibri had written on the table: *Siegea Perilisi*. The pen had been right about Gal; it knew she would be the one to steal the page from Morgan Fay. So it had to be right about the rest of them, reasoned Arti; the names the pen had given *all* the Book Knights must be true. *Even mine*, she thought, realizing how blessed she had been to share a place at the round table with such remarkable people. People who really cared about her. *True* friends.

*Forged together in truth, the pen and the will are one.*

"The pen's been trying to tell me all along what I want the future to be. What *my* will is." Arti could barely contain her excitement. "You," she said, getting a bewildered look from Gal. "Us. The Book Knights. We're the future I want."

Excalibri came to life in her hand, a warm glow emanating from its poles—the tiny pommel and ink-covered tip—and from the ends of the miniature guard resting across Arti's closed fist. It was the same light that had filled the motorhome when it wrote the names on the table, the same energy that just a short time ago transplanted the final page to the damaged *Grail Tome*.

Arti lowered Excalibri to the page, concentrating on each name the pen had inscribed on the round table, starting with the one across from her: Merlini Sagia.

She closed her eyes thinking about how much the old librarian cherished books and knowledge, how he had devoted his life to protecting the written word, the many years he had searched for Arti in the hope of stopping Morgan Fay's madness.

It worked.

Excalibri glowed brightly in her hand and started to travel across the page, leaving an inky trail in its wake. The Old Ferencian script curled and flowed as it transcribed Arti's will in perfectly formed letters, translating the message in her mind.

*There will be wisdom, those who will not forget the past. They will treasure and share knowledge for the better of all.*

Gal didn't know what the words meant, but she sat silently in her place at the table, watching intently as Arti wrote them, making sure not to distract her.

Arti focused on the next name, Lancea Coraggia, and the pen continued on its path.

*There will be courage, those who will protect the weak. They will fight only when they must, and always with honor.*

Gweneath Justea.

*There will be justice, those who refuse to give in to prejudice and fear. They will seek what is right at all costs.*

Siegea Perilisi.

*There will be those who answer the call when all hope is lost, honest and faithful friends, loyal to the end.*

Artia Bendi.

*With the fealty of others will come freedom, friendship, and love, to be cherished forever.*

Arti paused, holding the pen over a narrow ribbon of white at the bottom of the page. She knew she wasn't done, that there was still one thing left to say. She thought about Morgan Fay and the Corporation, Mordred and his Incendi. History could not be allowed to repeat itself—not under her watch. She smiled as Excalibri agreed, glowing brightly in her hand, and she lowered its point gently to the page.

*And shared by all, the power of words shall vanquish its enemies.*

At the instant Arti finished the sentence and lifted Excalibri from the paper, everything went quiet, and the light streaming in through the motorhome's window went off, as if someone hit a switch.

"Did...*you* do that?" asked Gal.

"I'm not sure," said Arti, stunned by the sudden change. She placed Excalibri back in its case, setting it down hastily beside the ink well. In that moment of looking away, the words she'd just written on the *Grail Tome's* final page vanished.

"Everything I wrote is gone!" Arti gasped, running her fingers across the page. "It's all gone!" She rotated the book so Gal could see, then started flipping back through its broad pages. "The whole chapter's blank. All of it."

Gal leaned over the tome and with her good eye noticed a tiny fragment of ink materializing at the top of *The History's* first page. "It's startin' over," she said, pointing a splinted finger at the budding mark. "It musta worked. It's back at the beginnin'."

"I think you're right," whispered Arti. She looked at the counter where the vidlink had been sitting. Like the words in *The History*, the device was gone.

Gal let loose a blissful hoot and was rewarded with a sharp twinge of pain in her head. Arti wasn't ready to join the celebration. Not yet. A minute ago her parents and Gwen had been running for their lives from Mordred. She prayed she'd written the page in time to save them.

Outside, Merl and Lance noted the sudden absence of noise and light around them, and the abrupt disappearance of the helicopter overhead. They nearly collapsed with relief, knowing it could only mean one thing.

"She did it!" said Lance.

"Yes," agreed Merl, with a deep sigh of relief. "The final page has been written."

A branch cracked, and Merl aimed his flashlight into the gloom. A figure emerged from the trees, pushing away a sapling's drooping limb, raising a hand to shield her eyes from the bright beam.

The old librarian's voice caught in his throat. "Gwen? Is that you?"

"Yes," she replied, out of breath. "Lance? Arti? Did they make it back?"

"We made it," said Lance, running to meet her. "Are you alright?"

Gwen nodded, still panting. "Mordred isn't dead. A minute ago, he was right behind us. But then it got dark and quiet, and he was...gone. Just...gone." She shook her head, looking for an explanation. "How's that possible?"

Whatever method of deception Mordred had used to mask his death in the tower, Lance made it clear he wasn't worried, that this time he was certain the man in black wasn't coming back.

"We won't see the Incendi again," he explained, looking gleefully at the motorhome's window. "Gal brought Arti the page. She just finished writing it."

Gwen's elation bubbled out in a slew of questions. "But how did she...and where was the...and when did it—"

"All in good time," said Merl, interrupting her. "You said 'us'." He looked past Gwen at the trees. "Is someone with you?"

The door to the motorhome opened, and the weak light from within spilled out into the clearing. Arti and Gal had rejoiced when they'd heard Gwen's voice and realized she was okay. As Arti helped Gal down the steps and steadied her against the side of the vehicle, she awaited the answer to Merl's question.

"Yes," said Gwen, and the smile she offered Arti made her spirit soar. "There's a couple of people real eager to see you."

Gwen turned back to the trees, and two forms emerged from the shadows behind her, holding on to one another as they approached. Though she'd been steadying Gal, it was Arti who staggered when she saw the faces of her mother and father enter the light. Her legs suddenly felt heavy, and she was worried she was going to faint.

"Arti!" they cried, rushing to embrace their daughter.

"We thought we lost you," said her mother, weeping. Joy colored her thin face as she madly hugged and kissed Arti's forehead and cheeks.

Arti's father wrapped his arms around both of them, eyes tightly clenched with emotion. He'd aged a great deal in two months, not knowing if his family would ever be together again. "But you came for us," he said. "Gwen told us what you did. We're so proud of you."

"I had help," said Arti, finding her voice, happily imprisoned in her parents' arms. "That's Merl," she nodded. "He's a librarian, and he knows magic. And that's Lance. He's a real Knight of Maren from Ference." Arti's parents smiled appreciatively at each of them, knowing the debt that was owed could not be paid.

"You've already met Gwen," said Arti. The look she gave the beautiful young woman said more than her words: "She's...amazing."

"And you must be Gal," said Arti's mother, smiling warmly at the girl standing quietly by herself. "Gwen told us you're Arti's best friend."

Gal leaned bashfully against the wall of the motorhome. She tilted back her lucky cap to answer, but Arti beat her to it.

"She's not my best friend." Gal frowned at the denial, a lump forming in her throat. A smiled curled Arti's lips. "She's a whole lot more than that. She's family."

Gal gritted her teeth to keep from crying. It might have worked if Arti's father hadn't knelt in front of her, gently taking her hand in his. "I always wanted another daughter," he said.

Arti reached for the only words that could capture the power of this moment, the only ending that seemed right.

"And they lived happily ever after."

# EPILOGUE

Far away from Arti Penderhagen's triumph in Main, a young man weaved his way through a forest on the Island of Maren, cradling a book in one arm, holding a lamp with the other. The night sky draped the naked tree tops like a black shroud, and he shivered in the cold damp of the Ferencian fall. Covered with wet leaves, the old stone path was difficult to follow, but his eagerness to complete his task and return to a heaping pot of stew in the warm castle kitchen kept his feet moving.

As a junior member of the Order of Librarians, Tomas was duty-bound to honor his elder's wishes, but his devotion to Vivian de Lac went far beyond the obligations of rank. She had been his teacher, his mentor, the one who had lifted him from the poverty of ignorance, offering him a life rich with knowledge. A life with a future.

And though books were Tomas's passion, he felt uneasy carrying this one, so ominous was its reputation. According to the library records, it hadn't been opened for centuries.

When he'd asked Vivian why, her answer was both frank and frightening: "To keep what's inside from getting out."

The tome's appearance and title only added to its malevolent reputation. Vertical bars were embossed on its black vellum cover, and a thick leather strap sewn into its back wrapped around the rough-edged pages, secured by a sturdy silver lock fastened to the book's face. The yellow letters above the lock had faded over the centuries, but he could still make out the Old Ferencian script: Guardea di Almi. *The Souls' Keep.*

Where the path ended at the base of a granite escarpment, he located an iron gate pressed against the rock face and hidden by a thick curtain of leafless vines. Setting the lamp and book down, he cleared away enough of the woody shoots to access the rusty padlock that kept the gate closed. Removing a pitted key from his pocket, he inserted it in the device and turned it, relieved to see the old lock's shackle release. Ancient hinges moaned as Tomas wrenched the gate open, but it only swung a short distance before getting snagged on the thick undergrowth. Retrieving the lamp and tome, he slipped through the narrow gap.

A few feet inside, the passage widened, and Tomas saw the foot of a stone sarcophagus with the name *Jean de Lac* engraved on its end. He recalled the ceremony for *The Bard of Lucinne* held in this place half a decade before. Like the letters on the casket, the dignity that Vivian and her nephew, Lance, had shown in their moment of grief was still etched deep in Tomas's memory.

Tomas and Lance had grown up together, the closest of friends, though their educations differed. With Vivian as his instructor, Tomas had spent his youth in service of the Order, studying and conserving the extensive collection of books in the de Lac library. Lance, on the other hand, followed in the footsteps of his forefathers, reciting *The Verses* and training in *the strike of words* under the watchful eye of his legendary uncle and master.

It was Lance who had given Tomas the message from Vivian a month ago, just before leaving for Old Tintagel in answer to his aunt's unexpected summons. As strange as her instructions seemed to Tomas, he followed them without question: *At midnight on All Souls Eve, take the book into the Tomb of the Knights of Maren. Hide it deep within the crypt. No one but Lance and I must know you've done this. Never return to it. Never speak of it again.*

The line of stone coffins continued, one after another, arcing off into the murky gloom of the catacomb. Resting next to Jean de Lac was his brother, Bayne, Lance's father. He died young, but Lance still talked about him often. It was too bad that he never got to see how skilled a fighter his son had become.

A third of the way into the deep cavern, one sarcophagus stood out among the others. It was ornately decorated with carved oak leaves and garlands. On its lid was the sculpted form of its occupant, Guillaume de Lac. Tomas had read many of the renowned author's works, most of them fascinating histories of the men to be found in the darkest depths of the tomb.

Tomas passed generation after generation of de Lac knights, finally arriving at the end of the rough-hewn shaft where the first of them, Marglen of the Lake, had rested for two millennia. The young librarian had never come this far before, had never seen The Founder's resting place. He held the lamp over the ancient sarcophagus, illuminating the king's effigy, careful not to defile it with his touch.

Marglen's arms were crossed at his chest, hands wrapped around the handle of a great sword, the blade of which ran the length of his chiseled body. The bearded warrior of old wore his crown proudly, content in his rest, satisfied that eighty generations of his line had served the Order of Librarians and the people of Ference so well.

As instructed, Tomas set *The Souls' Keep* on a ledge next to The Founder's casket. Holding the lamp out, he looked at the book one last time, wondering what reason Vivian had for storing it here. It was a question he intended to ask her.

Content that he had completed his mission, Tomas started back the way he had come. He'd only taken a few steps when he heard the low hiss of a woman's voice in back of him. He spun around, his heart racing with the kind of terror a child feels when they imagine a monster hiding in the darkness. Tomas stabbed at the shadows with the lamp but saw nothing there—just the stone caskets he had passed. Then he heard the phantom woman whisper again.

"No," she said, in what sounded like disbelief. "No, it can't be." The moment of silence that followed was pierced by her agonized scream. "No!"

Tomas staggered back from the terrifying lament, tripping over a stone on the tomb's rocky floor. He dropped the lamp as he fell, and its flame went out. In the sudden darkness, he scrambled blindly to his feet in the panic to escape. As his eyes slowly adjusted to the gloom, Tomas glanced back to the end of the tunnel where he had placed *The Souls' Keep*. A weak halo of light warmed the rough stone wall next to The Founder's coffin.

271

Tomas shuffled hastily toward the tomb's opening, probing his way through the darkness, desperate to get away from the book—and whatever or *whoever* was trapped inside it. The last thing he heard was another voice, this one belonging to a man.

"What's happened?" he asked feebly. "Where are we, Mother?"